A Chance Encounter

USA TODAY BESTSELLING AUTHOR
NIKKI ASH

A LOVE & LYRICS NOVEL

With one look, one moment, one kiss, one touch, he saw me.

A Chance Encounter Copyright © 2020 Nikki Ash

Cover Design: Jersey Girl Design
Photo: Sara Eirew Photography
Editor: Emily A. Lawrence

All Rights Reserved. This book contains material protected under International and Federal Copyright Laws and Treaties. Any unauthorized reprint or use of this material is prohibited. No part of this book may be reproduced or transmitted in any form or by any means, electronic or mechanical, including photocopying, recording, or by an information and retrieval system without express written permission from the Author/Publisher.

This is a work of fiction. Names, characters, places, and incidents either are the product of the author's imagination or are used fictitiously, and any resemblance to actual persons, living or dead, business establishments, events, or locales is entirely coincidental.

To my second chance,
thank you for never giving up on us.

Playlist

Independent – Webbie

Didn't know What Love Was – Kane Brown

Worship You – Kane Brown

Found You – Kane Brown

If the World Was Ending – JP Saxe & Julia Michaels

Be Kind – Marshmello & Halsey

I'm the One – DJ Khaled feat. Justin Bieber

Let Me Love You – DJ Snake feat. Justin Bieber

E.T. – Katy Perry feat. Kanye West

Wide Awake – Katy Perry

Nobody's Love – Maroon 5

Something Just Like This – The Chainsmokers & Coldplay

Little Do You Know – Alex & Sierra

Prologue

SOPHIA

"THREE REDHEADED SLUTS." I DROP THE SHOT GLASSES ONTO THE BAR TOP and the three women thank me.

"To redheaded sluts," one woman—a brunette—yells over the blaring music. "And may they all burn in the pits of fiery hell."

I feel ya, sister...

The other two women—both blondes—cheer in agreement as they lift their glasses, clinking them against each other, before they tip them back and swallow down their shots in one fell swoop.

"Hit us again!" the brunette chimes, smacking her lips together. "I refuse to leave here a second before I'm so drunk, I forget the asshole who cheated on me with that redheaded slut!" Her words hit me hard, but I push them down. I'm working, and I need to make money so I can enroll in college in the spring. I don't have time to focus on anything else. Focusing on other shit is what got me into this mess in the first place.

"You got it." I plaster on a fake smile and grab the three glasses, dropping them into the dirty bin, then go about making them all over again. More drinks equal drunker people, and drunker people equal bigger tips. And I like big tips.

I pour Jägermeister, peach schnapps, and cranberry juice into a shaker, fill it with ice, then grab the top to shake it up. As I'm pouring the drinks into three clean shot glasses, my eyes lock with *him*. He juts his chin out, and the corner of his lips curves into a smirk. The same smirk that lured me to him, that had me fooled. *Not anymore, asshole.*

After I set the ladies' drinks in front of them and add them to their tab, I make his drink of choice, then walk over and show it to him. "Whiskey sour… with a side of fuck you, you lying, cheating asshole!" I toss the drink at him, drenching his face and shirt with the caramel-colored liquid.

"What the fuck!" Freeman booms, jumping up and

A CHANCE ENCOUNTER

grabbing napkins to wipe his face off. "What the hell is your problem, Sophia?" He tosses the soaked napkins onto the bar top.

"My problem is, I saw you on television"—I come around the bar and point my finger in his chest—"with a redheaded woman, who's apparently your *fiancée*."

His eyes widen, and for a quick second, I think I see a hint of remorse, but then his blue eyes go arctic cold. He grabs my wrist and pulls me down the darkened hallway that's designated for employees only and into the storage closet, where we had sex for the first time, several months ago. "What did you think?" he hisses, once he's slammed the door behind us. "That what we've been doing meant I wanted to spend my life with you?" He chuckles evilly, the sound making me want to vomit.

"I thought..." I swallow thickly, knowing what I'm about to say is going to make me sound pathetic—but still I say it anyway. "I thought you cared about me."

He scoffs. "I thought you of all people know how the real world works. You're a bartender who lives in a trailer park with her white trash mom, and I was looking to get my dick wet."

His words do as he intended, cutting me to the bone. I confided in him, told him about my family, how my dad up and left when I was eight and started a new life with another family, leaving my mom and me to fend for ourselves. She lost our home, and we were forced to move into a single wide mobile home. He told me where I live doesn't define who I am. He said he believed in me. When I told him I want to go to law school, he told me I could do it. Now he's throwing my truths in my face.

This is not the same man who told me I was beautiful and made love to me in his bed, night after night. Who told me how thankful he was that he stopped into this bar one night on his way home from work. This guy is someone completely different. Closed off, cold. Devoid of all emotions.

"My fiancée is the mayor's daughter. She's a college graduate from Berkeley," he continues. "I told you I have plans, and those plans could never include someone like you." His eyes and tone convey disgust, and even though I'm a fairly confident person, I suddenly feel like a light is shining brightly over me, emphasizing every one of my flaws. "We're from two different worlds, Sophia. You were good on your back, but you're not wife material."

A CHANCE ENCOUNTER

Tears sting the backs of my lids, but I refuse to let them fall. Fuck him and the high horse he rode in on.

"Does she know what her *fiancé* has been up to?" I accuse, choking back a sob that's threatening to break free. "That he's had another woman in his bed for the last several months? Where does she think you are right now, only hours after announcing your engagement?"

I can't believe I ever thought this guy could be the one. When we would lie in bed, he made me feel special. It was all fake. He's all fake. And now, I'm fucked. *Literally.*

"One, that bed you slept in wasn't mine. It was a friend of mine's who's been out of the country." He barks out a humorless laugh. "You couldn't have possibly thought I was going to put a ring on your finger and introduce you to my family." He sneers. "And no, she doesn't know, nor will she ever."

"Well, maybe she should know." I straighten my spine and cross my arms over my chest, tilting my chin up toward the ceiling. "Maybe she should know that you not only slept with a *trailer trash bartender,* but you got her pregnant."

Freeman freezes in his place, his eyes dropping to my belly. "You're lying."

"I'm pregnant." I found out this morning and was planning to tell him. Then I found out he's in a relationship with another woman, whom he's now engaged to.

He cuts across the small space and pins me against the wall, his hand slamming against the wall next to my head "If this is true, you're getting an abortion," he says slowly.

"Like hell," I spit. "My body, my baby."

"Sophia, do. Not. Fuck. With. Me." He grabs ahold of my ponytail and yanks my head back, so I'm forced to look into his eyes. I flinch at the bite of pain but refuse to cower to him. "I've worked too hard for your slutty ass to fuck up my plans."

"I'm keeping the baby," I repeat, looking him right in his cold gaze. "But if you don't want to be the father, then you don't have to be." Growing up, my dad was like a broken record, telling me how he wanted my mom to have an abortion. As far back as I can remember, I've felt like a mistake and I refuse to let this baby growing in me ever feel the same way.

"Fuck!" he booms, punching his fist through the wall. The drywall crumbles on impact. He pulls back, but his eyes never leave mine. "I came here looking to get laid, but you just had to go and complicate shit."

He closes his eyes and his fingers drag through his hair,

tugging on the ends in frustration. When he reopens them, his features are cold, calculated. "You tell anyone, and I mean *anyone*, about this baby, and I'll destroy you and your family. That secretarial position your mom just got at Klein and Eisenhower—my father plays golf with them. One word from me that she's a recovering addict and she'll be unemployed."

My body stiffens at his threat. My mom is finally at a job that makes her happy. A job that doesn't involve her flinging fried food. How the hell does he know about that? I never told him... That must mean he looked into me—into my family. The thought makes my stomach roil.

"And your uncle Oliver who just got that promotion at the bank... One call and he'll be gone." Oh my God... Fear crawls up my esophagus, burning like acid.

Freeman steps toward me and grabs my chin, jerking my face up to look at him. "If anyone ever finds out we were together, that I share DNA with that baby, I will fucking destroy you. I'll have nothing left to lose and I will come after you. And after I'm done doing that, I will take great pleasure in ripping that baby from your arms, so you never see it again. My family has connections everywhere, and I will use every single one in my power to see to it that if my life implodes, yours does too. It's best you remember that." He backs up and pulls a couple hundred-dollar bills from his money clip and drops them on the floor in front of me. "I suggest you get that abortion, Sophia, but if you're stupid and don't, you better make damn sure no one ever links me to you or that baby." He walks out, and I run to the closest trash can, vomiting everything in my stomach. Then I vomit once more.

Once I'm almost positive my stomach is empty, I go back out to the bar. My hands are shaking and I'm lightheaded, but I'm still in the middle of my shift.

"Miss, I need another beer," a guy calls out. "Miss."

"I heard you," I snap, then quickly smile, not wanting to piss him off. I need the money now more than ever.

The rest of the night goes by in a blur, and when the club is closed and the bar is clean, I head home. I'm exhausted and my heart is aching. All I want to do is shower the night off and get some sleep.

But when I walk inside and find my mom sitting on the couch with a pink and white box in her hand, I know I won't be doing either of those things yet.

"Tell me this isn't yours," she says, tossing it at me. "Tell me you didn't just destroy your entire future!" She stands and grabs a cigarette from the pack, pushes it between her wrinkled lips, and lights it.

"It's mine," I admit.

"And the father?"

"He's dead." The lie flows from my lips easily, as I recall Freeman's threats.

Her brows rise in confusion. "Dead?"

"Dead," I repeat. Dead to me, dead to the baby growing in me, and to the world, he will always be known as an unnamed man who's dead.

"You going to have an abortion?"

"No." It was never a thought in my mind. Like my dad made sure to tell me he wanted my mom to have an abortion, my mom has told me a million times she considered it but couldn't do it. If she had, if she had listened to my dad, I wouldn't be here.

"You should," she says, shocking the hell out of me.

"You didn't."

"And look how hard this life has been on the both of us." She takes a puff of her cigarette and releases the toxic smoke into the air. My thoughts go straight to the health of the baby I'm carrying, and I back up a step—it's my job to protect the baby.

"Do you regret having me?" My voice cracks. Not once has she ever said she did. That was always my father.

She sighs. "I could never regret having you. I love you, but that doesn't change the fact that life's a mean, cruel bitch, who'll eat you up and spit you out. It hasn't been easy raising you. I wasn't able to give you a fourth of the shit I wish I were."

"But you loved me," I rasp. Isn't love enough?

"Love doesn't pay for formula or diapers or clothes or an education," she says, answering my unspoken question. She hates that she can't afford to help me with college, that even though I had the GPA and scores to go to a good school, because we can't pay for that, I'm instead going to a local community college, while my half-sister, my dad's other daughter, is going to Stanford because my dad can afford to pay for it.

"I'm keeping the baby," I tell her. "I'll figure it out."

She sighs in frustration. "We can barely afford to keep this roof over our heads." Tears well in her eyes. "Please, Sophia. Don't let one mistake ruin your entire future. I want more for you than this life."

A CHANCE ENCOUNTER

My heart both hurts and swells at her words. We've never been close. Not like I imagine a mother and daughter should be. She's been stressed and struggling for as far back as I can remember. But it warms my heart that despite that, she still cares about me and my future. She wouldn't kick me out on the streets with a baby in my belly, but that doesn't mean I should put this on her. This is my problem. And I'm going to need to deal with it on my own.

I take a shower, remaining under the hot water until it turns cold, then throw on a pair of cotton shorts and a tank top. It's hot tonight and we don't have working air conditioning.

When I'm putting my phone to charge, a text comes in from my cousin and best friend, Naomi: **Miss you, love you, need you.**

I glance at the time on my phone. It's four in the morning here in California, so it's seven there.

Me: Everything okay?

My phone rings and I hit answer. "What's wrong?"

"Jacob took a job in China. Told me he wanted a fresh start. We broke up."

"What?" Jacob is the reason Naomi moved across the country to New York. They were high school sweethearts, and he got an offer to work for some tech company in New York and asked her to go with him. "What are you going to do?" She works as a bartender like I do, in New York, but she can't possibly afford to live there without him.

"Dante said he'd help me out." Dante is her boss, and she's mentioned on several occasions how close they are. From the way she speaks about him, I almost think she has a thing for him, but she swears they're just friends—which raises the question as to why she's friends with her very much older boss.

"So, what, he'll be your sugar daddy?"

We both laugh.

"No, he said I can... work the stage." Shit, she's going to strip? She said they make more money, but Jacob wouldn't let her do it. "It won't be enough, but I'll find a roommate."

"I'm pregnant," I blurt out.

"What?" She shrieks. "How?"

"Well, when a man and a woman—"

"Bitch, now is not the time for jokes."

"I know." I sigh. "But if I don't joke, I'll cry."

"Is it the guy you mentioned you've been seeing? What's his name?"

A CHANCE ENCOUNTER

"No, he's dead."

We're both silent for a moment while I wait for Naomi to call me out on my lie. She knows me better than I know myself, and she knows damn well if the guy I was dating died, I would've told her.

"Dead?"

"Yeah, dead."

"Okay then. He's dead."

I exhale in relief, thankful she's going along with the lie so easily. I'm not sure I could continue the lie is she questioned me.

"Your mom know about the baby?"

"Yeah."

"Oh boy. How'd she take it?" Naomi's mom and mine are sisters. But while my mom struggled, Naomi's mom did things the right way—went to college, found a wealthy man to marry, bought a home in a nice area, and then had Naomi. My mom isn't jealous of my aunt Vicky—she's more envious, if anything. And any time she talks about my future, she always tells me she wants me to be like her sister—get out of this trailer park and make a life for myself.

"Not good. I know she'll help me, but I can't let her do

that. She's finally working at a job she likes and pays well, and I'm grown up. I can't put her through this… But I don't have anywhere to go… And bartending isn't going to pay for a baby. Shit, Naomi, maybe I'm in over my head here. Maybe I should have an abortion," I choke out, hating myself for even thinking that. I'm not against abortion by any means. Every woman has the right to do what she wants to her own body, but could I live with that choice?

We're both quiet for a moment before she says, "Move here."

"What?"

"Move here. I need a roommate and you need a place to live."

"Did you not hear I'm pregnant?"

"Yeah, I did. We'll figure it out together."

I think about my options for a moment, but the fact is, if I stay here, I risk running into Freeman, and while I'd like to believe he's not capable of acting on his threats, my gut tells me he is. Then there's my mom—I can't put her in a position where she feels she's obligated to help me raise my baby. But if I leave, I'll be across the country, away from Freeman, and my mom will be off the hook. She deserves to finally live her life for herself. She gave me eighteen years. It's not fair to put her through another eighteen.

"Okay, I'm in."

One

SOPHIA
SEVEN YEARS LATER

"TWO JACK AND COKES, A TOM COLLINS, AND A WHISKEY NEAT." I REPEAT THE order as I set them on the tray. "Anything else?"

"Nope, that's it. Thanks, Soph." Sterling grabs the tray and sashays over to the table with the drinks.

I go back to manning the bar, when a gentleman sits down, his eyes immediately raking down my body. I ignore it and place a napkin in front of him. "Welcome to Emerald's. What can I get you?"

"You," the gentleman says with a cocky smirk splayed across his face. I avoid rolling my eyes. He isn't the first, second, or hundredth guy to make that cliché remark, nor will he be the last. Do guys seriously think that'll work and us women will just jump into bed with them? Ugh. Why are men so stupid?

"I'm not available," I tell him pointblank, like I tell every guy. Never will I let a man pick me up in a bar again, nor will I allow him to even think he has a sliver of a chance. "But I can get you a drink." I wink flirtatiously to lessen the blow—because, hello, tips—and like always, it works.

He smiles. "Gin and tonic, please."

"You got it."

I go about making his order, serve it to him, then grab the ticket that just came in to make an order for a waitress. Once that's done, I check on my other customers, making sure they're good. The music throughout the club is thumping, and I find myself dancing as I walk over to greet my new customer who's sat himself at the end of the bar.

"How's it going?" Dante asks with an easy-going smile. He's the owner of the club and my cousin Naomi's boyfriend.

I make him his usual whiskey on the rocks and hand it to him. "It's fine. Tips aren't as good, but it is what it is." I shrug, making him laugh. The corners of his eyes crinkle, showing his age—fifteen years older than Naomi and me. At first, I was concerned about her dating an older man, but I

A CHANCE ENCOUNTER

quickly understood why she's attracted to him. He's good-looking, mature, responsible, and doesn't play games—all rare qualities in a man from what I've seen. My cousin has hit the jackpot with him—and him with her, because she's a damn good catch herself.

"Say the word and I'll put you back on that stage," he says, taking a sip of his drink. "I've already had a dozen men ask why you aren't on the floor tonight." Tonight is my first official night behind the bar. For the last six years I've been on the floor, serving, and on the stage, dancing, but since this is my last year of school before I apply to law schools, I feel it's best if I get off the stage and floor and keep my clothes on.

"It's not the stage that makes the money and you know it…" It's the private dances you get from showing your ass off on the stage. And working at the bar means no private dances, which means no percentage or tips that come with them. But I've been saving like hell, knowing I wouldn't be working the floor forever. It was a quick way to earn a good amount of money and it did what I needed it to do. I've just started my senior year of college, free and clear of any debt, and I have a good amount put away for law school. I probably should've stayed on the floor a little longer, saved a little more, so I'd have a more padded cushion, but I'm twenty-five years old and tired of taking my clothes off. Plus, next year I'm going to be applying for internships at law firms, so I need to get used to making less money.

Dante swallows the last of his drink and stands. "I'm heading to your place. Naomi conned me into bringing her pizza and ice cream."

I laugh. "She didn't con you into anything. You're pussy-whipped. Just admit it." Dante and Naomi have been dating for the last three years, since she gave in and gave him a chance, after she quit working at Emerald's to start her own business. He's obsessed with her, and it would be sickening to watch if I weren't so happy for the both of them.

"Yeah, I am." He smiles wide and nods, pulling a fifty-dollar bill out and dropping it onto the bar top. I would tell him that's too much for his drink and tip, but I already know he'll just wave me off. He owns the club—and several others—so technically he shouldn't even be paying, but he always pays and tips big. Naomi jokes that it's his way of contributing to the single mom college fund.

"Give my girls a kiss for me," I call after him, setting a napkin in front of a gentleman who just walked up and sat down.

"Will do."

I turn my attention to the gentleman. "Welcome to Emerald's. What can I get you?"

He drags his gaze down my body. "How about you, sweetheart?"

"RISE AND SHINE, SUNSHINE." I LIFT THE BLANKET AND THE CUTEST LITTLE pair of blue eyes pop open. She stretches her tiny body and her dirty-blond curls fan out across her pillow.

"It's so early," she whines, sounding more like a teenager than the six-year-old she is.

"It's seven o'clock and you have to get ready for school."

The mention of school has her perking up slightly. While she hates getting up early, often sleeping in as late as ten on the weekends—I know, I can't believe I lucked out either—she loves school.

"Fine." She sits up, wiping the sleep from her eyes with her little fists. "Can I have pancakes for breakfast?"

"If you get ready quickly, yes."

Her eyes light up. "With chocolate chips?"

"Only if you hurry. Brush your hair and teeth and get dressed." I pat her leg and stand. "I'll meet you in the kitchen."

"Okay."

While she gets dressed, I whip up a batch of chocolate chip pancakes, then go about getting my stuff ready for class today.

"Morning," Naomi chirps, gliding into the kitchen in a cute pink wraparound dress and nude heels.

"What has you so happy?" I follow her into the kitchen and grab two mugs, pouring us each a steaming cup of coffee.

"Felicia Mourning has hired me to do her wedding." She beams. When I raise my brows, having no clue why that's significant, she sighs. "Felicia Mourning is the fiancée of Drake Mourning, the NBA star who plays for New York. If she's pleased with my work, she'll no doubt recommend me to her friends. Plus, just having their names on my referral list will speak volumes."

Naomi runs a successful event planning business called An Affair to Remember, and she's determined to take it to the next level. "Congratulations!" I wrap my arms around her for a hug. "You're going to kill it. You always do."

"Thank you." We separate and she takes a sip of her coffee. "Dante said last night was kind of rough…"

"Bartenders don't make a fourth of what dancers make."

"The downfall of leaving your clothes on." Naomi quit stripping when she decided to open her own business. Her parents were so thrilled she was taking the initiative to do something with her life, they gave her the startup capital. She took it seriously and created a wonderful business for herself—paying her parents back with interest.

"Yeah," I agree, swallowing a sip of coffee as Kendall comes running into the kitchen and plops her butt into the chair. Her hair is still messy, but she's at least dressed in her school uniform. She dives into her food, telling me between bites how good it is.

After she finishes eating, I brush her hair and stick it up in a ponytail, and then we're off. I walk her to school, which isn't far from our apartment in Lennox Hills, kissing her goodbye and telling her I'll see her at three o'clock when school gets out. Working at Emerald's means I get to be home with my little girl. I take classes while she's in school and spend the afternoon with her. We get to have dinner together, and after she goes to bed, I head out to work.

Today, I only have one class, and when it's over, since it's relatively nice outside, I decide to do my studying at Bryant Park. It's not far from Kendall's school, so when three o'clock rolls around I can scoop her up and we can go home.

I find an available bench and am sorting through my books, when someone barks out a string of expletives. I look up and find a man, flailing his arms all around him, like he's fighting with the air.

"Jesus Christ!" he hisses, swatting at… something. I can't see what it is, but unless he's lost his mind, something is attacking him, I think.

"Are you okay?" I ask, standing… to do what? I have no clue.

"This damn bee won't go away."

I don't see a bee, but what I do see is an extremely hot man with a forest green beanie on his head, a white Henley stretched across his chest, and forest green pants hugging his obviously muscular thighs. His face is full of dark scruff, and his brown eyes are the color of melted chocolate chips.

In the moment of silence, the buzzing of the bee is heard, and I spot it. On his shoulder.

A CHANCE ENCOUNTER

"Don't move!" I jump into action, grabbing my sandal from my foot and slapping his shoulder the bee is perched on. It takes a couple tries, but finally the bee drops to the ground. The man spots it and proceeds to stomp on it with his large shoe-clad foot. Over and over again.

"I think it's dead," I tell him through a laugh. "But maybe stomp on it one more time… just in case."

As if realizing I'm still here, he locks eyes with me and smiles back, his perfectly white teeth practically sparkling against his naturally tanned skin. "You're my hero," he says, his grin widening. "I'm allergic to bees."

"I'm glad my sandal could be of assistance." I drop it to the ground and slide it back on.

"I'm Easton." He holds out his hand and I glance down at it, noting how large and masculine it is.

"I'm—"

"Excuse me," a petite woman says, cutting me off. "I just watched all of that." She waves her hand in the air. "It was brilliant! Please tell me you two are strangers and single."

"What?" Easton and I both say at the same time.

"The bee… You beating him with your sandal… The laughing. Do you two know each other?"

"No," Easton says, "but she did just save my life."

He winks playfully and I throw my head back with a laugh at the absurdity of the situation.

"And are you both single?"

We both nod at the same time.

"Well, if it isn't my lucky day!" She squeals. "My name is Rita, and I'm a photographer." She lifts her camera that's hanging around her neck. "I'm doing a special showcase next month at my gallery called Stranger Sessions. It's pretty much how it sounds. I find strangers and pair them up, taking pictures of them. I don't sell them, and they'll only be showcased on my website and in my gallery. I was searching for some strangers when I saw you two. So, what do you say? Will you do it?" Before either of us can answer, she adds, "And look how adorable you two are. You're even matching!"

I glance down at my lacy, white tank top and green pants and snort out a laugh because she's right. We're totally matching. "I'm down," I tell her, feeling adventurous. Taking pictures with a good-looking man is hardly a hardship.

But when my eyes meet Easton's, he looks sort of nervous. "I mean, only if you are… If you don't want to, we don't have to," I add, trying to backtrack, so I don't look like an idiot.

A CHANCE ENCOUNTER

His brown-eyed gaze locks on me for a brief moment before he says, "I'm down."

"Oh yay!" Rita exclaims. "Thank you. Just sign right here, stating you agree to allow me to post the photos on my website and in my gallery, and then we can get started."

Reluctantly, I tear my eyes from Easton and over to Rita and her iPad she now has out. I scan the document quickly, noting it reads as she explained, and sign my name.

Easton reads it a bit more carefully before he signs.

"Great. Now, go ahead and sit together. We're going to take some photos here first. Then, if the weather holds up, we'll take some over there." She points to the bridge. I glance up and notice the sky, which was clear a few minutes ago, is now a bit darker."

"We're taking them here?" Easton asks, glancing around.

"Yep, I'm all about the natural," Rita tells him. "Now, sit, sit."

Easton does as she says and sits on the bench. I put my laptop into my bag and set it on the ground next to the bench, then sit next to him. It's suddenly awkward as hell, and when we glance at each other, we both break out in laughter.

"Maybe sit on his lap," Rita suggests. "Act natural, like

you're a happy couple in love."

My eyes go to Easton's lap and he chuckles. "I won't bite," he murmurs, patting his thigh and making me laugh.

I roll my eyes playfully but stand and do as Rita said. Only when I sit down, it looks like I'm perched on Santa's lap—albeit a sexy Santa—and we both end up cracking up all over again.

I spot Rita out of the corner of my eye, with her camera up to her face, snapping pictures, but I ignore her, pretending like every move I make isn't being caught on film—and wondering what I was thinking agreeing to this.

But then, I turn my body to face Easton—his warm, mesmerizing, brown eyes filled with mirth—and I'm reminded why.

Distracted by his good looks, I almost slide off his thigh, but he quickly catches me, his hands landing on my butt. My own fly out to catch myself and land on his hard chest. Our eyes lock and it feels as though the entire world around us fades away. His fingers grip my hips, and he pulls me into his lap, so I'm straddling him. As my body glides across his, I feel a hint of hardness beneath his pants.

When I raise my brows, he chuckles. "There's a beautiful

A CHANCE ENCOUNTER

woman on my lap." He shrugs nonchalantly, not at all embarrassed. "What do you think is going to happen?"

My cheeks and neck heat up at his words, and his grin widens. And my goodness, is his grin sexy as hell. His eyes light up with laughter at my obvious embarrassment and I tug on his beanie, lowering it enough to cover his eyes. This only makes him bark out a loud laugh, so I playfully cover his mouth with my hands to shut him up.

He bites the inside of my palm and I jump slightly. "You bit me! Thought you didn't bite, huh?"

"I couldn't help myself." He shrugs a single shoulder, lifting his beanie back over his eyes.

We stare at each other for several beats, and then he reaches up and tucks a few strands of my blond hair behind my ear and murmurs, "You have pretty eyes. They make me think of the city in the summer time after a hard rain. Fresh and clean."

I swallow thickly, shocked. Nobody has ever complimented my green eyes before. "Thank you," I mutter, feeling suddenly shy.

"Good," Rita says, breaking the trance. "How about if we move this into the grass? Oh, what about these rocks?"

I'm about to climb off Easton's lap, when he clasps his hands under my butt and lifts me. He walks us over to the cluster of rocks, like I weigh nothing, perching himself up against them with me sandwiched between.

"Good, good," Rita says. "You guys are perfect."

My legs wrap around Easton's waist, and my hands tighten around his neck.

"I never got your name," he says.

"Sophia."

"Beautiful name for a beautiful woman." And just like that, once again nothing exists but Easton and me.

Our faces are now close, too close. My eyes drop to his mouth as his tongue darts out, wetting his fleshy lips. And then, before I realize what's happening, his mouth is on mine. Warmth floods through my veins. It's been years since I've been kissed, touched. His lips are soft yet strong. His tongue traces my top lip, then my bottom one. I'm frozen in place, unsure of what to do, until his tongue slips into my mouth, finding my own, tasting me, coaxing my tongue to duel with his. He tastes like cinnamon: spicy yet refreshing.

He pulls me closer, and my center grinds against his hard length, making him groan into my mouth. Our kiss deepens.

A CHANCE ENCOUNTER

My fingers run through the hair at his nape, while his massage the globes of my ass.

And then Rita yells out, "Wow! Perfect," slicing through the moment.

We separate slightly, both of us panting. Easton's forehead rests against mine, and his eyes meet my own. "Let me take you to dinner."

I'm already shaking my head before he can finish his sentence. He can't become a distraction. I have too much on the line. I don't do dating or boyfriends or commitment. I do school and work and Kendall. But then he presses a soft kiss to my mouth and my lady parts nearly light on fire.

"I can't do dinner, but if you're looking to fuck, I can do that," I blurt out, flinching at how crass I sound. But in my defense, he's hot and I'm horny… and it's been a long-ass time. Plus, he's not trying to pick me up at the club and I'll never see him again after today.

A drop of liquid lands on my cheek, and then another one on my forehead. And when I glance up, I see the sky has opened up above us. Easton looks up as well, his lashes now darker and thicker from the raindrops that are soaking them.

The rain continues to come down, but neither of us moves.

"Have dinner with me," he says again, his eyes pleading for me to say yes.

"I can't," I repeat, as the rain strengthens and a boom of thunder makes its appearance.

"We better get out of the rain," Rita yells. "It came sooner than I expected."

Her words remind me where we are: in the park, in the rain, being photographed.

I scramble off Easton and run over to grab my bag since it's housing my very expensive laptop, and look around for where I can find shelter. He sidles up next to me, grabs my hand, and pulls me across the park as the rain pelts us from above. We keep running, until we end up in front of a building. Easton guides us inside, where it's dry, and then his lips crash against mine, his skillful mouth devouring my own.

"I want you," I murmur, fully aware I've lost my mind and am now begging a stranger, who I've known for mere minutes, to have sex with me.

Without argument, he lifts me into his arms and carries me over to the elevator. Our kiss never breaks. Not when we enter the elevator, nor when he walks us to a door and, with a press of a button, opens it. Our kiss doesn't break when he

A CHANCE ENCOUNTER

lays me on the bed and I drop my bag onto the floor.

In the back of my mind, I'm aware we're in a hotel room, obviously belonging to him, but I pay it no attention, only focusing on how good he tastes. We kiss for several minutes, until he breaks the kiss and his shirt comes off, exposing his chiseled chest and defined abs. I sit up and drag my fingers down each of the hard ridges, until I get to his waistband.

Easton lifts my shirt over my head and his mouth dips to the top of my bra, peppering kisses along the swells of my breasts. He pushes my chest down, so I'm lying flat on my back, and then continues working his way over the material of my bra, stopping briefly to suck on a nipple through the lace. He runs his tongue down my belly and, once my pants are off, kisses each of my hipbones before removing my panties.

He spreads my thighs and parts my folds and then goes to town, eating me out. Needing to touch him in some way, I pull his beanie off his head and delve my fingers through his inky hair. His mouth works me over, until I'm screaming out my much-needed release, my eyes closing in pleasure as white dots flash behind my lids.

I haven't come down from my high, when Easton's mouth is back on mine. I can taste myself on him and it's an aphrodisiac. I pull his pants down and wrap my legs around his backside, tugging him toward me. With his mouth fucking my own, his thick length enters me hard and deep, filling me up in the most delicious way. His hands land on either side of my head, and my fingers wrap around his corded biceps.

"Fuck me hard," I beg. He obliges, thrusting his hips forward and sinking inside me before he pulls back slightly, only to do it all over again. He picks up his pace, his dick rubbing my insides in the best way possible, as he fucks me with complete abandon.

All too quickly, my second orgasm rips through me, and as I'm coming down, mentally noting how good he feels, it hits me... "Shit! Pull out!" His eyes go wide, and he jerks back. His dick springs at attention and ropes of cum shoot out across my belly.

"I'm so sorry," he breathes. "I've never gone without a condom..."

"It's okay. We just got caught up in the moment." In the kissing, the touching, the rain... But now the moment is gone.

"Wait here," he says, climbing off the bed. "Let me get something to clean that off with." He quickly returns with a warm washcloth and wipes the stickiness off my stomach.

A CHANCE ENCOUNTER

"Would it be okay if I used your bathroom?" I ask, glancing at the clock and seeing that I won't have enough time to go home before I have to pick up Kendall from school.

"Yeah. There's two. Use this one, and I'll use the other." He hovers over me and kisses me softly. "Once you're dressed, be prepared for me to convince you to have dinner with me."

Without a word, I grab my clothes and close the door behind me. I drop onto the toilet and go pee, while I'm pulling my shirt over my head and my pants up my legs. When I'm done, I look at myself in the mirror and notice my mascara is running from the rain. I quickly wipe under my eyes and fix my hair the best I can and then head back out, snatching my bag up as I walk past the bed and out to the living room. My eyes scan the area, and when I don't see Easton, figuring he's still in the other bathroom, I slip out of the hotel room. There's no way I'm waiting around for him to convince me of anything.

I meant what I said: I can't be distracted.

Two

SOPHIA
A LITTLE OVER A MONTH LATER

"YOU'RE WHAT?" NAOMI SHRIEKS.

"Shh… keep it down. Kendall is sleeping." My girl works hard at school and when she gets home, she's wiped out and in need of a little power nap. After she has a snack, she always passes out for about an hour or so. And once she wakes up, we'll tackle her homework.

"I just don't understand how…"

"Well, when a man and a woman—"

"Stop being a smartass, bitch!" Naomi playfully slaps my arm. "I didn't even know you were having sex! And why the hell aren't you on birth control?"

"Because I'm not having sex."

She quirks a brow up and her eyes dart to my belly. "Could've fooled me."

"Well, I wasn't!" I huff. "Until I did... It was only one time." I go about telling her the details. The deadly bee. How I saved his life. How the photographer approached us... "I was horny," I tell her in my defense. "And he was there."

"And now your ass is knocked up."

"He pulled out," I groan, dropping my head into my hands. A few days ago, I woke up feeling sick. I thought it was all the candy I ate, since I've been scarfing that shit down since Halloween, but when the sickness continued on for several days, I knew something was wrong.

"I can't believe this happened. I should've known better. Of course the best sex of my life ends with me knocked up. Now I'm going to have two babies by two different guys." I look up at Naomi. "There's gotta be a trashy reality show with this plot somewhere."

Naomi laughs. "You should really get on birth control. It's obvious you're very fertile."

I hit her with a hard stare. "Sure, I'll get on birth control... *after* I have this baby."

She covers her mouth with her hand to hide her smile.

"Good idea."

I close my eyes and groan, stressed out, sick to my stomach, and exhausted. We literally had sex one time and he pulled out. I went to the doctor the following week and requested to be checked for STDs, but it must've been too soon to show up on the tests that I'm pregnant.

"What are you going to do?" Naomi asks, her tone turning serious.

I sigh and flop back, my head hitting the back of the couch. "Have the baby..."

"I know that, but are you going to try to find the baby's father? You know, if he's still alive..." She side-eyes me, but I ignore her comment, as well as the look she's giving me. We don't talk about Kendall's lack of a dad ever.

"And how would you expect me to find him? All I know is that his name is Easton and that a little over a month ago he was staying at The Penthouse."

"Maybe he's still there..."

"Yeah, maybe." Although I'm not sure why someone would stay at The Penthouse for over a month, or who in their right mind could afford to... "Would you mind watching Kendall while I go over there?"

"Of course not."

A little while later, I'm strolling through the lobby of The Penthouse, a luxurious hotel situated in front of Bryant Park.

When the receptionist calls me over, asking if I'm here to check in, I shake my head. "I'm actually looking for someone who was staying here. I'm wondering if maybe he's still here. His name is Easton, and he was staying in room…" Shit, I don't remember his room number, or the floor he was on, or anyfuckingthing other than how good of a kisser he was and how delicious his dick felt inside me.

Jesus, focus, Sophia.

"That's all I have," I tell her. "His first name."

She frowns. "Unfortunately, with only a first name, I'm not able to give you any information. We take our guests' privacy seriously."

"I get it. Thanks."

I walk outside and dial my gynecologist's number, so I can get the pregnancy confirmed. Maybe the test is wrong and I'm not pregnant—but even as I think it, I know I am, and the gynecologist will only confirm it. And once she does, I'll be back to square one, raising another fatherless baby. And law school? Well, I can kiss that goodbye. There's no way I'm going to be able to take care of Kendall, a new baby, and take law classes, while working at a law firm.

And I have no one to blame but myself. I never should've had sex with Easton that day, especially without protection. I know firsthand what unprotected sex leads to. The first time, I was eighteen and could chalk it up to ignorance and innocence and naivety, but now, I'm twenty-five and have no excuse. What I did was reckless and stupid, and now I have to deal with the fallout. I handled it back then and I'll handle it now.

WHOOSH, WHOOSH, WHOOSH, WHOOSH.

"...and that's the baby's heartbeat. According to the measurements and your estimated conception date, you're roughly six weeks along and everything looks good."

A tear slips out of my eye and slides down the side of my face, wetting my ear. Six weeks pregnant... I really am pregnant, and once again without a father.

"Soph, are you okay?" Naomi asks, squeezing my hand.

It's then I notice the nurse is gone, and it's just the two

of us, and I've been crying for who knows how long. "I don't think I can do this again," I admit, hating the words as they come out of my mouth.

"You know I'm not going to judge whatever decision you make, but I'm here for you, and you're not alone."

"I know." I sit up and wipe my eyes. "But you have Dante now, and your business. And it's not just about taking care of the baby… This isn't how I envisioned my life. I wanted a husband and a family. A home." Tears stream down my face.

"You have a home… *We* have a home."

"I can't let you put your life on hold for me, again." When I showed up here all those years ago, I could only work for so long because I was pregnant. And once I had Kendall, Naomi busted her ass to make money so we would survive until I was able to go back to work. We worked opposite shifts, so someone was always home with Kendall, and if we both had to go in, Dante was great about letting her sleep in his office. But things are different now, and Naomi deserves to move forward and live her life, and not be held down by my stupidity.

"You're not asking," she says, brushing her knuckles down my cheek. "And as far as finding a husband goes, when the

A CHANCE ENCOUNTER

time is right, you will find him. And having two beautiful babies won't keep him away."

After I get dressed, I make my next appointment with the receptionist, and then we head out. After we pick up Kendall from school, we stop at the pretzel stand, buying us each a hot pretzel since it's freezing outside. When we get home, Kendall asks if she can watch some television, falling asleep only minutes after her show begins.

"I was thinking," Naomi says. "You mentioned that guy and you took photos, right?"

"Yeah…" I glance up from my laptop. "The photographer said she would be displaying them on her website and in her gallery."

"So, let's have a look. Maybe his name is on them."

"Maybe, but I don't remember the name of her gallery. Only that her name was Rita." I pull up Google and type Rita and art gallery New York into the search bar, then click on the first website that pops up.

"That's her!" I point my finger at the woman on the screen next to the headline: Stranger Sessions. I scroll through picture after picture until I get to the ones I recognize.

"Holy shit!" Naomi gasps. "These are effing hot." She

snags my laptop from me and continues to scroll. She's right. They are hot, and if you didn't see the headline, you would think Easton and I were a real couple. Rita did an amazing job capturing us. From our awkwardness, to the laughing, to us kissing like we needed each other's oxygen to breathe.

"Damn, girl. He's sexy," Naomi points out, when we stop at one of Easton holding me in his arms with his head thrown back in laughter, his Adam's apple jutted out, and his chiseled jaw on display.

"Yeah, sexy enough I got caught up in the moment and got knocked up. I'm never having sex again."

Naomi snorts. "Don't say shit you don't mean."

"Whatever."

"There's a number here, call her." She reads off the number as I dial it on my phone. It rings several times before a voicemail starts. "Hello, this is Rita. I'm out of the country until after the first of the year. Please leave a message and I'll return your call as soon as possible. The gallery is open Monday through Sunday from eleven a.m. until five p.m."

I hang up. "Well, that won't help. Any other ideas?"

"Not yet," Naomi says, "but I'll keep thinking."

"Thank you." I pull her into a hug. "I can't imagine my life

A CHANCE ENCOUNTER

without you."

"And you'll never have to."

We spend the rest of the afternoon hanging out, and once Kendall wakes up, I help her with her homework while Naomi makes dinner. Afterward, I give Kendall a bath, and once eight o'clock rolls around, I put her to sleep and then head out to work. As long as I'm not showing, I can continue to work at the club, but I have no clue what I'll do for money once my baby bump appears.

The club is bustling tonight, and I don't get my first break until just after midnight. Like always, I pull my phone out so I can text Naomi and check on Kendall. Only when my phone lights up, there are a million notifications.

I click on the first one and it takes me to a post on Facebook. I read it three times before my brain accepts what I'm seeing.

Freaking Naomi.

She posted a couple pictures of Easton and me—ones where you can see his face completely, but you can't see mine, only the back of my head—with the caption: **MIA: Please share so we can find this man. It's life or death,** and has tagged me in the post.

I roll my eyes at her dramatics and click on the post. It's already been shared twelve thousand times and there are just as many comments. I scroll through the comments and am stunned by what I see.

Are you stupid? Everyone knows who this guy is.

OMG! Is this Easton's girlfriend? Lucky bitch.

I bet she's not showing her face because she's ugly.

In response to that one, someone wrote: **Yep! Her profile doesn't have any pics of her. Definitely ugly.**

My heart rate accelerates. I've made it a point to keep my profile set to private. I highly doubt after seven years Kendall's sperm donor even remembers I exist, but I'm not chancing it. Aside from my name—which is only my first and middle name—and my profile picture—which is of some flowers I took a picture of in Central Park, nobody can see anything from me: not what I look like, where I live… nothing. And I prefer it that way.

I continue to read more comments, stopping at one that mentions his last name.

Duh! Everyone knows who Easton Blackwood is.

The comments continue on. Some nice and some mean,

A CHANCE ENCOUNTER

but they all have one thing in common. Everyone, but me and Naomi, seems to know exactly who Easton is.

I pull up Google and type Easton Blackwood. The first site is Wikipedia. Curious as to how popular this guy is, I click on it, and sure enough, the father of my baby's face pops up. It says he's a musician and—

My stalking is put on hold by my phone ringing.

"Hello?"

"Oh my God, don't kill me but—"

"I know, I saw."

"So, you know you're knocked up by a music sensation who's worth over a half a billion dollars?"

I gasp in shock. "I hadn't gotten that far yet, but yes, I'm aware the man I had sex with is famous. How do we not know him?"

"Probably because we listen to mostly country music."

"Hey, I listen to other stuff... Like Jordan Walker."

Naomi laughs. "You only listen to Jordan Walker because he showed up at the club that one time and gave you a lady boner."

"He was hella hot." I shrug even though she can't see me.

"You're getting off course..."

"Sorry."

"I listened to his music and it's good. He sings that song, "Lost." The one that Kendall loves to sing and dance to."

"Yeah…" I know exactly which one she's talking about, but I didn't know who sang it. When we're baking or cooking, I'll put my Apple Music on shuffle so we can dance to the music. But it doesn't mention who sings which song.

"He's on some world tour right now," Naomi adds, "and since it's sold out, because he's so famous, they've added several more shows."

I close my eyes and drop my head against the wall. How can this be happening? My mission in life has been to remain low, in the shadows, and not only did I get knocked up by someone famous, but he's also apparently one of the most popular musicians out there right now. This is like the definition of not low.

"This is bad," I say out loud. "So, so freaking bad."

"Maybe not…"

"How the hell not?" I hiss. "What am I supposed to do? Message him and be like, 'Hey, so remember back in September when you asked me to dinner while we were getting our picture taken, and I refused, begging you to fuck me because I was horny and you were hot, and then afterward, I ran out the door while you were in the bathroom... Well, I got knocked up, and surprise, you're the daddy!' Do you know how many women have probably pulled that same move on him? And even if he does believe me, who's to say he'll even want the baby."

We both go silent at my final words, knowing this is really my fear. My father didn't want me. Kendall's father didn't want her—even if I pretend he's dead—and now I'm pregnant by some famous guy, who has women falling all over him.

"If I tell him and he says he doesn't want anything to do with this baby, I'm scared it might be my breaking point," I admit softly.

"Oh, Soph." Naomi sighs. "There's a chance he might say that, but maybe he won't. You won't know until you try. Plus, it takes two to make a baby, which means he was just as much a part of this as you were."

"Yeah, I know, but I'm still nervous. He's probably going to think I'm after his money, and it doesn't help I work at a strip club."

"Don't you dare go there," Naomi says. "You're a single mom, who has worked her ass off to provide for her daughter and get through college. There's no shame in what you do for a living, and if anyone tries to tell you otherwise, you tell them where to shove it. Got it?"

I laugh softly, loving my cousin for having my back. "I got it."

"Besides, you're not even a stripper anymore. You're a bartender. And soon you'll be a lawyer."

"I have to get into law school first…" I figured out, that since my due date is in June, unless the baby comes way early, I can graduate on time, have the baby, and still be able to apply to law schools for the fall. I have no idea how I'm going to juggle everything, but I'm going to damn sure try.

"You'll get in," she tells me. "Have a little faith."

I release a harsh breath. "My break is almost over, and I'm starving. I'm going to grab something to eat. I'll see you in the morning."

"Love you, Soph."

"Love you more."

"Impossible."

We hang up and I click on the internet, backing out and clicking on the images. Hundreds pop up, of him with dozens of different women, at award shows, on the streets, in fancy cars, out at clubs, confirming my suspicions that he is in fact a ladies' man, and what's worse is he's everywhere, in the spotlight, where I need to stay out of. I click out of the internet then pocket my phone, needing to get back to work. I'll deal with this later.

Three

EASTON

"THIS WEEK WE HAVE A SHOW IN ST. LOUIS, THEN TWO IN ATLANTA. FROM there, we'll stop in Tampa for one show, and then head down to Miami." My sister hands me the printout of my itinerary, knowing I'm not going to remember any of this shit—even if it's on my calendar and in my reminders on my phone.

"When do we go back to New York?"

She eyes me speculatively, and I make a mental note to check my calendar myself so she doesn't ask me questions. "We'll be back the second week of December. You'll have a couple weeks off for the holidays, aside from the New Year's show you're performing at, and the charity concert you're attending as a guest, and then you'll have another four weeks on tour.

I nod and lean back against the couch in the tour bus. It's late, and I'm exhausted from having four shows in five days, but I can't complain because I only have that many shows because my fans are loyal enough to buy tickets—enough that my record label has added several shows to the lineup.

"Easton, what's going on with you?" she asks. "You've been acting different lately... antsy. And instead of wanting to go home, you're wanting to go to New York, which in itself is strange, since you hate that city."

I knew she'd catch on—Nicole notices everything. It's why she's part of my PR team as well as my assistant—and the best damn one I've ever had.

I consider telling her about what happened in New York, about the woman I met, who rocked my world in the short time we were together, but it's pointless. The only thing I know about her is that her name is Sophia. I had never done anything like what I did with her. From the photography shoot, to kissing her, to bringing her back to my room. That's not who I am. How I operate. I don't do spontaneous, and I definitely don't fuck random women. But when I asked her out and she turned me down and instead propositioned me, I was stunned. I was attracted to her, and for the first time

A CHANCE ENCOUNTER

in a long time, I went with my gut instead of thinking shit through.

I want to go back to New York in hope of finding her, but what are the chances in a city filled with millions of people that I'll ever see her again? I contacted that photographer, hoping she would have her last name, but she's out of the country. I don't really have a plan to find this woman, except to stalk Bryant Park... and that's not exactly an ideal plan.

"Easton!" Nicole barks. "You need to talk to me. Did something happen in LA that's making you not want to go home? What the hell is going on? As your assistant, I need to know... and as your sister, it's killing me not to know."

"He's in looovvve," Jordan, my best friend and opener, says with a laugh.

I chuck a pillow at him, smacking him right in the face. "I'm not in love." It's too soon for that shit.

Nicole gasps. "Oh my God, who are you in love with?"

"I just said I'm not in love. You're going to believe that fool over me?" Who am I kidding? Of course she's going to believe him. Because she's in love with, and engaged to, him. Two facts I pretend don't exist. It's the reason why she's on tour with us, when she usually only shows up occasionally, because she doesn't want to leave her fiancé—the two of them are attached at the damn hip.

"Well, you're something," Jordan says, throwing the pillow back at me. "The only times I've seen that look on your face was in the tenth grade when Rosalinda Pierce kissed you during spin the bottle and when Ashleigh said yes to marrying—"

"Don't go there," Nicole warns, cutting him off.

Jordan flinches, then shoots me an apologetic look, knowing the mention of my ex, Ashleigh, is a touchy subject for me. It's been years, but her betrayal still runs deep.

"Look, I'm not in love," I tell them. "I met a woman at the park and we kind of hit it off…"

"Wait a second." Nicole grabs her phone and types away. "It wouldn't happen to be this woman, would it?" She turns her phone around and on the screen is a photo of Sophia and me from the impromptu photo shoot. I know this because I have every one of them saved to my phone—have looked at them no less than a dozen times.

"It is, isn't it?" She shrieks.

"How did you get this?" I ask, as Jordan comes over and looks over her shoulder at the photo.

"Preston emailed me regarding them, asking if he missed a photo shoot and if he should post them on your social media and website. I was going to ask you about them, but I got sidetracked. What shoot are these from?"

"They're not from a shoot…"

Nicole raises a brow, and I sigh, knowing she's going to freak out when I tell her what I did. All press shit and photo shoots have to be approved by the label—luckily, the label is Blackwood Records, owned by our parents.

When I finish explaining what happened—leaving out the part about us having sex in my hotel room afterward because that shit isn't her business—my sister is speechless, and Jordan is grinning like a damn fool.

"Where did you find the photos anyway?" Maybe they'll lead me to Sophia.

"On social media. Apparently, you've been tagged in them, but I haven't had a chance to check it all out yet. I was working out the details for the New Year's Eve performance at Times Square for Jordan."

"You got in?" I ask him.

"Yeah, someone backed out," he says.

"That's awesome, man." I extend my fist and bump

knuckles with him. Jordan went the college route, majoring in music. After he graduated, he took a job working for my family's record label, in the studio. A few years later, he came to me and said he wanted to record but needed some guidance. He had a shit load of songs but needed help with the exposure, wanting to do it right. Of course I told him we'd help him. Unlike my music, which is more pop and contemporary R & B—think Justin Bieber, pre-finding Jesus days—meets Justin Timberlake, post-NSYNC—Jordan's is a bit more hip hop with a bit of rap thrown in—a Drake meets Dre vibe. I suggested we collaborate on a track and it blew the hell up. People wanted more. So the record label gave them more, and a year later, he's opening for me on my fifth tour. There's nothing better than doing what you love, except doing it with the people you love.

Jordan wraps his arms around Nicole and she snuggles into his chest. He kisses her temple and she smiles up at him. My heartstrings tug slightly, wishing I could find what they've found. What my parents, who've been married for over thirty years, found. I thought I found it once, but it turned out to be a lie.

"It says here, that woman, Sophia, is looking for you,"

Nicole says, snapping me from my thoughts.

"What?" She goes to hand me her phone, but I pull mine out instead. "Send me the link."

A second later, a text comes through from her. I click on it and it takes me to the post made a few weeks ago by a Naomi Stratton. Sophia is tagged in it. The post is a couple pictures of us and she's asking people to share it so she can find the guy in the picture—me—because it's life or death. What the hell…

I scroll through the comments, laughing at some of them asking how they don't know who I am. I was kind of shocked myself. I thought for sure she would say something, but when she didn't, and turned me down for dinner, I knew she didn't know me—which only made me want her that much more.

I click on Sophia's page, but it's all set to private, only showing her name, which reads Sophia Marie, which I'm guessing is her middle name and not her last. I send her a friend request and then click on the button to send her a message. As I'm contemplating what to write, I notice Jordan and Nicole are staring at me.

"I'm going to lie down," I tell them, standing.

"What? C'mon! You can't leave us hanging," Nicole says

with a pout.

"Let the guy have some privacy," Jordan remarks, snagging her phone from her and setting it on the table. When he kisses her, successfully distracting her, I sneak away into my room, closing the door behind me. Thankfully the tour bus is plenty big, and instead of having several bunks, this bus has two bedrooms and two bathrooms. It also has a completely functional kitchen, as well as a living room and dining area. Touring can get lonely as hell, so it's nice to get to share it with my best friend.

I stare at the screen for several seconds, considering what to write, but in the end, I go with playful.

Me: What's up, Dash? Heard you were looking for me...

I laugh to myself at the nickname, wondering if she'll get it. A few seconds later, it shows she's online, has accepted my friend request, and accepted my message request.

Sophia Marie: Dash?

That's it? She went through all that work to find me and she sends me a one-word response. Figures.

Me: Yeah, you know... Dine and dash... cause you dined on my dick and then dashed. ;)

A CHANCE ENCOUNTER

When she doesn't respond right away, I worry my joke was too much. I hardly know this woman.

The bubbles appear and I hold my breath, waiting to see how she's going to respond, praying she doesn't block me, and then her message comes through, making me laugh.

Sophia Marie: Ha ha. Hilarious. Didn't know you were expecting payment.

She has a sense of humor. Nice.

Me: Your number would've been payment enough.

She responds a second later with **You knew the score** and I shake my head. Fucking woman... she's unlike any other woman I've met. Most women are begging me for my number, sometimes even going to great lengths to steal it, not dipping out after sex without so much as a goodbye.

Me: Yeah, I did. Which is why I'm curious as to why you've been searching for me... You hungry, Dash?

There, the ball is back in her court. Let's see how she talks—well, writes—her way out of this one. While I'm waiting for her to respond, I click on her name and change it to Dash just to mess with her.

Dash: Oh my God. Really? Is this name sticking? Most

guys would call what we did, what I did after, a dream come true.

Her message is meant to be funny, and I could be wrong, but I'm sensing some underlying meaning behind her words. Maybe it's just the artist in me overthinking and analyzing shit.

Me: The name is sticking. And most guys are dumbasses.

Dash: I need to talk to you.

Well, okay then. Mood shift.

Me: I figured that, based on the "life or death" part of the post.

Dash: That was just Naomi being dramatic AF. No one is dying, but we do need to talk.

Me: I can call you now...

Dash: Probably better in person.

Shit, please don't tell me she has an STD. I got checked afterward but...

Me: I'm on tour, heading to St. Louis. I can fly you out.

The second I hit send, I wonder what the hell I'm thinking. I don't know this girl and I'm offering to fly her out... and do what? Hang out with me on my bus? At the concerts?

Dash: No can do. I'm in school.

Damn, how old is she?

Me: How old are you?

Dash: 16

What the fuck!

Dash: Kidding…I'm 25. I'm in my last year of college.

Me: You damn near gave me a heart attack!

I pull up my calendar to see if I have any time off to fly to New York and back, but I have a show just about every day. It doesn't help that we added extra nights.

Me: I'll be in NY in December for the holidays. I can meet you then.

Sucks I'll have to wait a few weeks to find out what she needs to tell me, but there's nothing I can do about it.

Dash: Okay, that'll work. Message me when you're in town and we'll meet up.

Me: What's your last name?

Dash: Davis

I try to think of a way to continue the conversation, not wanting it to end, but before I can come up with something else to ask or say, she adds: **I'm off to bed. Good night,** effectively ending the conversation.

I shoot back a good night, but it goes unread since she's already gotten off.

Four

SOPHIA

"I'M STUMBLING THROUGH THE DARK, LOST..." KENDALL BELTS THE LYRICS OF Easton's latest song, "Lost," at the top of her lungs while we mix the batter for the cookies we're making for her Christmas party she's having with her friends from school tomorrow. Today was her last day of school, and tomorrow we're meeting her friends and their moms at the ice-skating rink for a little Christmas party. All the girls are bringing something and will be spending the afternoon skating.

"... lost in the dark, with no chance of being found..."

I press pause on my phone, and she glares at me. "It was just getting to the good part." She huffs.

"How about we listen to some Christmas music?" I suggest. Because if I hear that damn song one more time, I might toss my phone out of our second story window.

"Okay!" She grabs my phone and types something in then the music starts… and Easton's voice fills the silence. Seriously? The guy has a freaking Christmas album?

I plaster on a fake smile, reminding myself that it's not my daughter's fault I'm freaking out over my upcoming meeting with Easton, and Kendall and I go back to mixing the cookie dough.

"Wow, isn't it festive in here?" Naomi says, as she and Dante walk in.

"We're making cookies!" Kendall squeals.

"I can see that." Naomi walks over and kisses her on the top of her head, before glancing at me. "How are you feeling?"

"Okay." I don't say anything more, knowing little ears are always listening. Since I'm just about to hit the twelve-week mark, I've decided to wait to tell anyone until after my next appointment. I'll be thirteen weeks and in my second trimester. I would hate to tell Kendall she's going to have a little brother or sister and then lose the baby and have to explain that to her. My last pregnancy, I wouldn't have thought like that, but this one has been different. Last week I was in the hospital for bleeding. I thought for sure I was losing the baby, and it was in that moment, I knew, no matter how hard it'll be, no matter how much my life is going to change, again, I already love this baby and want him or her. The doctor told me to rest, so I took a few days off, but I go back to work tonight.

"We have something we need to tell you guys," Naomi says, looking a little nervous.

"Well, tell us!" I prompt when she doesn't continue.

"We're... engaged!" She shrieks, holding up her ring.

"Oh my God!" I pull her into a hug. "Congratulations. When did this happen?" I grip her ring finger to admire the beautiful stone.

"Last night," Dante says.

"You did well." I give him a hug. "I'm so happy for you guys. Now you'll get to plan your own wedding." I waggle my brows, knowing how much Naomi has been waiting for this day to come. Every event she plans, she tells me how she would do it differently if it were hers. She has books of notes saved for the day she gets to plan her engagement party and wedding.

"Does this mean I get to be the flower girl?" Kendall asks, licking a spoon of cookie mix.

"Yes, you do." Naomi lifts her and spins in a circle. "And you won't have to wait long because we're getting married this summer."

I almost choke on my own saliva. "This summer? Like in six months?"

"More like seven. We're planning for after the Fourth of July. There's no way I'm getting married in the winter and I'm not waiting eighteen months…"

"Wow," I say, shocked.

"And there's more," Dante adds, his voice taking on an excited tone.

Naomi shakes her head so quickly, if I weren't looking at her, I wouldn't have seen it. Dante flinches, and my stomach drops.

"What else?" I direct my question at Dante.

"It's nothing," Naomi begins.

"Then tell me."

"Dante bought us a house. I had showed him a home I loved one day, not thinking he would actually buy it, but apparently it was for sale and the owners were anxious to sell. He closed on it yesterday. It was a surprise."

"Which is why he proposed," I say, putting the pieces

together. He bought her her dream home and then asked her to marry him. Can it get any more romantic than that? "When are you moving out?"

My mind is reeling. Our lease is up soon, and there's no way I can afford this place on my own, so I'm going to have to start looking for a new place to live. Which would be fine, except we live in New York where shoebox-size apartments cost thousands, and anything bigger will damn near cost you your soul, and then there's the fact that in a couple months, I'm going to start showing and I won't be able to work at the club anymore...

"Soph, breathe," Naomi says, "you're starting to hyperventilate."

"Mommy, what's wrong?" Kendall asks, her tone filled with worry.

"I'm okay," I tell her, grabbing a chair and sitting.

"This is why I wanted to talk to you about this later," Naomi says, glaring at Dante, who looks at me sheepishly. "I'm not moving out until after the holidays, and I'm going to pay my half of the rent and bills until the lease is up. We'll figure it all out, I promise."

I snap my head up at the sympathy in her words. She just

bought a home and got engaged. She should be excited, not worrying about me.

"I'm fine," I tell her, plastering a smile on my face—I seem to be doing that a lot lately. "I'm so happy for you. I was just in shock…"

"She was too," Dante admits. "She didn't know. If she had, she would've told you."

"I know." I nod robotically. "Seriously, I'm so happy for you guys," I repeat, needing her to know I mean that.

"Maybe you and Kendall could move in with us," Naomi suggests, like the best friend she is. This is exactly what I meant about wanting her to be able to move forward with her life. I knew if I chose to keep this baby, she would be all in, and if I asked her to, she would choose us over everything and anyone else. Because she has the biggest heart. But I can't let her do that. She deserves everything that's happening to her and I won't let her put us above her own future and happiness.

"I appreciate that, but we knew this day would come." My eyes meet hers. "I love you more than life itself, Naomi Stratton, and I've loved every moment we've spent living together, but it's time for you to focus on you."

Tears fill her eyes. "But, Soph…" Her eyes glance down at my still-flat belly, and I shake my head, not wanting to have this conversation now. Only Dante is observant and catches on quickly. When I took the days off after my hospital scare, I lied and said I had the flu.

"You're…" His gaze descends.

"Yeah." I nod. "I was planning to tell you soon. I'm going to have to put my notice in at the club." And then I'll be jobless. I've applied for a million different secretarial positions, hoping to snag one at a law office, to get my foot in the door, but I haven't gotten any callbacks.

"Bullshit," he says. "You're not putting in your notice. We'll figure this out."

"Ohhh, Dante said a bad word," Kendall says, breaking the tension in the room. "Now you have to do a chore."

Dante chuckles, as Kendall leans in and whispers into my ear, loud enough that everyone can hear. "Make him clean my room."

Naomi snorts out a laugh and Dante shakes his head. When Kendall is listening to music, sometimes they have bad words in them, so she likes to try to get away with saying them. Every time she says a bad word, I tell her she has to do a chore.

"Dante's an adult, so he can curse," I explain.

"Does that mean when I'm an adult, I get to curse too?" she asks, her eyes going wide in excitement.

Guess I walked right into that one...

"Yes, when you're eighteen."

She pouts. "That's so far away. Like a hundred years," she says, stepping back onto the stool to continue making the cookies, while we all laugh at her dramatics.

"I have to get to the club," Dante says, kissing Naomi. Then he looks at me. "We'll talk later."

Once he's gone, Naomi tries to talk to me about everything, but I shoo her away, just wanting to make cookies with Kendall. It's bad enough I have to have a serious conversation with Easton later.

Speaking of Easton, my phone dings with a message. We hadn't messaged since the night he contacted me, until two days ago, when he told me he would be arriving in town today and asked if I could meet him. I figured he would want a day to decompress, and mentioned as much, but he told me he's fine and would like to meet. Naomi said he's probably anxious to find out what I need to tell him. When she said he probably thinks I'm going to tell him I have an STD, I laughed and told her after I tell him the real news, he'll wish that's what my news was.

Easton: We're still on for 6:00?

Me: Yep. I'll meet you at the Starbucks off 3rd and 61st.

It's close to the club, so afterward, I can go straight to work.

Easton: See you then.

"You ready for this?" Naomi asks, glancing over my shoulder.

"No, but it is what it is." I shrug. Everything is changing. That's part of life and all I can do is roll with it.

Naomi, Kendall, and I spend the afternoon baking and decorating cookies. Once we're done, she keeps an eye on Kendall while I jump in the shower and get ready for work. My pants are already tight around my waist, so it won't be long before I'll need new clothes and a new job—I know Dante said we'll talk, but I'm not going to let him pay me when I can't work. I didn't save anything from my pregnancy with Kendall, so I'm going to have to go shopping soon.

After explaining to Kendall I have a meeting, which is

why I'm leaving early and Aunt Naomi will be putting her to bed tonight, I kiss her goodbye and head out. It's cold outside, and light flutters of snow are falling, but since I have on my thick, warm coat, and the roads are still dry, I walk to the Starbucks instead of flagging down a taxi.

When I arrive, I glance around and immediately spot Easton sitting in the booth with a hat and hoodie over his head, like he's trying to hide... And then it hits me, he was wearing a beanie that day in the park to hide himself because he's famous. And when he asked me when I could meet, he suggested we meet at his place, but I insisted we meet somewhere public. Shit, I didn't even think about that.

When he looks up and sees me, he stands, but I shake my head and pull out my phone to message him.

Me: I'll grab our coffees. What do you like?

Easton: I would argue I should be buying, but I appreciate you doing that so I'm not seen. Whatever you get is fine. Thanks.

I order two drinks and two pastries, then walk over to the other counter to wait for my name to be called. When the barista calls out, "Dash," I glance at Easton, who laughs.

"Here you go," I tell him, setting our drinks and food

down.

"Thanks." He takes the drink and has a sip, nearly choking on it. "What the hell is this?" he splutters.

"A cocoa cloud macchiato with extra chocolate drizzle." I've been craving chocolate like crazy this pregnancy.

"Does it even have any caffeine in it?" he asks through a cough. "Or is it just pure chocolate?"

"It has caffeine in it… but definitely more chocolate." I take a sip of my delicious drink. "Thanks for meeting with me."

He sets his drink down and gives me his attention, his brown eyes reminding me of the drizzled chocolate in our drinks. Maybe I can pick up marshmallows, and Kendall and I can make s'mores…

Easton clears his throat, and I jump slightly, remembering where I am. I blame the cravings, mental distractions, and detours on the pregnancy.

"Sorry." I take a deep breath, then begin. "As you know, in September, when we met, we went back to your hotel room and had sex."

The corners of Easton's lips curl into a sexy smile. "Yeah, I remember."

I ignore his comment, needing to get this all out before I chicken out. "It had been a while since I had sex and since I wasn't actively having sex, I wasn't on birth control." His eyes go wide, the cogs in his brain turning. "I didn't mean for this to happen and I don't want anything from you," I continue quickly. "I just wanted you to know that I'm pregnant, in case you want to have something to do with the baby when he or she is born. And also, I would like to add, in my defense, you went in without a condom and I was the one who reminded you to pull out, so if you try to say I tricked you, that will only make you look like an asshat.

"And I know you're thinking that since you pulled out, I shouldn't be pregnant, but there is such a thing called precum, and plus, you could've easily come before you pulled out. You're the only person I've had sex with, but I'm sure you hear that a lot, so if you want a paternity test, I'm completely okay with that... Or maybe you don't want anything to do with the baby and in which case—"

"Whoa," he says, cutting me off. I suck in a sharp breath, needing the intake of oxygen from my longwinded speech. "I know what went down. I was there. It was just as much my fault as it was yours."

I breathe out a sigh of relief and nod.

"So, you're pregnant? It's been confirmed?" He swallows thickly and his Adam's apple bobs in his throat. My thoughts go back to our time together and the way it did that when he was fucking me. I wanted so badly to lick my way up his throat...

He clears his throat, again, and I shake away my sexual thoughts. "Yes, it's been confirmed. I have my three-month appointment next week if you'd like to go. I'm due in June. But like I was saying, if you don't want anything to do with the baby, I'll understand, but I think—"

"Can you stop doing that," he growls.

"Doing what?" I squeak out.

"Giving me a damn out. This baby is as much mine as it is yours."

Five

EASTON

HOLY. SHIT. I KNEW THIS WAS A POSSIBILITY. THERE ARE ONLY TWO REASONS A woman contacts you after sex: she either has an STD or she's pregnant. I haven't personally experienced either one, but I know a lot of guys who have. Still, hearing her say the words is a shock to my system. It's one thing to think it, but it's another to actually hear it. And if learning she's pregnant isn't enough, it's clear the woman in front of me is freaking the hell out. So, instead of me processing what all of this means, I'm trying to figure out how to calm her down.

My hand goes to her shaking one, and I squeeze it, hoping it will help calm her. I didn't mean to snap at her, but she's making judgments without asking. I get she's nervous, but like I told her, I was there. I know what went down, and I know she wasn't trying to trap me. I never stick it in without a condom, but I was so wrapped up in her, well, I forgot to literally wrap it up. And that's on me as much as it's on her.

"I don't know what piece of shit guys you've been hanging out with," I say, making sure my voice remains calm, "but I was raised to take responsibility for my actions. I don't want or need an out."

She bobs her head, then removes her hand from mine, taking a sip of her coffee. "I understand, but taking responsibility can be done in different ways. I'm not asking you for any money, but if your way of taking responsibility is through money, I'm okay with that."

Da fuck?

"So, what you're saying is, you looked me up and saw that I have money, and instead of wanting me to be a dad to this baby, you want me to pay you off?"

If she thinks that's going to happen, she has another thing coming.

Her eyes go wide. "What? No," she chokes out. "That came out wrong. This conversation is not going as I planned." She releases a harsh breath. "What I'm trying to say is that if you don't want to be a dad, you don't have to be. You should probably think about it for a little while because being a parent is a life-long commitment and I would rather you say now you don't want to be in this baby's life than a few years from now after he or she is attached to you."

"Who hurt you? Was it your mom or your dad?"

Her eyes bug out, telling me I've hit the nail on the head. One of her parents didn't want her and now she's deflecting that hurt and fear on me.

"It doesn't matter," she says defensively, standing.

I assume my question has pissed her off and she's going to leave, but instead she unbuttons and removes her coat, draping it over the back of the chair. Underneath, she's wearing a tight black shirt and even tighter pants. She doesn't look pregnant, but her stomach isn't as flat as it was a few months ago.

She sits back down and her arms cross over her chest. Naturally, my eyes land on the swells of her breasts that are spilling out of the top of her shirt. The memory of kissing my way along her flesh hits me hard and I have to force my gaze back up to her face, which doesn't help any. Because when I look at her, all I see is her plump red lips that tasted delicious when I sucked them into my mouth, her emerald eyes I got lost in as she begged me to fuck her harder. Her blond hair is perfectly straight today, in a high ponytail, but that day it was down in waves, splayed out across my pillow. When I went to sleep that night, I could smell her sweet scent on my sheets. Unlike the last time I saw her, today she's wearing a bit of makeup. The natural look on her was beautiful, but with makeup on, she looks downright sexy—it's as if she's somehow two different women. Both equally attractive.

"What?" she asks, catching me checking her out.

"Nothing. You look gorgeous today. Different from the day at the park... More done up."

"Oh." Her teeth bite down on her bottom lip and a slight blush creeps across her neck and cheeks, giving her creamy complexion a little bit of color. "That's because I have to go to work after I leave here. The day you saw me I only had school."

I nod. "So, where do we go from here?" I ask, getting us back on track. "I want to be in this baby's life."

She smiles softly, and I'm thankful it seems she's done trying to convince me otherwise. "My doctor's appointment is next week. You could go with me if you want. I guess we could start there." Her teeth go back to gnawing on her bottom lip, and I have a feeling she has something else she wants to say.

"What?"

"Well, it's just that… for right now, I'd like to keep this between us. I'm still in my first trimester and I've already had one scare…"

That has my attention. "What do you mean a scare?"

"I had some bleeding." She waves it off like it's not a big deal. "Anyway, I just think it's best if we don't tell anyone yet, in case something happens or if you change your mind."

She has got to be kidding me right now. It seems to be one step forward and two back with her. I swallow down my anger, not wanting to upset her, especially knowing that she's had issues with her pregnancy and her accusation stems from something personal—which I'll get her to talk about soon enough—and take a deep, calming breath.

"I'm going to tell my family. We're close and I don't keep things from them. But as far as posting it or announcing it for the world to know, I won't do that until you're okay with it."

She sighs, in what looks like relief, and I mentally shake my head. So. Damn. Different. Most women would want to be shouting that shit from the rooftops. Using it to gain exposure. But not Sophia. She wants to keep it on the down-low.

"Thank you," she says, standing again. "I have to get to work, but I'll message you the information for next week."

I spot the logo on her shirt: Emerald's. Where do I know that name from? And then it hits me. It's a high-class gentleman's club. She works at a strip club?

"Is that where you work?" I ask, nodding toward the name on her shirt.

She stiffens, then grabs her coat to put it back on. "Yeah."

"If you need money…"

Her eyes light on fire and I know right away it was the wrong thing to say. "Don't you go there." She points her finger at me. "I'm a bartender and I have no problem paying my own damn bills. You want to be in this baby's life, fine. Good. But that does not mean you have any right to judge any aspect of my life, including where I work. Got it?"

I raise my palms in surrender. "I didn't mean it like that. You said you had a scare, and this baby is mine too. I just want to help in any way I can."

"I don't need anything from you," she says, snatching up her coffee and pastry she never ate from the table. "I'll see you later."

A CHANCE ENCOUNTER

She turns her back on me and exits the coffee shop, leaving me sitting here speechless and in shock. I consider going after her, to talk to her, to make sure she makes it to work okay, but stop myself. Sophia Davis is independent as fuck and I'm going to have to remember that if I want to make any progress with her.

Which makes me wonder... What progress do I want to make with her? Sure, I want to be able to talk to her about our baby, and I definitely want an active role in our baby's life. But before I found out she was pregnant, I wanted to find her and get to know her, and not as the mother of my baby, because I didn't know she was pregnant. I was hoping to find she was still single and we could get to know each other. And I still want that. Only now it's going to be that much harder because I'm going to have to convince her I want her for her and not because she's pregnant with my baby. Fuck, do I have my work cut out for me.

I step outside and the snow is falling hard. White shit covering the ground everywhere. I groan, hating this damn city. It's why, even though my parents live here the majority of the time, I live in LA full-time—where it's warm and there's no damn snow and I can drive my own vehicle. Looks like I'm going to have to get used to it, though. I've refused to buy a place here, only staying at hotels or with my family when I visit, but now things have changed, and I'm going to be here more often as long as Sophia and my baby are here, which means I'm going to need to look into buying a place.

Instead of going back to my hotel, I find myself at my parents' house, knocking on their door. Yes, knocking on their door, because at any given time, they could be naked since they can't keep their hands off each other.

Mom answers the door with a wide smile on her face. She's still dressed in her work clothes—a smart pantsuit and heels—her brown hair up in one of those tight bun things, making her look every bit the shrewd businesswoman she is.

"Well, isn't this a pleasant surprise," she says, pulling me in for a warm hug. Alicia Blackwood can be a hard-ass. When she's at work, she runs a tight ship as the VP of Blackwood Records, next to my dad, who is the president. She doesn't take shit from anyone, saying it's ten times harder for a woman to get the respect she deserves. But as a mom, she's the complete opposite. Warm and comforting. She's the definition of home.

"I need to talk to you and Dad."

A CHANCE ENCOUNTER

She opens the door so I can go in. "Sean, Easton is here and needs to talk to us."

Moments later, my sister and Jordan appear, along with my dad. "What's going on?" Nicole asks, concern etched in her features. I didn't know she and Jordan were here, but I guess it's for the best. I can tell everyone at once.

"I'm starved," Dad says, already dressed down in a white Blackwood Records long-sleeved shirt and black sweats. "Can we talk over dinner?"

"Why wasn't I invited to dinner?" I ask with a pout, as we walk into the kitchen and I smell Mom's famous empanadas. She's Venezuelan, moved to California with her family when she was ten. Even though she's lived in the U.S. for the majority of her life, she loves to make dishes from where she's from, dishes her mom used to make when she was alive, and none of us complain one bit, because those dishes are delicious as hell.

"You were," she says. "Check your phone." I pull it out and sure enough, there's a group text with her inviting everyone to dinner.

"My bad. I was meeting with someone, which is what I need to talk to you guys about." I help Mom finish placing the food on the table then we all have a seat. Everyone goes about making their plates of food, and I waste no time grabbing several empanadas and loading my plate up with some beans and rice.

"Hey, save some for us," Jordan says, snatching the spoon for the rice from me.

I take a huge bite of food and moan at the deliciousness.

Everyone eats in blissful silence for a few minutes before Dad speaks up. "What did you need to talk to us about, Son?"

I swallow my food and take a sip of my water to wash it down. "A few months back, while I was in town visiting for Dad's birthday, I met a woman."

Mom's gaze swings over at me, her food forgotten.

Nicole smiles knowingly.

My dad and Jordan keep eating.

"I kind of, umm…" I clear my throat. "I got her pregnant."

Mom and Nicole gasp, and Jordan's and Dad's jaws drop.

"You did what?" Mom yells, before she starts going off on me in Spanish. I don't know everything she's saying, but I have no doubt she's cursing me to hell.

"What were you thinking?" Dad asks, running his hand along his face.

A CHANCE ENCOUNTER

"You didn't mention you slept with her," Nicole adds.

"You knew about this?" Mom's gaze darts over to my sister.

"I knew he met someone," she says. "They took photos together that were spread all over social media."

"Oh Lord," Mom groans. "You took pictures with her? What were you thinking?"

"Not those kind of photos," I clarify. "We had all our clothes on."

"So what does she want?" Dad asks, going into manager mode. "And are you sure you're the dad? You're going to need to get a paternity test."

"I'll make an appointment with Daniel," Nicole says, already typing away on her phone. Daniel is the family's personal attorney. The label has a firm on retainer, but because it could be seen as a conflict of interest, we use a separate firm for our personal needs.

"She doesn't want anything," I tell them. Eight pairs of eyes land on me, all displaying various looks of disbelief. And I get it, in the world we live in, everyone wants something— but Sophia isn't from our world and she's different. Don't ask me how I know that when I've only met her twice, but I can feel it.

89

"Is that why she was looking for you?" Nicole asks.

"She was looking for you?" Mom's brows knit together in confusion.

"She didn't know who I was when we… had sex, and now that she does, I don't think she's too pleased. When she told me, she flat out said she doesn't expect me to be in the baby's life and that she's fine with that. When I offered her some money, she yelled at me and pretty much told me where I could shove it. She also asked me not to tell anyone about the pregnancy."

"What the hell?" Mom hisses. "Of course if the baby's yours, you'll be in his or her life, and how dare she get upset at you for trying to do the right thing." I can hear it in her tone she's not fond of Sophia, and the last thing I want is for my family to dislike her, so I explain…

"I think she's just scared and maybe cynical. It seemed like she comes from a home where one of her parents didn't want her." Mom's face softens. "It was as if she didn't want me to feel obligated. Like she was scared I would say I want to be in the baby's life and then later dip."

"I'm not going to give you a lecture on safe sex," Mom says. "It's too late now and I've done that enough over the

A CHANCE ENCOUNTER

years. Besides, you're a grown man. But what you need to understand now, is that this baby is a life-long commitment. No matter what happens from this point on, you and…"

"Sophia. Her name is Sophia Davis. She's twenty-five, lives here in New York, and is in college."

"You and Sophia will be in this together," Mom says. "It's why your father and I always encouraged you both to get married before having babies. Having a successful relationship in our world is already difficult as it is. Raising a baby with someone you don't even know…" She shakes her head, and I hate that I've disappointed her. This isn't how I wanted shit to go down. I've always been careful. I might be seen with various women at events and social gatherings, but I'm picky about who I sleep with, and up until now, I've always used protection. I don't know what it is about her that had my head spinning, but when we went back to my hotel room, I was not in my right mind.

"You have a lot to think about," Dad says. "For one, you live in California, and she lives here. I can't imagine trying to be a dad while living across the country from you guys and your mom." Growing up, my parents always made sure to provide a stable homelife for us. My parents are people I look

91

up to, strive to be like, and I take their actions and words to heart.

"I know," I tell him. "I was actually thinking about that on my way over here. I'm going to buy a place here. I was also thinking I could record my next album here, so I'm close."

Mom smiles softly. "We'll definitely be happy to see more of you."

"I'll put in for studio time," Nicole says, typing on her phone.

"I know this isn't ideal," I tell everyone. "But before I found out she was pregnant, I wanted to get to know her. I don't know what the future holds, but I would like to explore our options. Who knows? Maybe she is the one for me."

"Just be careful," Jordan says, finally speaking up. "If you pursue a relationship with her and it doesn't work out, you're still stuck parenting with her."

"Truth," Dad adds, taking a bite of his food.

"Invite her over," Mom says. "We'd love to meet her." She leans over and pats my arm. "It will all work out. Just know, no matter what happens, we've got your back."

Six

SOPHIA

I'M SITTING IN THE EXAM ROOM, WHEN EASTON WALKS IN WITH THE NURSE, who is looking at him like he's the one who invented sliced bread. He's dressed in a black hoodie with the single word LOST across his chest, holey jeans, and a pair of black Nikes. The moment our eyes meet and he smiles, my belly does a weird flip-flop thing that I ignore. Easton is good-looking, for sure, and the chemistry we share is undeniable, but it's also what got us into this mess in the first place. Right now, I have too much on my plate to add a relationship into the mix.

This morning he called to let me know that since I'm uncomfortable with anyone knowing about the baby yet, he'll have it set up with the doctor's office for him to come in through the back, discreetly, so he isn't seen. His attorney also sent over a request for a paternity test. Apparently, you can find out if your DNA matches through a blood sample and a cheek swab. Easton let me know that as well during our conversation, so I wouldn't be blindsided by it. I have no doubt he's the dad, but I don't blame him for making sure. He explained it's not court ordered, so if we ever went to court, another one would have to be done. I was a little overwhelmed by the conversation, but I understand where he's coming from. We might've had sex, but we don't know each other.

Along with the paternity test, his attorney sent over NDA forms for the staff, including the doctor, to sign. I wanted to be embarrassed at that, but I know he's only doing it to support my decision to keep everything out of the media for now. Eventually it's going to come out, but I haven't thought that far ahead yet. I've spent the last seven years staying out of the public eye, and it wasn't difficult since I'm insignificant, but now that I'm pregnant with Easton's baby, who's a big freaking deal, it's going to be more difficult, and that scares me to death.

"You can have a seat right here," the nurse says to Easton, "and the doctor will be in soon." She excuses herself, leaving

A CHANCE ENCOUNTER

us alone. Instead of sitting down, Easton rounds the exam chair, sidling up next to me. He leans in and kisses my cheek, shocking the hell out of me. The kiss is quick, his lips not lingering, but it's enough to smell his signature scent of cinnamon.

"You look beautiful today," he murmurs before finding his seat. "How're you feeling?"

It takes me a second to get my head on straight, but once I do, I answer him truthfully. "I'm okay. Tired." I shrug. I'm used to it. I'm a pregnant, single mom going to school and working full-time. It's to be expected.

Easton frowns. "If there's anything you need…"

"I'm good," I tell him with a smile.

"I told my family. They want to meet you."

Great… I can imagine how that conversation went. After Easton told me he planned to tell his family, I looked him up. His dad is a famous musician who started his own record label. His parents have been happily married for thirty-two years, and his mom works for the label. He has one sister, who is his right-hand. It's hard to know what's real or fake on the internet, but one thing's for sure, his family is close. Unlike mine…

Don't get me wrong. After Kendall was born, my mom visited, and she visits once or twice a year. She sends Kendall gifts for her birthday and Christmas, but between me stripping and putting off college, she was disappointed, and it created a huge fissure in our already fragile relationship. Now that I'm back in school, it's gotten a little better, but we're nowhere near as close as the media portrays Easton's family.

Before I can respond, there's a knock on the door and then the doctor walks in. "Good morning," she says, "I'm Dr. Burger. We met earlier."

"Thank you again, for helping us keep this discreet," Easton says, turning on the charm.

"Absolutely." She smiles, then turns her attention on me. "And how are you doing today?"

I open my mouth to answer, but Easton beats me to it. "She said she's tired." He ignores me when I glare his way, his eyes trained on the doctor.

Dr. Burger laughs. "Being tired is common during pregnancy. Her body is growing a baby. Aside from being tired, how are you feeling?"

"I'm fine."

"No more bleeding?" She goes about checking me out,

and I should probably be self-conscious since I barely know Easton, but after giving birth once already and him having seen me naked, I don't have it in me to care.

"Nope. Everything is good." I'm having trouble sleeping at night from the stress, and as a result, beyond exhausted, but there's nothing she can do to help with that.

"Your blood pressure came in rather high," she says, laying me back and raising my gown. "Are you under stress?"

I glance at Easton, whose gaze is searing into me, before I close my eyes while she presses around my belly. "Maybe a little," I admit.

She squirts some gel on my stomach, making me open my eyes back up. "Stress isn't good for you or the baby," she says in a motherly tone. "I know it's not completely avoidable, but high blood pressure early on can lead to other issues."

"I understand."

"What kind of issues?" Easton asks, stepping over next to the bed.

"Preeclampsia and premature birth," she says, answering him, while she clicks on the monitor and then grabs the ultrasound wand.

"I'll do my best to lower my stress," I promise her.

"Good. Now let's take a look at your baby."

"I didn't know I had an ultrasound scheduled for today," I note. I already had one when I first found out I was pregnant, and from what I was told, I wouldn't have another one until twenty weeks.

"Normally we don't do them until twenty weeks," she says, voicing my thoughts. "Insurance companies only approve them in between if there's a medical reason…"

"Is there something wrong with my baby?" I ask, suddenly freaking out. She said my blood pressure was high, but I didn't think it was enough for her to suspect something is wrong with my baby.

"I asked for one," Easton says. "I wanted to see *our* baby."

I flinch at his choice of wording—realizing I insinuated the baby was only mine, which wasn't my intention—and am about to apologize, when his first statement hits me. "You asked for one? Why?" I blurt out. "Do you not believe me? You're getting a DNA test! My insurance isn't going to cover this…"

"I requested an ultrasound because I missed the first one and wanted to see our baby."

And now I feel like a complete bitch. "Oh."

"And I'm covering the cost," he adds.

"Oh," I repeat like an idiot.

Thankfully the doctor saves us—more so me—from this awkward exchange by speaking up. "And here's your baby."

Both of our eyes move to the screen where the 3D image of our baby is on display, and my heart soars. He's so tiny, but you can see his head and hands and feet and the umbilical cord. His tiny little heart is beating, the sound filling the room. Tears prick my eyes, blurring my vision, and I quickly wipe them away, not wanting to miss a second of the baby on the monitor.

When I notice Easton is quiet, my gaze flicks over to him. He's staring at the screen, frozen in his spot, his eyes glassy. A single tear slides down his cheek, and the dam that was holding back my tears breaks.

His eyes meet mine. "That's our baby," he rasps, another tear falling. "Thank you."

His words are my undoing. "I'm so sorry for going off on you." Tears slide down my face. "I'm just such an emotional, hormonal, crazy person lately." My sobs intensify and Easton takes my hand in his.

"It's okay," he says. "It's to be expected. You're carrying our cute little boiled egg. I can't even imagine what that would be like."

"Our what?" I choke out through a half sob, half laughter.

"I looked it up. Thirteen weeks is the size of a boiled egg. Last week he was the size of a man's right testicle." He grimaces. "I'm kind of glad that week is over because it was weird thinking about him as half of a ballsac."

The doctor snorts out a laugh, reminding us she's still in the room.

"I think you're supposed to compare the baby to something cute, like fruit. Maybe a kiwi or a strawberry."

"Fruit's cute?" His nose scrunches up in the most adorable way. "If it helps, next week he'll be the size of a Rubik's cube. That's kind of cute, right? All the colors and it's a kid's toy…"

I burst out laughing, as more tears stream down my face. "Thank you," I tell him, squeezing his hand. "I needed that laugh."

He smiles down at me and then leans over and kisses my forehead. "Everything's going to be okay," he murmurs so only I can hear, and for the first time since I found out I was pregnant, I feel like maybe he's right. Because it's clear, even though I don't know Easton well, he's nothing like Kendall's sperm donor.

We both dry our eyes and then Easton tells the doctor she can continue.

She smiles warmly at us both. "He *or* she is doing well. Measuring perfectly in line with your due date." She explains a few things to us that are on the screen, capturing a few still images, and then removes the wand, the image of the baby disappearing.

"I want you to focus on removing stress from your life," she says, standing and handing me some paper towels to clean the gunk off my belly. She pulls some papers from the machine and hands one to me and one to Easton—pictures of the baby.

Easton grins down at them with the most beautiful, proud smile, and my heart cracks. This is how a man is supposed to react to a baby, how I wanted Freeman to react. I'm so happy this baby will have a father in his or her life, but at the same time, my heart breaks for my daughter, who will never know what that feels like.

"Sophia," the doctor prompts. "Did you hear me?"

"Yes, sorry. Eliminate stress. Got it."

She moves the top of my chair to a sitting position.

"Good. I'll see you next month." To Easton, she says, "It was nice meeting you."

Once she's gone, I climb off the bed and disappear behind the curtain to clean up and get dressed. When I come out, Easton is still standing there, staring at the photos.

"You okay?"

"Yeah, I just can't believe I'm going to be a dad." He sniffles and folds the paper up, depositing it into his back pocket.

After I put on my coat, we head out to the check-out counter. I make my appointment for four Fridays from today, since by then I'll be back in school and Fridays are my only days off, and then Easton leads me out the back door, where he has a car, driver, and bodyguard waiting.

"Do you have anything going on?" he asks. "I was thinking we could go to lunch…"

I glance at the time on my phone. Kendall is at a playdate and I don't have to pick her up for a couple hours, so I don't have any excuse. Plus, I do want to get to know him, but agreeing to go to lunch with him will run us the risk of being seen…

"I was hoping we could talk," he adds. "We could go back

A CHANCE ENCOUNTER

to my hotel, where we won't be bothered, and order room service."

"Okay, that sounds good."

When we arrive at the hotel—a different one than the one he took me to before—his driver pulls up to a back entrance, and we slip in through the back door. The elevator is for the penthouse only, so nobody is on it but us. I can't help but remember the last time we were on an elevator together... the way he had me pinned against the wall. When my eyes meet his, he smirks, and my cheeks heat up, knowing, based off the searing look he's sending my way, he's thinking about the same thing. I shake the thought from my head. Now is not the time to be thinking about sex.

"Are you planning to stay here for a while?" I ask, as we step off the elevator and walk toward his door. "It must be expensive to live out of hotels all the time." Then I flinch, remembering he's worth hundreds of millions of dollars and probably thinks I'm an idiot.

"Actually, I'm looking for a place to buy." He opens the door and gestures for me to enter first. The place is how I would picture a penthouse in New York—everything gaudy and lush, expensive-looking. Makes you afraid to touch anything in fear of breaking it.

"Really? Because of the baby?"

"Unless you want to move to California," he says with a hint of humor in his tone.

The mention of that state causes chills to run up my spine. I haven't been back since the day I left, and I have no desire to ever return. Freeman hasn't contacted me since he walked away, and I've made sure to stay off the radar. His threats back then were scary as hell, and since then, he's come up in the world, just like he planned. I'd hate to think of what he's capable of doing now—and I have no intention of finding out.

"New York is my home," I tell him, sitting on the couch.

"Yeah, I figured." He hands me a menu, and once I check it out and pick what I'd like, he places the order. When he hangs up, he sits diagonal from me in the oversized chair, and we stare at each other in awkward silence for several long seconds before we both crack up at the same time.

"I'm sorry," he says. "I've never been in this situation before."

"What?" I mock-gasp. "You mean you don't go around knocking up strangers all the time?"

He chuckles. "This is definitely a first." He edges forward. "But I have a confession to make…" His eyes lock with mine and butterflies attack my belly. "Before I found out you were pregnant, you were on my mind. I couldn't get you out of my head, since the day you dined and dashed." He laughs softly, and I groan, knowing he'll never let me live that down. "I even called the photographer to try to get your full name," he adds.

"I called her too."

"She's out of the damn country." He takes my hand in his and rubs circles along the center of my palm. "Obviously I didn't know at the time you were pregnant, but I had a solid plan. I was going to stalk Bryant Park, specifically that bench, every day until you showed up again."

I can't help but laugh at his craziness.

"I'm serious," he says with a playful smile. "I wanted to beg you to let me take you out on a proper date, and I wasn't going to stop until I found you." His other hand cups the side of my face. "I still want to take you out on that date."

"Easton…" I shake my head.

"Before you say no, just hear me out, please." His beautiful brown eyes plead with me, so I nod. "I know you're busy with school and work, and you made it clear that day you weren't interested in going out with me, but there's something between us. I felt it that day in the park, when you were in my bed, and I know you did too. And now that you're pregnant, I think we owe it to ourselves to at least see where things go."

I swallow thickly, hating that even though his words are so sweet, my insecurities are still coming out. I know he said he felt it before he knew I was pregnant, but I can't help wondering if maybe he's pushing so hard because I *am* pregnant.

"And what if it doesn't work? What if you get to know me and realize it was nothing more than sexual chemistry? What then?"

"Then we do what everyone else who has a baby together but aren't together does, we co-parent. But we have several months before the baby comes, and I'd really like to get to know you. Even if we don't end up together, you're my baby mama." He hits me with a lopsided grin. "We'll be in each other's lives until we die, so I think we should still get to know each other."

A laugh escapes. "Until we die, huh?"

"Damn right, woman. You're stuck with me for life."

A CHANCE ENCOUNTER

There's a knock, and Easton gets up to answer the door. I meet him in the kitchen so we can plate up our food. It all smells so good, and my stomach growls in anticipation.

"So, what do you say?" he asks, once we're seated at the table.

"I can't make any promises," I tell him truthfully. "And you're right, I do have a lot going on…" *More than you know…* I still need to tell him about Kendall, but once I do, it's out there. He's going to ask questions, and I'm going to be forced to lie. Because a secret is only a secret if no one knows. And I have to make sure, for my daughter's well-being, nobody ever knows who her sperm donor is.

"But I felt what you felt," I add, "and I would like to explore the possibility of something more." His face lights up. "But…" His face falls. "I think we should take things slow over the course of my pregnancy and when the baby comes, we make a decision. If we aren't compatible, we co-parent and move forward separately."

Easton's face lights back up. "So, what you're saying is I have roughly six months to convince you that we're perfect for each other."

I laugh. "Or you have six months to realize I'm crazy and

plan your escape."

"Oh, I already know you're crazy," he deadpans. "But I have a feeling you're my kind of crazy." He grins and takes a sip of his drink. "I hope you're prepared…"

"For what?"

"To be wooed."

"Wooed?" I laugh.

"Yep! Wooed. It's the term my grandfather used to use when he was alive. One thing you need to know about us Blackwood men. We're great at wooing."

I groan, wondering what the hell I've gotten myself into. But also, deep down, I'm kind of excited because I'm twenty-five years old and I've never been wooed.

Seven

EASTON

Dash: I can't. I'm not feeling well. Sorry.

I SIGH, SETTING MY PHONE DOWN, WONDERING IF SOPHIA'S REALLY NOT FEELING well, or if she's using it as an excuse to not come over. After our lunch date at my hotel, I felt like we were making some progress. She told me about school, how she's planning to one day become a family attorney, and I told her how music has been my entire world since I was little. We made small talk while we ate and it was nice. Shortly after, she said she had somewhere she had to be and promised we'd get together soon.

The last couple days, we've been texting—I gave her my number so we wouldn't have to message on Facebook anymore—and she's been opening up more.

When I asked her what she's doing for Christmas, and she mentioned her roommate and cousin, Naomi, would be out of town for the holidays because her fiancé was taking her to visit his parents, I invited her over, so she wouldn't be alone.

"Is she coming?" Mom asks, sitting next to me.

"She's not feeling well."

"You don't sound like you believe that."

"I think she's scared. She doesn't really talk about anyone but her cousin, Naomi, and I wonder if maybe she's all alone."

Mom nods. "The deli on the corner is open. They make the best chicken noodle soup."

"You're okay with me leaving?"

"We'll wait for you. If she's really not feeling well, you should be there, and if she's okay... maybe you can convince her in person to join us."

After letting everyone know I'm leaving, but will be back in a little while, I stop by the deli, pick up some soup as my mom suggested, and then head over to Sophia's apartment. When I arrive at her door, I knock and wait for her to answer. I should've warned her I was coming over, but I was afraid she'd come up with some excuse for me not to.

A CHANCE ENCOUNTER

I hear stomping in the apartment, and a second later, the door swings open. I'm expecting to see Sophia, so I'm taken aback when instead, a tiny little girl, with curly blond pigtails, dressed in red and white striped pajamas is standing at the door.

"Hi, who are you?" she asks, her bright blue eyes meeting mine with curiosity.

"I'm—"

"Kendall Naomi Davis!" Sophia yells, walking down the hallway. "You know better than to open the door to a stranger, and especially without asking who it is!"

"Uh-oh." The little girl's mouth forms an adorable O. "Mommy said *all* my names. I think I'm in trouble." She slams the door closed in my face, and I stand here in utter fucking shock. She just said Mommy... and I'm pretty sure she's the spitting image of Sophia.

I'm still wrapping my head around what the hell just happened, when the door opens back up, this time by Sophia, who's looking sexy as hell in a pair of pink sweats and a tiny white tank top, exposing her midriff. Her stomach still isn't round, but there's a clear bump, and she's not wearing a bra, so her nipples are poking through the thin material.

She clears her throat, and my head pops up. Damn woman is a walking, breathing fucking distraction. "What are you doing here? And how do you even know where I live?" Her questions come across sounding more nervous than accusing, and I have a feeling the three-foot mini-version of her, who I didn't know about, is why.

"I saw your address on the paperwork at the doctor's office, so I memorized it. And I'm here because you said you weren't feeling well." I hold up the brown bag. "So I brought you soup."

Her shoulders slump, and her face falls, and I know she was lying. She feels fine, but she's been hiding something kind of big. "Thank you," she mutters, taking the bag and gesturing for me to come in.

"Is there a reason why you didn't mention you have a daughter?" I ask, once we're inside. I keep my voice low, so her daughter doesn't hear.

"How do you know she's my daughter?"

"One, she referred to you as Mommy, and two, aside from the blue eyes, she's practically your mini-me."

A smile spreads across her lips. "Yeah, I guess she is."

"Mommy, can I come out now?" the little girl calls out.

A CHANCE ENCOUNTER

"Yes, you may."

Pitter-patter of feet are heard and then she appears. "I'm sorry for opening the door," she says to her mom, eyeing me curiously.

"It's okay," Sophia says. "Kendall, this is Easton." She kneels in front of her daughter, so they're eye-level. "Remember last night how I told you I'm having a baby?"

Kendall nods emphatically. "I'm going to be a big sister!"

I smile at her excitement.

"That's right. Well, Easton is the baby's daddy."

Kendall is quiet for a brief moment and then her eyes meet mine, still full of curiosity, but also something else. "Are you my daddy too?" It's then I recognize what her eyes are filled with: hope. And just like that, the wind is knocked from my lungs and it's hard to breathe. I open my mouth to answer, but thankfully Sophia beats me to it.

"No, Sunshine," Sophia says with a hint of shakiness in her tone. "You know how your friend Karina has two mommies or how Sandra only has a daddy?"

Kendall nods, but the earlier excitement and curiosity are gone, and now she merely looks resigned, and fuck if my heart doesn't feel like it's just been punctured with a steak knife and is bleeding out.

"Families come in all shapes and sizes," Sophia says. "But you have me and Aunt Naomi and Uncle Dante." I expect her to continue, because most people have some type of extended family, but she stops, and my earlier thoughts are confirmed. It's just them.

"And I may not be your dad," I add, "but I'd like to be your friend."

Kendall gnaws on her bottom lip, just like her mom does, as she contemplates my offer. And I find myself holding my breath, waiting to see if she'll accept or not. And not just because I can already tell Sophia's world revolves around this little girl and if she doesn't like me, I don't stand a chance with her, but also because when she asked me if I was her dad, I wanted to be able to say yes. Because with one look, just like her mom, she's got me wanting to give her the world.

"Do you like music?" she asks softly.

"Yeah, I love music."

"What's your favorite song?"

"'My Only One.'" It's Jordan's new single that's topping the charts as we speak.

Her face scrunches up. "That's Mommy's favorite song."

A CHANCE ENCOUNTER

She shrugs. "My favorite is 'Lost.'"

Hell yeah, I knew I liked this kid. "That's a really good song," I agree.

Out of the corner of my eye, I see Sophia roll her eyes, telling me she knows it's mine.

"I know!" Kendall exclaims, her face becoming animated. "Mommy hates it, though."

I bark out a laugh as Sophia splutters, "I don't... hate it."

"Yes, you do," Kendall tattles, planting her little fists at her sides. "You always turn it off."

"Because you play it over and over again," Sophia argues. "I'm just trying to give other songs a chance."

Kendall rolls her eyes—just like her damn mom—and I laugh harder. These two are adorable together.

"But it's the best!" Kendall says. "I'm going to go get it so we can listen." She takes off running down the hall, leaving Sophia and me alone.

"You're not sick, are you?" I raise a single brow, daring her to lie to me.

"No," she admits sheepishly. "I'm sorry. I should've been upfront with you about her, but I'm protective of her, and everything kind of happened so suddenly. It's like one minute it's just us and the next there's a baby on the way and then you're sliding into my life…" She sighs. "If you want to rescind your idea about the possibility of us, I'll understand. It's one thing to take on a woman who's pregnant with your baby." Her hand goes to her belly. "But it's another to take on a child who isn't yours."

"Where's her dad?"

"He's dead." I wait for her to explain further, but she stops there, not giving me anything more.

I step over to her, placing my hands on her hips. "You're right. You should've told me. Not because it would change how I feel or what I want, but because we're supposed to be in this together, and it's not going to work if you keep shit from me."

"I know. Letting someone in is new for me, but I'll try harder."

"Come to my family's for dinner, please. It's Christmas Eve. My aunt and uncle and cousins are there. They've got a couple kids, so Kendall will have a blast. There'll be tons of food and desserts, and we all watch *The Grinch*…"

"I love *The Grinch*!" Kendall squeals, running back out with a small iPad in her hands. "Santa Claus is coming tonight!

And I've been so good so he's going to bring me toys."

Sophia smiles down at her daughter before looking back at me. "Are you sure your family will be okay with two more?"

"More than okay. They're looking forward to meeting you."

After they both change—Sophia, in a red sweater, jeans that hug every curve, and knee-high black boots, and Kendall, in a cute red Christmas dress, red and green striped leggings, and black fluffy boots—we take off to my parents' place. I texted my parents and sister while they were changing to let them know they're coming—and to tell them about Sophia's daughter—so they aren't shocked as shit when we walk in.

Since it's cold as hell outside, we snag a cab, and about fifteen minutes later, we arrive at my parents' house, which is situated in Greenwich Village. It's a four-story single-family home, and the kind of house I've been looking at the last couple days. In New York, since everything is piled on top of each other, the only way to get the space you want, is to purchase a multi-level home. I prefer my spacious two-story home in Calabasas, but since Sophia's made it clear this is her home, I've come to terms with the fact that I'll be making New York my new home base.

When we walk inside and head up the stairs to the living room, we're met with an onslaught of greetings from my family. The majority of our extended family lives in California, but my dad's sister lives here with my uncle and cousins, who have kids of their own. So, even with only a small portion of our family here, the house is still loud and full. I introduce Sophia and Kendall to everyone—except my sister and Jordan, since they're in the other room at the moment—and Mom lets everyone know dinner is almost ready.

"Is there anything I can help you with?" Sophia nervously asks.

"Oh no, sweet girl," Mom tells her. "It's all done. I just have to heat a few things up. Go sit and enjoy yourself." I sigh in relief, that even though I know Mom and Dad have their reservations about Sophia, they were warm and welcoming.

So she's not too overwhelmed, I pull Sophia over to the couch to sit down, and notice Kendall shyly follows, instead of running to play with my cousin's kids. Kendall pulls her iPad out of her backpack and sticks her earbuds into her ears. A second later, she whispers something to her mom, who shakes her head, making Kendall pout.

"What's wrong?" I ask.

A CHANCE ENCOUNTER

"My iPad needs Wi-Fi to play music, but it needs a password."

There's music playing in the surround sound, the lyrics scrolling across the television, and it gives me an idea. "Want to play karaoke while we wait for dinner?"

"What's that?" Kendall asks.

"You don't know what karaoke is?"

"Nope," she says, shaking her head.

"It's when you play a song and sing to it like you're the person who sings it. Lyrics pop up on the screen and you follow them."

Her eyes light up. "I can't read too much, only like a hundred words, but I know every song."

Sophia's shoulders shake with silent laughter.

"Every song?" I ask.

"Yep."

"All right, let's see."

I grab the remote and am switching through the songs to find a good one, when my sister and Jordan make their appearance.

"Oh my God!" Sophia gasps.

I spin around to see what's wrong. "Are you okay?" I glance

down at her stomach. "Is it the baby?"

Her eyes dart over to me. "What?"

"Are you okay?" I repeat.

"Yes, I'm okay," she hisses. "Jordan Walker is in your home."

My sister snorts out a laugh and Jordan grins like a fool.

"Yeah, I know. He's my best friend."

My sister clears her throat. "And my fiancé."

I ignore her, focusing on Sophia and the damn sparkle in her eyes. "Wait a second. Hold up." Everyone's gaze turns on me. "You knew who Jordan Walker was just by looking at him, but you didn't recognize me when we met at the park?"

My family, who are all apparently listening, laugh.

"Kendall told you 'My Only One' was my favorite song," Sophia says.

"Yeah, but that doesn't mean you know who he is... And how the hell do you know him and not me?"

"Bro," Jordan says, dropping a hand to my shoulder. "Jealousy does not look good on you."

"I'm Nicole," my sister says to Sophia, "Easton's sister."

"I'm Sophia. It's nice to meet you." Sophia's cheeks tinge pink. "Sorry for fangirling over your fiancé. I met him a while

A CHANCE ENCOUNTER

back at the club I work at, and that night because he was there, they played his music. I'm more of a country girl, but I totally fell in love with his music."

"It's all good," Nicole says, pulling her in for a hug. "It was worth it to see my brother's face when he realized you knew Jordan and not him."

"What the hell were you doing at Emerald's?" I ask Jordan.

He laughs and then his face goes serious, his gaze going to Sophia. "I totally remember you," he says. "Nic, remember when we met with Diddy about that liquor endorsement?" She nods. "She was our waitress."

"Oh wow! What a small world," my sister says. "I've heard a lot about you from my brother. It's nice to meet you."

"Are we going to sing or what?" Kendall asks, dropping her hand to her hip. At least *she* doesn't care about who Jordan is.

"Yeah, but be prepared to get your butt kicked," I warn her.

"How do I get my butt kicked?" she asks.

"Whoever sings more words correctly wins," I tell her.

"Okay." She nods.

When I get to one of my newer songs, Jordan laughs. "You can't play your own song, man, that's cheating."

"What song?" Kendall asks.

"'Lies,'" I say, curious if she knows it.

"That's not your song." Her little brows draw together in confusion. "I have it on my iPad and Mommy has it on her phone."

"Sunshine," Sophia says, "Easton is a singer. 'Lost' and 'Lies' and all those other songs you like are his."

Kendall's brows shoot up to her forehead. "They're not just your songs. They're everyone's songs. You have to share." It's then I realize that even though she loves my music, she doesn't really understand I'm the man behind the words.

Everyone in the room stifles their laughter, while Sophia tries again. "You know when you listen to the songs, there's someone singing them?"

"Yeah."

"Well, the person who's singing them owns the songs. They sing it in a studio and record it and then they upload it so everyone can hear it. Easton is the one who sings 'Lost' and 'Lies.' It's his voice on the songs."

Kendall's features morph into understanding, but then she says, "I'm still going to beat you."

"At my own song?" I laugh.

A CHANCE ENCOUNTER

"I know *all* the words to 'Lies,'" she says, throwing her hands in the air in frustration.

This time everyone laughs.

"All right, kid," I tell her, clicking play. "Bring it on."

Eight

SOPHIA

"IT SAYS, 'I'M LOOKING FOR A LOVE.'"

"No, it doesn't," Kendall argues, as we walk up to our apartment with Easton. "It says, 'I'm looking for a *dove*.'"

I look back at Easton, who's sighing in playful exasperation. After they karaoked the hell out of 'Lies,' where Easton won, Kendall demanded to sing another song. She beat him in another one of his older songs when he tripped up on the chorus. The tiebreaker had to wait until after dinner because Easton's mom, Alicia, called us all into the dining room to eat.

I was nervous about how it would go, but everyone was nice and welcoming. They asked a little about me and Kendall and the baby, like when I'm due and how I've been feeling, but nobody got too personal. The food was delicious, and the conversation flowed smoothly amongst everyone. It was the first time in a while since I've sat at a family dinner like that, and it made me crave more of it. Kendall even warmed up to Easton's cousin's kids, and by the time we had dessert and sat down to watch *The Grinch*, she was sitting next to them, drinking hot chocolate. I sat next to Easton during the movie, and maybe it's because everything caught up to me, but about thirty minutes in, I passed out on his shoulder, not waking up until he was gently nudging me awake to let me know the movie was over.

But before we could go, Kendall insisted on that tiebreaker. She and Easton sang the lyrics, word for word, except for one line. It's obviously 'I'm looking for a love...' because why the hell would a grown man be looking for a dove, but Kendall disagrees, and it's kind of hilarious to listen to them argue over it.

When we step up to our front door, Easton stops in his place. "Just for you, I'm going to sing a special version where he's looking for a dove."

Kendall rolls her eyes. "He *is* looking for a dove."

Easton laughs and shakes his head but doesn't argue.

A CHANCE ENCOUNTER

"Make sure you get to sleep fast so Santa doesn't skip your house." He playfully ruffles her hair. "Have a good night."

"Wait," Kendall says. "You have to stay. I made the baby a special present and you have to see it too."

Easton's eyes go wide. It's clear he doesn't know how to say no to Kendall, so I'm going to have to be his backup. "Sunshine, it's Christmas. Easton has his own family to celebrate with."

"Actually, I don't have any plans," he says.

Kendall jumps up and down. "You can watch me open my presents, but you're too big, so you don't get any. Mommy is too big, so she doesn't get any either." She turns to me. "Can he stay, Mommy?"

"Sure," I tell her, opening the door. "Go get your pajamas on and brush your teeth. Quick."

She runs inside and goes straight to her room. Once she's gone, I turn to Easton. "You're on the couch tonight, and since you're here you get to help me put the toys together."

"Isn't that Santa's job?" Easton jokes.

"It sure is, and tonight, you're Santa."

"Hmm... And what do I get out of this?"

"The same thing Santa gets..." I step close to him, so

our faces are almost touching. "Milk and cookies, and the satisfaction of knowing a little girl will be extremely happy on Christmas morning."

Before I can back up, Easton snags the bottom of my shirt and pulls me toward him, until our bodies are almost flush with each other. "As Santa, it's my duty to make sure *everyone* is happy. Tell me, Dash, what is it *you* want for Christmas?" I roll my eyes at his damn nickname for me.

"For Kendall to have a good Christmas," I answer without thought.

He shakes his head. "I asked you what you want. What will make *you* happy?"

I swallow thickly at the heavy-ass question now resting between us. It's been so long since I've thought about myself. I go to school, work, take care of Kendall. All things that make me happy but aren't necessarily done for me. They're done for us, for our future, so I can provide for my daughter. Give us a stable home. But I can't remember the last time I did or bought something to make *me* happy.

"I don't know," I answer honestly.

"Then that's something we're going to have to work on. After all, I *am* Santa." He smirks playfully. "Which means it's

A CHANCE ENCOUNTER

my job to make sure you get everything you want." He leans down and softly presses his lips against mine. I'm shocked at first—it's our first kiss since I've agreed to see how things go—but within seconds, my head catches up and a swarm of butterflies explode in my belly.

"So fucking sweet," he murmurs.

"It's probably the candy cane I ate," I say dumbly.

"No, it's all you." He kisses me one more time, this time his mouth lingering a little longer on mine. "And if I recall correctly, your lips aren't the only sweet part about you."

At his words, the apex of my thighs clench in anticipation.

Without waiting for me to respond—which is good since he's stunned me silent—he saunters into the house, not even looking the least bit affected by that kiss or his words.

"I'm ready!" Kendall yells. "Can we put the cookies and milk out for Santa now? I wonder how many he'll want. Two or three?"

"I have it on good authority," Easton says, glancing back at me with a mischievous grin. "Santa *loves* sweets. I'd say give him three."

"Okay!" Kendall runs into the kitchen to grab the cookies we made and set aside for Santa.

After setting out the milk and cookies, Kendall goes to bed without issue, since she knows Santa won't come until after she's asleep. Once I know she's asleep, I grab the wrapped presents from my closet and bring them out with Easton's help, setting them under the Christmas tree.

Then I have him help me grab the three unwrapped boxes. "These are the things we need to put together."

Easton grabs the first box. "What's this for?" He eyes the vanity with a stool and mirror on the box.

"So she can put her makeup on and do her hair and paint her nails."

His brow furrows. "She's six. She doesn't need makeup or nail polish."

"She's a girl. Girls love makeup at all ages."

"What's next? Dating? You gonna tell me girls do that at all ages too? She should be playing with Legos or dolls at her age."

I laugh at his dramatics, then go serious. "No dating yet. But she did say she thinks Nicholas Sawyer is cute."

"What?" he gasps, dropping the box. "That guy is a fucking tool. She isn't going anywhere near any guys, with or without makeup on, until she's forty. Especially since she has such horrible taste."

I double over in laughter. Nicholas Sawyer is a new up and coming artist, who's in his teens and is also known as a ladies' man. He's taken to his newfound stardom by getting into trouble and in turn, his face has been splashed across every tabloid in the grocery stores. Kendall loves his music, but she never said he was cute.

"You better get used to it," I warn. "If this baby is a girl, there will be two girls running around in makeup, crushing on boys like Nicholas."

Easton's face contorts into a look of horror. "It's a boy."

"You don't know that," I tell him through my laughter.

"Yes, I do, because there's no way I could handle two girls." He mock-shivers. "It's a boy and he's going to keep all the other boys away from Kendall. End of story." He grabs the pamphlet and opens it up. "Now, grab me a drill please, so I can put this stupid pink thing together."

I'm still laughing when I bring him my toolbox and set it down in front of him.

"What the hell is this?" he asks, eyeing it.

"My tools. I don't have a drill, but I have a bunch of screwdrivers and stuff."

"It's pink," he deadpans, holding it up. "And glittery."

"It's cute," I argue.

"This shouldn't even be allowed to be sold." He stands and pulls the parts out of the box. "We're going to need to get you some real tools."

"No need." I shrug, walking around the mess laid out on the floor so I can help him. "I have you now. Part of being a boyfriend means putting stuff together." I step over a piece of pink plastic and am about to step over another, when I lose my balance. My foot slips across the wood floor and my hands are torn between catching my fall and protecting my belly. Before I can decide which to do, strong arms encircle my waist. Easton and I still go down, but he lands first on the hard floor, taking the brunt of the fall, while I stay wrapped up safely in his arms, my body landing on top of his.

In the same breath, he carefully rolls us over, cushioning the back of my head and hovering above me. "You okay?" he breathes, his eyes filled with concern.

"Yeah." I bob my head. "Thank you."

"You called me your boyfriend."

"Huh?"

"You said part of being a boyfriend means putting stuff

A CHANCE ENCOUNTER

together."

"Oh." Shit, I did say that.

"I like the sound of that," he admits, kissing the corner of my mouth. "And I also like knowing I'm the man you *want* to put shit together."

He pulls us up into a sitting position. "Now, you sit here, where it's safe, while I put *this* shit together. Kendall told me she wakes up extra early on Christmas, so I imagine we've only got a few hours."

"Aye, aye, captain." I mock-salute.

I watch him for a little while putting the item together in silence, then get bored. "How old were you when you knew you wanted to be a musician?"

"I was young, probably Kendall's age. I grew up in the studio and on the road with my parents, listening to my dad sing, watching him perform. I loved it all and knew one day I would follow in his footsteps."

"What if you couldn't sing?" I ask, curious.

"Then I would've done something else in the music industry, like write music or produce." He flips the page on the directions and squints at it in confusion.

"How about I read the directions while you put it

together?"

"Sounds good." He hands me the paper.

I read him the next direction and he gets started on it. A minute later, he says, "How about you?"

"Huh?"

"You said you wanted to be a family attorney the other day. When did you know that's what you want to do?"

I can't tell him about Freeman and the fear I felt when he threatened to take my baby away, so I give him half the truth. "My dad left when I was little. He owns his own business, so he lied about what he makes and got away without paying child support. My mom struggled because of it. I want to help people in her position, so they don't feel helpless."

"I'll never be that guy," Easton says, stopping what he's doing. "No matter what happens, I will always be a father to our baby and make sure you're taken care of."

I nod, knowing he's telling the truth. I can feel it in my bones that Easton is nothing like Freeman and my dad.

"What's your favorite color?" I ask, switching gears.

"Definitely not pink," he says dryly, lifting the tiny screwdriver. "What's the next step?"

I read it to him, and he follows what I say. "What's your

favorite food?"

He glances up at me with a wolfish grin. "You."

"Oh my God, stop!" I smack him with the pamphlet. "You only ate me out once. How do you even remember what I taste like?" My face heats up the second I realize what I just blurted out.

Kill. Me. Now.

Easton's grin widens. "Trust me, it would be damn near impossible to forget what your sweet pussy tastes like. But don't worry, I plan to taste you again, and soon, just to make sure my memory serves me right." He lifts the vanity up. "All done."

Jesus, how does he say shit like that without being affected at all? Meanwhile, my body is thrumming in anticipation, remembering the last time he went down on me and looking forward to the next time.

I clear my throat. "It looks great." I grab it, along with the stool, and set it over by the tree, then hand him the next box.

While he's opening it, I ask, "So, seriously, what's your favorite food?"

"Hmmm… I guess bacon."

"Bacon? Really?" I love me some bacon, but I'm also

pregnant.

"Yeah. Add bacon to anything and it makes it better. A burger, chicken sandwich, mac n cheese. All good, but add bacon and bam! It's delicious."

"Mmm... I can totally see that."

He hands me the new set of directions and I read off the first step.

"What's your favorite food?" he asks.

"Being pregnant, my cravings change on the regular. But right now, it's anything chocolate... Donuts, ice cream, candy bars."

"How about chocolate covered bacon?" he jokes.

"That actually sounds freaking delicious," I admit, making him laugh.

"What's your longest relationship?" he asks, after I read him the next step.

Shit, this is not a conversation I want to have. I was over here talking about favorite foods and colors and he, of course, has to go and delve deeper. I think for a second. Does Freeman even count as a relationship when he was cheating on his fiancée? No, it doesn't. Which means the only relationship I've ever been in was with my seventh-grade boyfriend,

A CHANCE ENCOUNTER

Jonathon Duran, for like three weeks. Jesus, my love life has sucked. "Eh, not long," I say vaguely. "You?" I ask, quickly diverting the attention back to him.

"A little over five years."

"Wow! How old were you?" That's a pretty long relationship.

"We started dating when we were seventeen. She was by my side when I released my first album and it blew up. We graduated high school and she took classes online while touring with me. The day she graduated from college I proposed. Six months later, I ended our engagement."

"What happened?"

His eyes leave the Barbie mansion he's putting together and meet mine. "She was keeping secrets, hiding shit. And instead of being honest, she lied about it all."

I swallow down my guilt over my own secrets and lies. This would be a good time to tell him, but I can't do it. I can't risk it. *Ever.* My secret is one I have to take to my grave because once it's out, it can never be taken back. And I can't ever chance losing my daughter. It's my job to protect her. And I will do that until the day I die.

"I gave her so many chances," he adds, "but she couldn't

do it... Couldn't be honest. And in turn, she lost my trust. We went our separate ways, and she now works for a competing record label."

"The song 'Lies'..." The lyrics run through my head. They're about his ex.

"Yeah," he says, "I wrote it after we broke up."

"But it's a new song."

"The album Lost is new because I sat on it all for a while. I needed time to get past her betrayal to be able to sing those songs... To be able to have them out there for everyone to hear."

"Do you write all of your songs?"

"Yeah. Some I write and then they get tweaked to appeal to my audience, and others they approve of without changing anything, but all my songs come from me."

"That's pretty cool. I'm going to have to listen to your songs now so I can learn *all* about you."

He chuckles and pulls me down into his lap. "You're more than welcome to listen to any of my songs, but you don't need them to learn about me. You have me right here and I'll tell you anything you want to know. I'm an open book." He kisses my lips softly, and I close my eyes, hating that no matter what

I tell him, what I share with him, I'll always have at least one secret I have to keep from him.

"DO YOU HAVE A PRINTER?" EASTON ASKS WHEN WE'RE ALL DONE SETTING everything up and getting rid of any evidence of the items being put together here instead of at the North Pole. It's nearly three in the morning and I'm thankful Easton is here. The vanity and kitchen were both a lot harder to put together than I anticipated.

"Yeah, it's in my room, and it's probably for the best if you sleep in my bed…" His eyes light up. "Not like that." I slap his chest playfully. "If you're on the couch, Kendall is going to ask if you saw Santa and as smooth as you are, I don't see you getting out of that one."

While he uses my laptop and printer, I take a quick shower and get dressed for bed, and when I come out, he's done. His shoes and socks are off, but he's still in jeans and a shirt, since he didn't bring any clothes with him. I would offer him something to wear, but I don't have anything.

Plus, it's probably for the best if he keeps his clothes on. Less temptation that way. The few times he's kissed me, I've had visions of things going further, and that's not exactly congruent with my idea to take things slow... Then again, neither is labeling him my boyfriend this soon.

As I crawl into my comfy bed, my eyes are already fluttering shut in exhaustion. I'm a little nervous about sharing a bed with Easton, but when he climbs in as well and pats his chest for me to lay my head, I sigh in contentment. Using him as a human body pillow, I wrap my arm around his torso and close my eyes, listening to the beat of his heart. It's been a long time since I've been in bed with a man, and the first time I've just *slept* with one.

"I liked seeing you with my family tonight," he says, running his fingers through my hair.

"I liked hanging out with them," I say back, snuggling into his side. "And I also liked hanging out with you. Getting to know more about you."

"Good." He drops a kiss to the top of my head. "Because I really like hanging out with you too and getting to know you. And you being on board will make it that much easier to woo you."

A CHANCE ENCOUNTER

I chuckle softly through a yawn at his word choice. "Better get some sleep. In case you forgot, a very excited child will be up way too early to open her presents."

"Just think, next year we'll have *two* kids opening presents."

"Yeah," I agree, my eyes closing of their own accord.

And as I fall asleep to the image of the four of us on Christmas morning, I mentally question why that idea doesn't scare me in the slightest. But I already know the answer. It's because it's with Easton. And for some reason, even though it feels like things are moving a hell of a lot faster than I planned, the idea of a future with him doesn't scare me like I thought it would. In fact, it does the opposite.

Nine

EASTON

"SANTA CAME! SANTA CAME!" KENDALL SQUEALS FROM THE SIDE OF THE BED. I glance at my phone and see it's only four thirty in the morning. Holy shit, it's early. When she said she would be up early, she wasn't kidding. I look over at Sophia, who's fast asleep, curled into a ball with her hand absentmindedly around her belly. It's insane to think that in a few months we're going to have a baby. The thought should probably freak me out, but it doesn't.

When Kendall yells again and Sophia doesn't stir awake, I put my finger up to my lips to quiet her. "Let's give your mom a few more minutes to sleep."

"I'm up," Sophia rasps, stretching her limbs. Her shirt rides up her belly and I see the beginning of a bump. My fingers twitch to touch her flesh, to feel connected to the baby growing in her.

"You only got an hour of sleep," I whisper.

"The life of a parent." She shrugs. "I'll sleep when I'm dead." She climbs out of bed and, even though I know damn well she's exhausted, plasters on a big smile. "Did I hear Santa came?"

Kendall nods excitedly. "He did! And he brought me so many presents. Like five hundred."

We spend the morning watching Kendall open her presents. Because neither my sister nor I have any kids, it's my first time watching a child's Christmas morning through an adult's eyes, and even though I know the presents didn't come from Santa, it's just as magical experiencing it all through her. Every toy she opens, she swears it's exactly what she wanted and spends time checking it out before moving on to the next thing, until everything is unwrapped and the area looks like a wrapping paper room that exploded.

"Oh! I forgot about my stocking," she exclaims when there's nothing left to open. "And I have the present for the baby!" She runs into her room and comes out with a wrapped present. "Here." She hands it to her mom, who smiles softly.

A CHANCE ENCOUNTER

She opens it up and inside is a tiny little green and white knitted hat. "I made it with Aunt Naomi. It's for his head."

"*His*, huh?" I ask.

"Yeah. It's a boy," she states matter-of-factly.

Sophia laughs. "It's beautiful. And even if *he's* a *her*, she can use it." She grabs her daughter and lifts her into her arms for a hug. "Thank you, Sunshine."

"You're welcome." She kisses her mom's cheek.

"It's perfect," I add. "Thank you."

"You're welcome."

She climbs off Sophia's lap and grabs her stocking, dumping it out all over the floor. Candy and toys litter the area, as well as a piece of paper.

"What's this?" she asks, handing it to her mom.

Sophia reads it, then darts her attention over to me. "Easton..."

"Don't look at me. It was all Santa." Unfortunately, the only shows left are long distance. So, I got them tickets to my show in Los Angeles. It's on a Friday night, and I'm planning to fly them out and afterward show them around where I live, since I'll be done with the tour.

"What is it?" Kendall asks, taking the paper and attempting

to read the words.

"They're tickets to see Easton in concert," Sophia tells her.

"What's that?" Kendall asks.

"He performs songs like 'Lost' and 'Lies' in front of a big crowd. Santa brought you two tickets to go."

"Wow! Cool!" Kendall's gaze meets mine. "Can I sing too? I know all the words."

"You can sing too," Sophia says, "from your seat. He'll be on stage, though."

Kendall's brows knit together. "Why can't I go on stage?"

Sophia explains to her how a concert works, pulling up one of my previous concerts to use as an example.

"Hey, Kendall, can you give your mom her stocking?" I ask, when the girls are done discussing the concert and Kendall understands.

"Oh, Santa doesn't bring me anything," Sophia says. "I'm too big."

Kendall is already at the stocking and peeking inside. "Mommy, you have papers in your stocking too!" She pulls them out and brings them over to Sophia. "What did you get?"

Sophia glares my way then opens the papers, reading

A CHANCE ENCOUNTER

them to herself before telling Kendall. On one is a monthly pregnancy pampering package at a local spa my mom loves. She can go in every month for the next year and they'll give her a massage, facial, pedicure, and manicure. On another one is a gift certificate to an upscale maternity store. And on the last paper is a certificate of purchase for a pregnancy box. According to the website, they deliver a monthly box full of stuff a pregnant woman would want, like snacks and stuff for cravings. I found it in a pregnancy forum and thought it might be something she'd like.

Sophia reads it all to Kendall, explaining what each thing is. Because Kendall is little and doesn't really get it all, she simply says, "Cool," then runs off to play with her toys.

When she's gone, Sophia glances up at me, her eyes filled with tears, and I worry I fucked up. Until a beautiful smile stretches across her face and she comes over and hugs me. "Thank you," she murmurs into the crook of my neck. "Did you do all this last night?"

"I bought it all before and had it printed out to give you when I saw you, but when I realized I would be here, I printed it all again so you would have it this morning. Now, Kendall's was done last night. But only because I didn't know about her until then." I hit her with a pointed look.

"I feel so bad I didn't get you anything," she mutters softly.

"Trust me," I say, kissing her forehead. "You've given me plenty."

"HONEY, I'M HOME," A FEMININE VOICE RINGS OUT. SINCE SOPHIA AND KENDALL are both passed out—Kendall in her new mini pullout couch and Sophia with her head in my lap, stretched out across the couch—I know it's neither of them. After we made breakfast, we spent the morning putting the rest of Kendall's toys together. Then, while Sophia made lunch, I bagged up all the garbage and set it outside to take down to the dumpster. Kendall started to get cranky, so we put a movie on for her that she got for Christmas, and both girls, within minutes, fell asleep.

"You're not my honey," the woman says, glancing from Kendall, to Sophia, to me.

"I'm not," I agree. "I'm Easton."

"Oh, I know who you are," she says. "I recognize your

A CHANCE ENCOUNTER

pretty face from the photos."

"You must be Naomi."

"That'd be me," she says, as a guy comes in, closing the door behind him. "And this is my fiancé, Dante."

"Nice to meet you both," I tell them.

"This is Easton," she tells her fiancé, catching him up. "He's the guy who knocked up Soph."

I cringe at the crassness of her words. Yeah, it's true that's what I did in the literal sense, but wording it like that feels like she's cheapening what's growing in Sophia's belly—a beautiful miracle.

"Looks like a lot has changed in the few days we've been gone," Naomi continues, leaving her bags at the door and having a seat on the other couch with Dante.

"Naomi, don't," Sophia says, sitting up and rubbing her eyes. I expect her to move away from me since we're around other people and we haven't established what we are yet, so I'm shocked, and happy, when she stays where she is and leans into me, resting her head on my shoulder. I wasn't sure how this would all go down, but spending the last twenty-four hours with her helped crumble the wall that was between us. We still have a long way to go, and a lot to learn about one another, but I really feel like we're on the right track.

"Don't what?" Naomi asks innocently.

"Give Easton a hard time." She scrubs her palms over her face. "How was your trip?"

"Good. How was Kendall's Christmas?" She pouts. "This was the first Christmas of hers I missed."

"I'm sure when she wakes up, she'll show you everything and it will feel like you were here." Sophia laughs, but it sounds forced.

"I know, but it's not the same."

My phone goes off, while the girls are talking. It's a text from my mom asking what time I'll be over for dinner and if I'm bringing the girls. I mentioned this morning when I called to wish them a Merry Christmas that I spent the night playing Santa and she told me she really likes Sophia and Kendall and looks forward to getting to know both of them.

"Hey, Dash, do you have any plans for dinner?" I ask when there's a lull in the conversation.

She mock-glares at the nickname, at the same time Naomi asks, "Dash?"

"Yeah," I tell her, glancing over at Kendall to make sure she's asleep. "Because she dined—"

"Easton!" Sophia yells, covering my mouth with her hand. "You are not allowed to call me that around anyone else, or really ever! And you are definitely not allowed to share the meaning behind it."

Naomi cracks up laughing, not needing me to explain. "Oh my God. That's good. Dine and dash."

Dante chuckles. "I need to go home to handle some stuff for the club. You coming?"

Naomi shakes her head. "I need to start packing." She sighs, and I feel Sophia stiffen next to me.

"You going somewhere?" I ask, curious since she just got home.

"Dante bought us a house," Naomi explains with what sounds like a hint of sadness in her tone. "We're moving in next weekend."

"Damn, woman," Dante says. "You make it sound like it's the end of the world. Excuse me for wanting to spend my life with you… in the same home." He stands and walks toward the door, and Naomi follows.

"You know that's not how I feel," she says. "I'm just going to miss my best friend."

"And I offered for them to move in as well," he says,

clearly frustrated.

"And we appreciate that," Sophia jumps in. "But this is your new chapter," she says to Naomi. "And as much as we'll miss you, it's time." She moves slightly away from me, so I'm able to see her face, and I notice her smile is fake. "Plus, your house isn't far and you're still going to babysit Kendall while I work... So, really, not much will change."

"Thank you for understanding," Dante says, flashing a grateful smile at Sophia.

"I'm sorry for being a brat," Naomi mutters to Dante. "I'm grateful for the house and I love it. I'll just miss my girls."

"I know, babe," he says, kissing her. "It's a transition, but you'll see that like Sophia said, not much is going to change. Soph," he says, looking up. "I'll see you at the club."

"Will do, Boss!" Sophia chirps.

"He owns Emerald's?" I ask once he's gone.

"Yeah. He's a great boss. I've been working there since a little after Kendall was born. And thankfully, he's agreed to give me more hours since my time is limited before I start showing. With Naomi moving, I have to find a new apartment for Kendall and me."

I don't like the fact that she's working at a strip club while she's pregnant, but I bite my tongue, already aware of how independent she is.

"Why don't you just stay here?"

Sophia snorts out a laugh. "Umm, because this place is way more than I can afford. Besides, our lease is almost up. I don't want to have to sign another year lease here. My goal is to get an internship at a law firm. It'll pay shitty, but I'll get the experience. That's why I'm saving up now, so I'll have money in the bank to supplement my income." I love how motivated she is. Based on her age, she had Kendall young, which would jostle anyone's plans, yet she remains focused and determined to give them a better life.

"Hey, Soph," Naomi cuts in, walking back in from saying bye to Dante. "Want to order something for dinner?"

"Sure," Sophia says with a warm smile. "Want to stay for dinner?" she asks me.

I was supposed to ask her about going to my family's for dinner, but with her time limited with her friend, I'm sure she'd rather spend time with her.

"I have to go to my parents' for dinner." I give her a chaste kiss on her lips. "Want to do something tomorrow?" Tomorrow's Sunday, so I know she's off.

"Sure." She plasters on a fake smile that I've come to know she only does when she wants everyone to think she's okay when she's not. "Thank you for last night and today and the gifts…"

"You don't have to thank me, but you're welcome."

After saying bye to Naomi, I go back to my hotel to shower and then head over to my parents' house. The entire time I'm there, I can't help but wish I'd invited her and Kendall to dinner. For one, I already miss them, which is crazy since I just spent the last twenty-four hours with them. But also because I'm afraid she mistook my lack of invite for not wanting them to go.

When her fake smile flashes in my mind for the millionth time, I shoot her a text: **I should've said this earlier… My mom invited you over for dinner, and I was going to invite you, but then Naomi asked about ordering in and you both seemed upset about her moving and I didn't want to interfere. But I wanted you here. Both you and Kendall.**

A couple minutes later, she sends a text back: **Thank you. My overly emotional pregnancy hormones were in overdrive and overthinking. You did the right thing, but thank you for explaining. I'll see you tomorrow, right? You can come over for**

A CHANCE ENCOUNTER

breakfast and we'll hang out.

Hanging out is fine, but it's not wooing status. I only have until New Year's and then I'm back on the road again for the final leg of the tour.

As I'm trying to figure out what else we can do, my phone goes off, reminding me of the Music for the Cause charity event that's happening Thursday night. It's an annual event that takes place here in New York and all the proceeds go to help the art programs that lack funding.

My dad is performing, and since I donated a significant amount to the charity, they gave me tickets. It would be the perfect way to introduce them into my world. Kendall will love the music and the three of us can spend time together. My family will be there as well...

Since it's a black-tie event, they'll both need dresses on short notice, and instead of driving myself, I should rent a limo so they get the full experience. I text Nicole everything I need, so she can make it happen, then text Sophia to let her know I'll be over in the morning with breakfast. I don't tell her about the event, leaving it as a surprise.

I have five days to woo the shit out of her and I plan to make every day count.

Ten

SOPHIA

"IS THAT FOR ME?" KENDALL ASKS AS EASTON WALKS IN CARRYING A HUGE BOX wrapped in Christmas paper.

"It is," he tells her, setting it down. "And this is for you." He pulls a small box out of his front pocket and hands it to me.

"A late Christmas present? Why, thank you," I joke, sitting on the couch next to him.

As Kendall rips open the wrapping paper, Easton leans over and kisses my cheek. "Missed you, Dash."

"You just saw us yesterday. That's hardly enough time to miss someone."

"You're telling me. I only spent one night with you and my bed already felt lonely as hell."

My throat goes dry at his admission, and I consider whether I should tell him that last night, when I went to bed, it took me an extra-long amount of time to fall asleep because I couldn't stop thinking about him and how good it felt the previous night to fall asleep in his arms.

But before I get the courage to admit that to him, Kendall finishes unwrapping her gift and asks, "What's this?"

"It's a karaoke machine," Easton explains. "It has two microphones, and you can plug your iPad into it to play your music. You can also use Bluetooth to connect it to the television to show the words."

Kendall shrieks, like, legit, shrieks in excitement. "A karaoke machine? Wow! And it's pink! Can we open it now, please?"

"What do you say?" I prompt.

"Thank you!" She runs over to Easton and hugs him. "This is the best present ever!"

I mentally roll my eyes. She says that about every present.

"You might want to open yours," Easton says, ripping the box open and pulling the machine out.

I do as he says and find a pair of earplugs.

"What's that, Mommy?" Kendall asks.

A CHANCE ENCOUNTER

"The best present ever."

"SO, I HAVE A FAVOR TO ASK YOU," EASTON SAYS, WHEN I WALK BACK INTO THE living room from putting Kendall down for a nap. She jammed out with Easton all morning and after lunch crashed. It was cute to watch them sing and dance. Easton even showed her a dance he does at his shows and she had a blast learning it. I'm not going to lie, about four songs in, the earplugs went in, and I spent a good hour reading a book, something I haven't done in a while, since I've been busy with school.

"Hit me with it." I drop onto the couch and stretch my legs out across his lap. He grabs the bottom of my foot and tickles it. "Hey!" I whisper-yell. "No tickling the feet. I'm hella ticklish."

He laughs, but stops, taking my foot and gently massaging the sole. I groan in pleasure, my eyes rolling back slightly. "I have to find a place to buy here, so I was hoping you would come with me to check them out."

My eyes pop open. "Me?" I hardly know anything about

buying homes in New York. I've lived in the same place for the last seven years, and before that, I lived in my mom's trailer for most of my life.

"Yeah." He drops my foot and grabs the other. "I'm buying it so I can be here for you and the baby. I know we haven't talked logistics, but I'm hoping we'll spend some time there as well. The baby will have a room, and I was thinking I could decorate one for Kendall. You'll be in school and working at whatever law firm you get hired at. I told my parents I'm going to record my next album at the studio here. That way I'm able to be here and don't have to travel back and forth."

He releases my other foot and scrubs his palm up and down his scruff—his telltale sign when he's nervous. "I don't really know what I'm doing," he admits. "So, I'll need some help, but I want to be a good dad."

My heart picks up speed. This is really happening. We're going to have a baby together. The last time around it was just Naomi, me, and Kendall, but this time I'll have Easton. And he's already thinking about what kind of father he'll be. And not just that, he's also thinking about me and my daughter. He really wants to do this... all of us.

"I can help you pick something out. But really, babies don't

A CHANCE ENCOUNTER

need much." I glance around my shoebox of an apartment. I should probably be embarrassed that my entire home could fit into his parents' living room twice over, but I'm not. I'm proud of the home and life I've created for my daughter. It might be small, but it's warm and inviting, and it's *home.* "Kendall's lived here her entire life and she's happy. Children just need to feel safe and loved, and really, you can provide that anywhere."

Easton lifts my legs and edges closer, shifting me slightly so I'm on his lap. His fingers grip the back of my head and his mouth descends on mine. The kiss is slow and soft, but filled with passion, and when he pulls back, I'm damn near out of breath.

"What was that for?" I breathe. He's kissed me a few times, but nothing like that.

"For being a good mom. For finding me so I won't miss out on being a dad… and just because I can." He grins playfully. "Now that I know you're on board with me kissing you, I plan to do it every chance I get."

He brings his mouth back to mine, and our tongues unite. His fingers tangle in the back of my hair, and mine find their way around his neck. The kiss deepens, and he pulls me around so I'm straddling him. Our tongues move frantically against each other. He tastes like his signature cinnamon scent that I've learned is from the cinnamon mints he keeps in his pocket and pops into his mouth throughout the day.

As I'm running my hands down his shoulders and chest, considering removing his shirt, the front door swings open and in walks Naomi. "Whoops. Sorry," she says, not looking the least bit sorry, while I scramble to get off Easton, who's chuckling.

"How'd the meeting go?" I ask, sitting next to Easton.

"Good. Thankfully she's not a bridezilla, so I think everything will go smoothly." She's referring to the NBA player's fiancée who's hired her to plan her engagement party and wedding.

She's telling us about some of the crazy stuff she wants, when Easton's phone goes off. "The realtor can meet us in about an hour."

"Realtor?" Naomi asks.

"Easton is buying a place here to be close to the baby."

"And you," he says. "This isn't just about the baby." He kisses me firmly on the lips.

My neck and cheeks warm up, knowing Naomi is

watching. Thankfully she doesn't comment on it. But when I glance over, I notice she and Easton are sharing some kind of look. "What?"

"Nothing," they both say in unison. *Okay...*

"Where's Kendall? Sleeping?" Naomi asks.

"Yeah. I'll wake her up so we can go."

"Or she can stay with me. I'm home the rest of the day. You two can go look at places and grab something to eat—kid-less."

"You sure?" Kendall will no doubt be bored looking at homes.

"Yep. Go on. Get out of here."

"All right, thanks." I stand. "Maybe while we're out, I can see what apartments are out there and available."

After I finish getting ready, we head out. Easton is driving his own vehicle today. He tells me it's his dad's, since his are all still in California, so it's easy to get from place to place. He's gotten it approved by the realtor to get the codes from each home, so we can look at them without her—the perks of being rich and famous, I guess.

We stop at a deli he likes and grab a late lunch. I'm worried about being seen, but it seems he's off the radar here. While we're eating, he hands me his phone with all the listings pulled up. The realtor has sent him over a dozen that meet his criteria.

"We should probably narrow them down. They're spread out all over New York. Where's your studio located?"

"Off Madison, near Bryant Park."

"Okay, so let's look at the homes in that area first."

"Where are you planning to look for places?" he asks, popping a chip into his mouth. "I want to be near you."

I laugh. "Your budget is a little different than mine. Plus, I'm hoping to stay in my area. Kendall loves her school and if I move out of that zone, she'll have to switch schools."

Easton nods.

We go through his criteria and narrow it down to five places to look at. The first two are nice—not my taste, far too much white—but he says they're not what he's looking for. The third place is gorgeous, but it's four floors like his parents' place, and when I point out that will be a lot of up and down with a baby, he agrees.

We walk into the fourth place and it's beautiful. Three stories—living room, dining room, kitchen, and full bath on the first, three bedrooms and two bathrooms on the second, and the master bedroom, en suite bathroom, and an office on the third. Everything is dark wood and stainless steel.

"What do you think?" he asks.

"I think if I were rich, I would buy this place," I say in awe. "It's even in Kendall's school district," I joke.

He smiles warmly. "Yeah, it's nice."

"Nice?" I splutter. "It's gorgeous. Did you see the breakfast nook in the kitchen? And the walk-in closets? If you don't buy it, I just might have to."

Easton laughs. "This place is definitely a possibility, so don't go trying to outbid me yet. Where to next?"

We look at the last place, and like all the others, it's beautiful. But my favorite is still house number four.

"What do you think? There are more places we can look at." I'm exhausted, my feet hurt, and I'm ready for bed, but I don't tell him that.

"I think we've looked at enough places today," he says, as if reading my mind. "It's late. Let's get something to eat for dinner and then go home."

"That sounds perfect."

When we get back to my place, it's already after eight. Kendall is fast asleep and Naomi is in her room. I knock to let her know we're here, and then Easton drags me into my room, closing the door behind us.

While I'm getting changed into something more comfortable, his realtor calls to see how it all went. I overhear him talking to her, and since I'm only hearing one side, I don't know all that's being said, but when he mentions the price of the place, my heart stops. It's so easy to forget that Easton is rich when he's hanging out at my house and playing karaoke or watching movies. But the fact is we're way different—and I'm not only talking about our tax brackets.

"She's going to place an offer on the house in Lennox," he says, hanging up.

"Are you sure that's necessary?"

He shoots me a confused look.

"I just mean, from what I overhead, it's expensive, and you mentioned you own a home in California... and I imagine you'll eventually go back."

His brown eyes harden slightly. "I do have a home in California, but you said your home is here, so that means mine is too."

"Like permanently?" I hear the insecurity in my voice, but I can't stop the words from spilling out.

A CHANCE ENCOUNTER

"As long as you're here, I'm here."

"I get that, but it's a lot of money to spend, and what if we don't work out?" I swallow thickly at the thought, but I have to be realistic because I'm already falling for him and if it ends the way it did with my father or Freeman, I'm going to be devastated. I always knew my father didn't want me, and looking back, Freeman never made any promises. They were all in my head. I was young and naïve, and I assumed we were on the same page. I was way, way wrong.

He steps over to me, his hands landing on either side of the dresser, since I'm leaning against it. "Wherever you are is where I'll be. I'll repeat that a hundred times, or a thousand, if that's what you need from me." He dips his head slightly and his lips brush softly over mine. "I'm here and I'm not going anywhere, so whatever preconceived notions you have in your head need to be wiped out. This isn't just about the baby growing in your belly. It's about us."

He lays a kiss to the corner of my mouth and then the other corner, sending a shiver of desire through my body. "I want to get to know you, Dash…" His lips descend, and he nips playfully along my jawline. "In every way possible," he murmurs, pressing a feather-like kiss to the shell of my ear.

My core clenches at his seductive words and touch.

When he lifts his face to look at me, his eyes are blazing with passion.

"I want you," he rasps, his eyes not leaving mine. "Your mind, your body, your heart... I won't stop until every single part of you is mine."

"You have me," I breathe. "I'm yours."

He shakes his head. "Not yet, but you will be."

His mouth crashes against mine, his tongue darting out and seeking entrance, at the same time he reaches around, squeezing the globes of my ass, and lifts me onto my dresser. He spreads my legs and steps between my thighs, pulling me to the edge.

Greedily, he possesses my mouth. His tongue caressing my own. My fingers drag through his hair, gripping the ends and tugging him closer. I'm turned on, craving him, but no matter how deep the kiss goes, it's not enough.

I grind my center against his front, using the hard-on in his pants for my pleasure, but it's still not enough. I groan in annoyance and Easton chuckles into my mouth.

"I got you," he murmurs against my lips. He breaks our kiss and lifts my shirt over my head, exposing my bra, then unbuttons my pants, tapping my thigh to lift so he can remove them. Since I've already taken off my boots when we got home, he slides them down my legs and drops them onto the floor, leaving me in only my bra and panties.

He steps back and rakes his gaze down my body. "Fuck, you're so beautiful," he says, his tongue darting out to wet his lips. "I've been dreaming about the day I get to taste you again."

He drops to his knees, aligning his face with my center, then leans in, inhaling my scent through the cotton material. I squirm, needing him to make me feel good. "Please," I beg.

His eyes dart up. "I'm going to make you come," he says, "but you need to be patient. It's like eating a dessert. I'm not about to rush through it. I want to enjoy it, savor it, every bit of it."

Holy shit! My thighs clench together in anticipation.

Easton hooks the sides of my panties and pulls them down my legs, then stands. With his strong hands gripping the tops of my thighs, he kisses me fervently. He sucks on my bottom lip, then trails kisses down my neck, suckling on my flesh. When he gets to the tops of my breasts, he reaches around and removes my bra, dropping it to the ground with the rest of my clothes.

He cups my breasts, gently massaging them, and because they're sensitive from my pregnancy, zaps of desire shoot through me. I moan in pleasure. "I need... *more*, please, Easton."

"I know, baby." He licks one of my nipples then wraps his lips around it, sucking on it, until my back arches, my chest jutting out. He licks the other nipple, while he pinches the one he just licked, and I swear it feels like I'm about to come from that alone.

Desperate to get more out of him, I reach down and try to undo his pants, but he backs up slightly and shakes his head. When I pout in frustration, he smirks. "Let me enjoy my dessert, Dash."

He drops back onto his knees and spreads my legs. He runs his finger along my folds, teasing and playing. I want to yell that adults don't play with their damn food and to eat me already, but then his tongue lands on me and the back of my head hits the mirror as my eyes roll upward.

He pushes my thighs wider, and his wet tongue runs up my center, lapping at my juices, until he gets to my clit. Then all his attention stays on it, licking, laving, flicking my clit,

A CHANCE ENCOUNTER

until my climax overtakes me. My legs shake and my overly sensitive clit throbs, but Easton doesn't stop until I've come completely undone.

"I knew it," he says, standing. "I *knew* I remembered you tasting this fucking good." His mouth brushes against mine for a quick kiss. No tongue is used, but I can still taste myself on his lips. When he pulls back, he's grinning. "Good, right?"

"Eh." I quirk my head to the side. "It's okay... But I'm strictly dickly if you catch my drift." I wink flirtatiously, and he barks out a laugh.

"My turn." I push him back and hop off the dresser, dropping to my knees. I quickly unbutton his jeans and tug them, along with his boxer briefs, down his legs. His dick springs forward, and I take a moment to appreciate it. It's long and thick and neatly trimmed.

Unable to wait a second longer, I lift his dick, so it's lying flat against his belly, and run my tongue along the underside of his shaft until I get to the mushroom head. I do that again and again, licking him like my own personal ice cream cone. When he's hard as steel, I flick my tongue across the tip, tasting the precum, then take him all the way into my mouth.

"Jesus," Easton breathes, pulling me up and forcing me to

release his dick.

When the corners of my lips dip down, he chuckles. "Sorry, but when I come, it won't be in your mouth."

He lifts and carries me to my bed, laying me on the mattress. He shucks his pants off and removes his shirt, exposing his toned body. As he climbs up the bed, I admire his fit physique appreciatively. He kicks my legs apart and situates himself between my thighs. "For weeks after we were together, I was thinking about you," he admits. "Trying to figure out ways to find you." His muscular arms drop onto either side of my head, caging me in, while he supports his own weight.

He kisses the tip of my nose. "I was only with you one time and you had me addicted." Our lips touch, and he thrusts into me. We both groan as he fills me completely.

"This is the way it should've been," he murmurs, withdrawing and then driving back inside. His body moving against mine in a slow, delicious rhythm.

"What?" I breathe, closing my eyes. Another orgasm is building, and every time he swivels his hips, my body tightens around him.

"The first time we were together," he says, "I should've

A CHANCE ENCOUNTER

taken my time…" He kisses the sensitive spot under my ear, and my body winds a little tighter in response.

"Explored every inch of you." He suckles on my neck, and I clench in anticipation. I'm hovering over the precipice and it won't be long until I fall.

"Tasted every part of you." In the same intimate way our bodies are connected, his mouth connects with mine, and like a rubber band wound too tightly, I snap and fall over the edge, screaming out my orgasm as it rushes through me. Thankfully Easton kisses me, muffling the sound. He picks up his speed, fucking me deeper, harder, and all too soon he's following me over that delicious edge.

"Stay the night," I say, once we've both gotten a handle on our breathing.

He pulls out of me and plants a soft kiss to my lips. "I'm not going anywhere."

And maybe it's the orgasm that has my head all fucked up, but for some reason, I believe him.

Eleven

SOPHIA

"HEY, SOPH, CAN YOU GRAB ME A BOTTLE OF DON PERIGNON?" MICHELLE ASKS, walking around the bar to grab some glasses and a bucket of ice.

"Did you input it?"

"Yeah."

I glance over at the printer and see an order hanging out. "Got it."

I check to make sure Clarissa is manning the bar before I run to the back to grab the chilled bottle. I ring it up on Michelle's tab, then hand it to her.

"Thanks!" she says, placing it into the bucket, then taking it over to her table.

"What does a man need to do to get a little service around

here?" a masculine voice asks.

I snap my head to the side and see Easton sitting at the bar with a sexy smirk splayed across his face. He's been here both nights I've worked this week, showing up around an hour or so before closing. The first night I got defensive, thinking he was either going to judge or berate me, but he did neither. Instead, he ordered a drink, hung out, chatted with me when I had time to chat, then after I was done closing down the bar, he took me home and spent the night with me.

We haven't had sex again since Sunday night—when he gave me two of the most amazing, mind-blowing orgasms of my life—because I've been too exhausted after working seven-hour shifts on my feet, but he holds me in his arms and plays with my hair until I fall asleep.

He told me today while we were hanging out, he'll be leaving for the last part of his tour on New Year's Day and my first thought was how much I'll miss him while he's gone. He's quickly become part of our life, part of our routine. Even Kendall wakes up and goes in search of him to play karaoke with her.

"Jack and Coke?" I confirm. It's what he's gotten the last two nights, but I just want to make sure.

A CHANCE ENCOUNTER

"Yep," he says with a soft smile.

After I make and serve him his drink, I check on my customers, before I head back over to him. He always sits at the end of the bar, in the darkened corner where he can't really be seen, and for that I'm grateful. The last thing I need is him being put on blast. The club has a strict no cell phone/recording policy, but who knows what would happen if people got wind of Easton frequenting. Because of me wanting to go to law school, Dante is nice enough to always pay me under the table so it can never be traced back to me working here, but if Easton gets caught here and is linked to me, all that effort to protect my reputation will go down the drain.

I lean against the bar and he stretches across it, kissing me quickly. "How's work?"

"Good." I shrug. Between the holidays and snow, it's been on the slow side. It'll pick up after the first of the year, but until then the tips are sucking. "I finished signing up for my last semester of classes during my break." It's crazy to think after this semester is over, I'll not only be a college graduate, but I'll also be a mom to two.

"Congratulations," he says, taking a sip of his drink.

"Hey, Soph," Clarissa calls out. "Dante said to tell you,

you can take off. It's slow and I can close up."

I glance at the clock and see it's 2:00 a.m. With how dead it is, I won't miss out on much money, so I might as well get home a little early and get some extra sleep. "Thanks!" I clean the dishes then grab my till and bring it to the back to cash out. Once I'm done, I meet Easton by the front door.

He puts the hoodie on his leather jacket up and grabs my hand, guiding us outside into the cold. Since he drove, we jump into his car, and he takes me home.

After I check on Kendall, who's asleep, and say hi to Naomi, who's packing, I quickly shower and change into my pajamas. When I come out, Easton is changed into a pair of sweats and a T-shirt he keeps here now.

"Naomi looks ready to move," Easton notes, sliding into the bed.

I lie on my side, flopping my leg on top of his. "Yeah."

"How will it work with her watching Kendall?" He runs his fingers through my hair and my eyes flutter closed in contentment.

"During the week, she'll stay here since Kendall has school, and on the weekends, she'll spend the night there."

"How many days a week do you work?"

"Six. The club is closed on Sundays."

Easton sighs and I can tell he wants to say something, but I'm thankful he doesn't. The last thing I need is to feel guilty for the number of nights I work. "Law school isn't cheap," I explain, "and they offer no financial aid. Once I graduate, after I'm home for six weeks with the baby, I'm going to look for a job at a law firm, but they pay crap." I laugh humorlessly. "Who would've thought a strip club would pay better than a law firm…"

Easton laughs as well, but it sounds forced. I hold my breath, waiting for his lecture to come, but I'm shocked when instead he says, "I'm going to miss you, Dash." He kisses the top of my head and I snuggle into his chest. "I'll be counting down the days to when you and Kendall come to my show."

"I'm going to miss you too," I tell him, as I breathe in his delicious scent, hoping to memorize it. I went years without needing a man and now I can't imagine going days, let alone weeks without Easton.

"MORE PRESENTS?" I ASK, WHEN EASTON WALKS THROUGH THE DOOR HOLDING three boxes in his hands, two of which are wrapped with large red bows. "In case you haven't noticed, Christmas was over several days ago." I know he knows this because he helped me take down my tree and put all the ornaments away while Kendall explained the meaning behind every single one to him.

When he woke up this morning and said he had to run an errand and would be back soon, I didn't expect him to come back with gifts.

"Wow! Presents!" Kendall squeals before he can answer me.

"Kind of," he says, setting them down, along with a bag that was hanging on his arm. "But first, breakfast." He grabs the top box and opens it up, exposing a dozen donuts, so gorgeously decorated it's almost a shame they're about to disappear into our bellies.

"Oh! I want this one!" Kendall exclaims, pointing at the one with white frosting and blue and silver snowflakes. "It's so pretty!" Easton goes to grab it, but before he does, Kendall changes her mind. "Wait, I want that one!" She points to a chocolate one with red and green sprinkles. "It looks like it tastes yummier." Easton grins and is about to grab it, when she changes her mind *again.*

I watch as she goes through each one, explaining why that donut is the best, and Easton patiently listens and discusses them with her, like it's a life-altering decision. It's no secret Easton is a delicious specimen of a man. Between his good looks and charm, he has women eating out of his hand. I've searched him and have seen the posts and comments from women all over the world begging for his time and attention. Yet, here he is, standing in my kitchen, discussing donuts with my daughter. The handsome face, the soulful brown eyes, and the abs that look and feel like they're carved out of stone are all great, but I've come to the conclusion that there's nothing sexier than a man giving a child his undivided attention.

Even when my dad was around, I never felt like I had his attention. He treated parenting like a chore—both my parents did—and because of that, too many times, I felt like I was a burden, a regret, a mistake they had to deal with. I told myself I would never allow my children to ever feel that way, that no matter how tough things got, they would know they're my world. That they're wanted and loved. And seeing the way Easton treats my daughter when she isn't even his, gives me hope that he'll be a hands-on, loving father to our baby.

"All right, so we're going with half of the chocolate one with red and green sprinkles and half of the one that looks like Santa?" he confirms.

"Yes!" Kendall grins in excitement.

Easton grabs a knife and cuts the donuts in half, setting them on a napkin, then pulls a bottle of milk out of the bag.

"Thank you," Kendall says, already stuffing her face.

"How about you?" he asks, stepping closer to me. "You hungry, Dash?" He leans in so Kendall can't hear. "I saw you unwrapping me with your eyes…"

"I was watching you talk to Kendall," I argue, fully aware I was doing exactly as he accused. I can't help it, though. I know what's under his *wrapping paper* and, even though I'm exhausted as hell, I want nothing more than to unwrap him again. Tonight is our last night together before he leaves—he has the New Year's show tomorrow night and leaves right afterward—and since Emerald's has been slow, Dante gave me the rest of the week off, so after Kendall goes to bed, I plan to do just that.

"Uh-huh. Just know that any time you're hungry for me,

A CHANCE ENCOUNTER

I'm available."

"I already had you." I shrug. "Twice. You were good, but these donuts look way more delicious." I grab the other half of one of the donuts he cut up for Kendall and take a huge bite. "Ycp," I say, moaning loudly. "Definitely more delicious."

He chuckles, grabs his own donut, and sits down at the table. "We'll see," he says with a mischievous sparkle in his eye, making my lady parts clench in want.

While we eat, we make small talk about Easton's upcoming trip. He tells us all the cities he has left to visit, and Kendall asks if I can print her a map to hang on her wall, so she can see where he's going. Easton promises to pick up something for her in every city he's in, which reminds Kendall...

"Is it time for presents now?" she asks.

"Who said the present is for you?" I ruffle her hair, making her pout. "Go throw your garbage away and clean your hands and mouth."

"Well, then, who is it for?" she asks, grabbing her plate and cup and dumping them into the sink. She stands on the stool and washes her hands, then returns.

"I told you it's only kind of a present," Easton says with a laugh. "So there's this concert tonight. It's for charity, to support music in the schools, and I have seats, so I was thinking the three of us could go."

He hands us each a box, and Kendall immediately starts pulling at the ribbon to get it open, while I stay frozen in my spot. We talked about this... About staying under the radar. He agreed.

Kendall gets her box open and inside is a gorgeous pink tulle dress and matching pink, sparkly shoes. She shrieks, of course loving it all.

"I'm going to go try it on!" she yells, already running down the hallway.

"You going to open yours?" Easton nods toward the box in front of me.

"What are you doing?" I ask, ignoring his question.

His brows knit together. "I'm hoping to take you and Kendall to a concert."

"In public? Where everyone will see us with you?" My heart stutters in my chest. This can't be happening.

"Nobody is going to know you're pregnant. You're barely even showing. And you're further along now anyway." He takes a step toward me and I take a step back, needing space to think. I thought I had more time to figure things out, but here he is, trying to pull me into his world… his very *public* world.

"What's going on?" he asks, his voice full of concern.

"What's going on is that I don't want my daughter and I splashed across the tabloids. I want my private life to remain private." I can't do this. I can't be who he needs me to be. Not with my secret… The thought devastates me. What the hell was I thinking? That's the problem… I wasn't.

"That's impossible with the life I live," he says, "but I can assure you, I'll do everything in my power to protect you and Kendall, always."

He speaks with such conviction, I believe him. I have no doubt he'd make sure we're safe and seen in a positive light. The problem is it doesn't matter what light we're seen in. Once we're out there, people will dig, and if they dig, I run the chance of my past getting dug up. And I can't take that chance. I care about him, I might even be falling in love with him, but I have to put my daughter's welfare first, always. I'm her mom and it's my job to make sure she's loved and safe.

"You said you didn't want anyone to know about the baby," he continues. "You didn't say anything about not being seen with me." Hurt flashes in his eyes, and I hate that he thinks this is about him, but I can't explain the truth to him. I have to stick to my story. It's how I'll ensure my family and daughter are safe from Freeman. I've seen the person he's become. He's worse now than he was seven years ago. The power has gone to his head and I can't even imagine what he's capable of.

"Well, I'm saying it now." I jut my chin out in defiance, trying to sound aloof, when inside, my heart is cracking, shattering, the pieces falling all over the ground. "I don't want to be in the spotlight."

"Sophia." He sighs, his tone filled with confusion. "It's impossible to remain hidden. Paparazzi follow me everywhere."

"Then I guess we don't go anywhere!" I shout in exasperation. I don't know what I'm doing right now, what I'm saying. It feels like my world, the one I've done everything in my power to keep in a bubble, is about to explode, and I can't let that happen.

"Ever?" he gasps.

"I don't know!" Tears of frustration prick my lids. I knew this day would come eventually, but I ignored it, pushed it to the side and allowed myself to get lost in him, which was

A CHANCE ENCOUNTER

easy to do in our own little bubble. But now he wants to pop said bubble... "This is all just happening so fast," I blurt out. "I need... I need some time to think." I want him, but I can't change who he is. And if I have to choose between him and my daughter... It's her, it's always her.

He shakes his head and is about to respond, when Kendall comes running out in her gorgeous dress. "I'm ready! I look like a pretty princess! Right?" My heart plummets because I'm going to have to tell her we're not going anywhere.

"You look beautiful," I tell her, forcing a smile on my face.

"You look like the prettiest princess in all the land," Easton murmurs, trying like hell to hide how he's feeling.

"Sunshine, can you do Mommy a favor?" I ask.

"Uh-huh."

"Can you go play in your room for a few minutes while I talk to Easton?"

Her face falls, but she nods and walks away.

Once she's in her room, Easton bridges the gap between us. "Don't do this," he pleads. "Don't push me away."

"I'm sorry," I mutter. "I can't do this."

"Do what?"

"Us." Our eyes lock and hurt dims his brown eyes. "I need

space."

He huffs. "Fine." He shakes his head. "Space granted."

He turns his back on me and walks out the door, and I fall to the ground, afraid I've just made the biggest mistake of my life.

Twelve

EASTON

"EASTON! WOW!" CARMEN, THE HOSTESS AND A GOOD FRIEND OF MY SISTER'S, gushes. "You sure know how to put on a show." She dramatically fans herself while I put my coat back on. I took it off to perform, but it's cold as fuck outside.

"Thank you," I tell her, smiling for the camera, since I know millions of people are tuning in to watch the New Year's Eve show. No matter what's going on in my personal life, I've been taught to put on a front for the public eye. Otherwise, they'll eat you alive.

"So, while I have you, I have to ask the same question I've been asking everyone tonight…"

Her lips quirk into a flirty smile and I know what's coming. It's a question I've been asked in some way, shape, or form too many damn times to count over the years since I ended my engagement with Ashleigh. The media has been salivating for me to throw them a morsel. After my engagement ended, I dived into my music headfirst, focusing on my career and future. Sure, they'd catch me at an event with someone on my arm, but it was never anything worth mentioning. And I made sure to never give them anything they could use against me.

"Are you ringing in the new year with anyone special?"

Usually, when I'm asked this question, I laugh and say something funny. But right now, I don't have it in me to make jokes. Because for the first time in years, I want the world to know that I've met the woman I want to spend my life with. I want them to know about how much I've fallen for her, how sweet and beautiful she is. I want to shout to the world that she's carrying my baby. For them to know how wonderful of a mother she is to Kendall. And how, just like her mother, her daughter has stolen a piece of my heart.

But I can't say anything to anyone. And the way Sophia was acting, I'm not sure if she'll ever be okay with me talking about her.

"Easton," Carmen prompts, snapping me from my

A CHANCE ENCOUNTER

thoughts. "Does your silence mean yes?"

Shit, I was spaced out and my guard dropped. I have to save this shit before people start speculating…

"Carmen, you know if the day ever comes when I find a woman worth mentioning, you'll be the first to know." I wink playfully, making her flush and giggle and, thankfully, move on to her next question.

As I robotically answer the rest of her questions, I can't help the bitter taste in my mouth. I know my response was the right one because that's what Sophia wants, but it still feels shitty, like she and our baby are some dirty little secret. When the truth is, they're anything but.

Once the interview is over, I head out, not in the mood to party. Because it's crazy in New York tonight, my sister hired a car service, and Joel, one of my bodyguards, escorts me to the car.

"Sir," he says, opening the door for me.

"Thanks, man." I bump his fist. "I'll see you in the morning." We're leaving early as hell, since we have a show in Toronto the following night.

"Where to?" the driver asks once I'm in and the door is closed.

"My hotel, please."

Once the car takes off, I pull my phone out and type out a text to Sophia. I haven't contacted her since she asked for space, but I have something I need to say...

Me: I was interviewed tonight and I hated not being able to tell the world about you and Kendall and our little Rubik's cube. I'm falling for you and I want everyone to know how much you mean to me. How excited I am to become a dad. I know my world is scary, but I'll always protect you. I promise.

It shows she's read my text and then the bubbles start. A few seconds later, her text comes through.

Dash: I saw the interview. I know you would...I just need some time to think.

Her lack of response has my heart sinking in my chest. She's scared, for whatever reason, and is pushing me away, and in a few hours I'm going to be back on a tour bus traveling for the next month. Whatever wall she's put up will only have time to rise higher and become more impenetrable. But I don't know what to do, how to stop this from happening.

"It's almost midnight," a man says on the radio, catching my attention.

A CHANCE ENCOUNTER

"When I was growing up, my parents used to tell me whoever you're with at midnight is who you'll be with all year," a female says in response.

The guy laughs. "Well, then, looks like we'll be seeing a lot of each other next year."

I glance at the clock—it's nine minutes until twelve. "Change of plans," I tell the driver. "I need you to take me to Lennox Hills." I give him the address of Sophia's apartment and he inputs it into his GPS. It shows seven minutes. I'll be cutting it close.

When he pulls up, I yell for him to wait and run up the stairs to her apartment. Not wanting to wake Kendall up, I knock softly, but hard enough Sophia will hear it. A second later, the door opens. Sophia's dressed in my gray sweats and LOST hoodie I left here, and my heart swells. She might be pushing me away, but she's wearing my clothes. That has to count for something, right?

"Easton," she breathes. Her hair is up in a messy bun and her face is splotchy. She's been crying. Whatever is going on with her, she's struggling. I don't like to see her upset, but I would be lying if I said I wasn't glad on some level to see that she's upset. It means she's struggling with her decision to push me away. Unless…

"Are you and the baby okay?"

She nods.

"And Kendall's okay?"

"Yes," she says. "Everyone is… okay. What are you doing here?"

"The person you're with at midnight is the person you'll spend the year with," I tell her, stepping into her space. "The odds are already against me, so I figured this might help tip the scale in my favor."

Without asking for permission, I entwine my fingers in her hair and kiss her hard. In the background, the man on the television announces that it is midnight, officially the new year.

I expect Sophia to resist, but she doesn't. Her body sinks against mine and she kisses me back. Her lips are soft and plump, and she smells intoxicating. She must've showered recently because I can smell her signature body wash she uses. I keep my mouth pressed to hers, inhaling her scent, trying to memorize the way she smells, the way she feels, the way she tastes. I'm going to need this memory to get me through the next month, until I can come back and somehow beg her to be with me.

The kiss ends and Sophia's glassy eyes meet mine. "Easton," she chokes out.

"Shh, baby, it's okay," I tell her, running my knuckles down the side of her cheek. "I get it. You need time, and I'm going to give you that. I just needed to see you before I left."

She nods and several tears fall. I wipe them with my thumbs, hating that she's hurting. Hating that I have no clue how to make this better for her. I have a feeling she's keeping something from me, but I don't know what. And until she tells me, there's nothing I can do.

"I'll see you soon, beautiful." I kiss her forehead and then step back into the hallway. "Take care of our baby, all right? And tell Kendall I'll be back soon."

She flashes me a watery smile. "I will," she rasps. More tears fall and I want to catch them all, but I have to go. I have to give her her space. And I know if I don't leave now, it'll only be harder on both of us. So, I do the hardest thing I've ever had to do and walk away.

"HEY, MAN, WE'RE GOING OUT FOR DINNER. YOU COMING?" JORDAN ASKS FROM the doorway of our adjoining hotel rooms. We're in Chicago for a few days, so we've checked into a hotel. We do that when we're in one city longer than a single night. Gets us out of the bus and keeps us from going stir-crazy. I should probably go so I can eat something, but I'm not in the mood to be around people, especially ones like my sister and Jordan, who'll drill me with questions.

"Nah, go ahead. I'll grab something here."

He sighs but doesn't bother to argue. "All right, we'll see you in a little bit," he says before closing the door behind him.

I pull out my phone and send my nightly text to Sophia. I've been texting her every day, twice a day, since I left: once in the morning, wishing her a good day, and another in the evening, asking how her day was. Her responses are always short, never giving too much away, but she at least responds… I'll take what I can get.

Kendall, on the other hand, I talk to every day. We FaceTime and I tell her the new city I'm in and she tells me how school is going and the drama of the day in first grade.

Me: Hey, Dash, my calendar notified me that you're officially 15 weeks today (I'm sure you already know

A CHANCE ENCOUNTER

that, though). Congrats! I looked it up and the baby is the size of a light bulb. Not much of a difference from the baseball he was last week... My favorite week is still the Rubik's cube. I hope you're having a good day off. Miss you.

I wait a few minutes, but she doesn't respond. She started back at school a few days ago, so between Kendall, work, and school, I imagine she's busy, but she generally responds pretty quickly, unless she's at work. But it's Sunday, so I know she's off. Hell, it's her *only* day off.

When I still haven't heard from her after a half an hour, I decide to call.

"Hello?" a small voice says—Kendall.

"Kendall, is that you?"

"Yes, Easton, is that you?"

"Yes," I say through a laugh. "What are you doing with your mom's phone?"

"We were watching a movie and she fell asleep. Her head hurts."

"Is your aunt Naomi there?"

"Nope, just me and Mommy."

"I'm going to FaceTime you, okay?"

"Okay."

She hangs up, and I call right back, this time with video. "Hi!" she yells, her adorable little face coming over the screen. "Where are you today?" I can see her walking down the hall and into her room, where Sophia set up a map for her like she asked.

"I'm still in Chicago, Illinois."

"Still? You've been there forever."

I chuckle. "Only a few days. I'll be here tomorrow too and then we'll go somewhere new."

"Okay."

"Can you bring the phone to your mom?" She said she's sleeping, but I can't imagine her sleeping while Kendall is awake by herself.

She nods and starts to walk again. When she gets to Sophia's room, it's dark, so I can't see anyone.

"Mommy, Easton's on the phone and wants to talk to you."

"What—Shit! I mean shoot. Did I fall asleep?" Sophia asks, her voice sounding groggy.

"Yeah. I heard the phone ringing, so I got it and it's Easton."

A CHANCE ENCOUNTER

"Thank you, Sunshine," Sophia says. There's a rustling and then Sophia says, "Hello?" I can't make her out, but I'm almost positive she has her ear against the phone, thinking it's a phone call.

"It's on FaceTime," I tell her.

"Oh, hold on." There's more rustling and then a soft light turns on and her beautiful face appears. "Hey." Under her eyes are dark and her face looks slightly puffy. Her hair is in a tangled mess on top of her head, and she looks like she's been run over by a train. She's still beautiful, don't get me wrong. She's always beautiful. But there's something wrong.

"You okay?" I ask, wishing I were there. Hating I'm hours away.

"Yeah." She clears her throat and plasters on her signature fake smile. "I worked late and woke up with a bit of a headache."

I want to tell her I'll give her money so she can stop working, but I know she won't accept it. It's like she has something to prove. She has to do it all herself, so she can say she did it on her own.

"Can you take something for it?"

"Yeah, I did." She squeezes her eyes together, like she's in

199

pain, then reopens them.

"Have you been in bed all day?" I ask, worried.

"For the most part. It's been snowing and raining all day, so we've been watching movies. I can't believe I fell asleep." I hear the guilt in her words and want to say something to lighten it, but I don't know what to say, so I ask the same thing I always ask her...

"Is there anything you need?" I already know she'll say no. I'm pretty sure she'd rather die than take help from me, but I'll keep asking in hope one day she'll say yes.

"I'm okay, but thanks."

"What are you up to this week?" I ask, hoping to keep the conversation going. This is the first time we've spoken since I left.

"The usual. School, work... Oh, Friday I have my four-month checkup."

Damn, it's already been a month since her last appointment? I run through the days in my head. We have a show here tomorrow, one in Colorado the next day... One in Utah Thursday... "I'm off Friday," I blurt out. "I can go."

Her eyes widen. "Aren't you far away?"

"I can fly." I don't know where I'm getting a flight from,

but I'll make it happen, no matter what it takes. There's no way I'm passing up a chance to see her, and since it's an appointment for the baby, she won't say no. "What time is it for?"

"Ten o'clock. But it's just a routine—"

"Dash," I say, cutting her off. "I want to be there. It's bad enough I'm away for the next month."

"Okay, well, it's up to you." Her voice is resigned, and it breaks my heart. "I need to give Kendall a bath and put her to bed..."

"Yeah, of course." I force a smile. "I'll talk to you soon?"

She nods once, then ends the call, leaving me frustrated as hell.

A second later, my phone rings and I quickly answer it, thinking it's Sophia calling me back. "Hey."

"Hey, sweetheart," my mom says.

I sigh into the phone. "Hey, Mom."

"I'm going to try not to take offense that you aren't more thrilled to hear from your mother."

I chuckle lightly. "It's not that..."

"It's that something's wrong," she finishes for me. "Your sister told me you've been sulking since you left. You're freezing her and Jordan out, keeping to yourself. What's happened, Easton?"

"Sophia and I got into an… argument, I guess. She doesn't want anyone to know she's connected to me. She wants her life to remain private."

Mom is quiet for a moment before she says, "Are you sure the baby is yours?"

I can see where she would make that assumption. If the baby wasn't mine, Sophia wouldn't want to announce it to the world and later look stupid, but…

"The baby is mine. I got the results back a few days ago." I never doubted it, but now we know officially.

"So, she's just uncomfortable?"

"That's what she says. She's also going to school and working full-time, and taking care of her daughter, and of course, she won't let me help in any way."

"Sounds to me like she's an independent woman. I knew I liked her." I can hear the smile in my mom's voice.

"Mom," I groan.

"I know, I get it. You're feeling helpless. But you have to understand this is a huge change for her. Your lifestyle, your money, the spotlight. You grew up with it, but for someone

A CHANCE ENCOUNTER

who's never been around it, I imagine it's a bit overwhelming."

I get what she's saying, which is why I'm trying to give Sophia some space, but it doesn't mean I have to like it or be happy about it. And I sure as hell don't have to agree with it. "I just wish she'd let me in instead of pushing me away."

"What if I talk to her?" Mom offers.

"You don't think it'll make it worse?" I don't want Sophia to think we're ganging up on her.

"I'll just call her to see how she's doing and go from there."

"All right, cool. Thanks, Mom."

We talk for a few more minutes, and once we hang up, I text her Sophia's number. I'm hoping this doesn't make it worse, but at this point, I don't have much to lose, and I'm not sure if it could even get any worse.

I pull up my schedule, even though for the first time I pretty much have it memorized, and start trying to figure out how I'm going to make it from Utah to New York for the appointment and then to Washington the following night for a show. It's going to be hard, and everything will have to line up perfectly, but I'm determined to make it happen.

Thirteen

SOPHIA

I PUT THE PHONE DOWN AND CLOSE MY EYES, NEEDING A MOMENT. I MISS Easton so damn much. Every day, I miss him. His smiles, his laughter, his touch. I miss him. And if I'm honest, between school and work and Kendall, I don't have time to miss him. But it doesn't stop me from doing so.

I thought if we didn't talk, the ache in my heart would go away quicker. But then he had to go and text me every morning and night, reminding me what I'm missing. What I'm giving up. When he FaceTimes Kendall and they talk, I listen, my heart clenching in my chest, wishing I could talk to him. Lean on him. Depend on him. Seek comfort in him. I shouldn't miss someone as much as I miss him, especially since our relationship had only just begun before I tore the rug out from under us, but I can't stop how I feel.

I pull myself up, and my head spins slightly, my surroundings blurring. I grab onto the nightstand to steady myself and thankfully, everything comes into focus. I've only been back to school and work for a week, but it's a lot. And then add the fact that Naomi moved out, and Kendall and I have to be out by the end of next month, and I'm a ball of stress. I know this is just a small moment, and I will get it all figured out, but right now, it feels like everything is piling up on my shoulders.

"Kendall, it's time to take a bath," I tell her, stepping into the doorway of her room. She's coloring a picture at her table.

"Already?" She pouts.

"It's almost bedtime. You have school in the morning." I walk over and kiss her forehead. "How about I pour some pink bubbles and we'll make it a bubble bath?"

She cheers and jumps up excitedly.

While she takes her bath, I go through some stuff for school. It's going to be a busy semester and with me trying to work more hours to save money, I'm going to have to stay on top of it.

I'm reading through some notes when my phone rings. I

don't recognize the number, but it's a New York area code, so I answer. "Hello."

"Hello, Sophia, it's Alicia, Easton's mom. How are you?"

Easton's mom... Why is she calling me? "I'm okay. How are you?"

"I'm good. I know this seems kind of random, but I asked Easton for your number. I hope that's okay."

"Of course," I tell her. She's going to be the grandmother of my baby.

"Great. Easton mentioned you're working and going to school, so I know you're busy, but I was wondering if you would like to come over for dinner one night this week."

Tears prick my eyes at her generous offer, and I want nothing more than to accept, but I can't. Because if I do, then I'm reopening the can of worms I'm trying to keep a lid on by ending things with Easton. Damn it, why does everything have to be so complicated? Why can't I just live my life and not have to worry about assholes like Freeman who don't worry about anyone but themselves.

"I appreciate the offer, but I'm just so busy..."

"Surely you have to take a moment to eat."

"I do, but it's usually on my way to work or on my way to

school…"

"Then I'll come to you."

She'll what? Jesus, she's as persistent as her son. "I don't—"

"What time do you work?" she asks.

"Um, eight."

"Perfect! I'll come over tomorrow at five, then. Any allergies?"

"No," I choke out, trying to think of a reason to tell her no. This can't happen. I'm trying to keep Easton at arm's length and now his mom is encroaching. "But—"

"Great. See you tomorrow night! *Besos.*"

The call ends and I'm left wondering what the hell just happened. Only I don't have too much time to wonder because I need to get Kendall dried off and ready for bed, and then I need to finish going through my notes. It's going to be a long night…

KNOCK, KNOCK, KNOCK.

"Mommy! There's someone at the door!"

"I know, Sunshine. Just give me a second," I yell across

the apartment. I don't know if it's something I ate or the pregnancy or if I'm maybe catching something, but I've spent the day throwing up. My body is sore, my head is pounding, and it feels like I'm dying.

I quickly brush my teeth, then go out to answer the door. When I open it and see Alicia standing there with bags in her hands, I curse my life. I forgot she was coming over for dinner. I glance down and groan at my lack of appearance. I'm in Easton's sweats because they're the only thing that now comfortably fit me—since I've had no time to go shopping— and a tank, sans bra. Between throwing up and it snowing and raining outside, I've been a damn mess all day, and her coming over completely slipped my mind.

"Mommy, who is it?" Kendall asks, knocking me from my thoughts and reminding me of my manners.

"Please, come in." I open the door wider so she can pass through. "I'm not going to lie. I forgot you were coming over. It's been a… busy day. If you can just give me a minute, I'll put some clothes on."

"You don't need to do that for me," Alicia says with a warm smile as she walks inside.

I see Easton's hoodie on the arm of the couch, so I grab it

and throw it on, then follow her into the kitchen.

"Kendall, do you remember Easton's mom, Alicia?"

"Yes," she says. "Easton is in Chicago."

Alicia grins. "He is?"

"Yeah, want to see where it is?"

"Sunshine, I'm sure—"

"I would love to," Alicia says, cutting me off.

We follow Kendall to her room, where she proceeds to explain to Alicia each place Easton has been so far. "I'm coloring him pictures every day he's gone so he knows what I did," Kendall tells her. "Do you want to color a picture with me?"

"Kendall, I don't think—" But before I can finish my sentence, a wave of nausea overtakes me and I run to the bathroom, barely making it in time. I'm in the middle of dry heaving, when a cool washcloth is placed around my neck, instantly cooling my heated flesh.

"Why don't you take a bath, while I color with Kendall?" Alicia offers.

"I don't have time to take a bath," I choke out. "I have to feed her and give *her* a bath and then I have to get dressed to…" I can't finish my sentence because I'm all of a sudden overcome with emotion clogging my throat, making it hard to speak, to breathe. Tears blur my vision, as the weight I'm carrying becomes too much.

Alicia wraps her arms around me while I sob into her shirt, more than likely drenching it. She runs her fingers through my hair and tells me it's okay, while I cry in her arms. I can't remember the last time someone held me like this, comforted me... But it feels good, therapeutic even.

When it feels like I'm finally all cried out, I glance up, embarrassed and mortified. She must think I'm crazy... "I'm so sorry," I begin, but she's already shaking her head.

"Don't you dare apologize," she says, wiping my tears from under my eyes, the same way her son did not too long ago. "You're pregnant and have a lot going on. Sometimes we just need a good cry."

"Yeah," I breathe. "It's just been a rough few days."

"We all have those, but the key is to let people help." She smiles softly, no judgement in sight, reminding me of Easton. "I'm here, so how about you let me help?"

I nod, knowing I'm at my limit today and my day isn't even close to being over. "Okay, thank you."

"Now, as I was saying before. Why don't you take a bath—"

"I would love to, but I have to go to work in a couple hours and—"

"Work?" She gasps. "No, that's not happening. You're not feeling well." She places her hand on my warm forehead. "You're going to call and let them know you're sick and won't be in tonight and then you're going to take a bath while I color with Kendall and feed her."

She raises a brow, daring me to argue, and as much as I want to, because I really need the money, I don't, because she's right. I'm not feeling well and I'll be no good to anyone at work.

"Okay, thank you."

"No need to thank me. That's what family is for." Her words cause me to choke up. Family... When I told my mom I was pregnant, *again*, she told me I was ruining my life and that she was ashamed of my choices, then hung up on me. We haven't spoken since...

After I call Dante to let him know I can't come in tonight and let Naomi know she's off the hook from watching Kendall, I fill the bath up and get in, putting my head back and taking a few minutes to relax. I can't even remember the last time I got to take a bath in peace.

A CHANCE ENCOUNTER

I'm barely awake when my phone dings with an incoming text. I open my eyes and click on it to see who it is.

Easton: Hey, Dash, I hope your headache has gone away and you're having a better day today. My flight is scheduled for Friday. I can't wait to see you. I won't have long, but I was thinking maybe we could go get Kendall from school together so I could see her too... Just a thought. If I'm overstepping, let me know. I miss you guys. Have a good night at work.

His text has me in tears all over again. He's trying so hard, and I keep pushing him away. I want so badly to tell him the truth. To tell him that my pushing him away is to protect Kendall. He cares about her. He'll understand. But what if he wants to try and play hero and says something to someone? Or he doesn't understand and then he knows and can tell anyone...

No, I can't risk it. I can't tell anyone, ever. But I'm not sure I can go on like this either. It feels like my life is at an impasse and I need to figure out which way to go next. And no matter what I choose I'm screwed...

I send Easton back one of my standard responses, so he doesn't worry, then lay my head back again and close my eyes, wishing and praying for the right answer to come to me—knowing there isn't one, and at some point, I'm going to have to face my life and deal with it head-on.

"SUNSHINE, COME EAT," I GROAN, SETTING THE PLATE OF FOOD ON THE TABLE.

"Okay!" Kendall comes running over, iPad in hand, where she's been watching video after video about skiing since yesterday, when Easton told her he was in Colorado, where—unlike New York City—there's a benefit to the snow—snowboarding and skiing. Now she's obsessed and keeps asking when we can go.

"Peanut butter and jelly?" She pouts—I know, I have a weird child who isn't a fan of the classic sandwich every kid is supposed to love. "Can I have soup?" she asks, referring to the homemade chicken soup Alicia fed us—which was delicious, until I threw it all up—before she insisted I go to bed, while she stayed and hung out with Kendall, putting her to bed.

I woke up the next morning to her making us breakfast—which I wasn't able to keep down. She made so much soup I was able to give it to Kendall last night for dinner, which was good since I was so sick and weak, I didn't have it in me to make anything else. I was forced to call out from work again. I'm pretty sure I have the flu or some kind of bug, and I've put a call in to my doctor to see if there's anything they can give me to help it along.

"I don't know how to make that soup," I tell her, dropping my head into my hands. And even if I did know how to, I don't have the energy to do so. My body is weak and it's hard to simply function. I wasn't even able to go to school the last two days.

"But, you know—" She begins to argue, but is cutoff by the knocking on the door. Shit, did I forget to tell Naomi I wouldn't need her to watch Kendall? She's been so busy with the upcoming wedding she's planning, we've barely spoken.

When I pull myself from my seat to answer the door, the room spins. I grab the side of the table, so I don't fall, as my head goes fuzzy and my vision goes in and out.

"Mommy!" Kendall yells, as I drop to the ground, my back hitting the cool wood floor. I try to answer my daughter, to tell her to call nine-one-one because something is clearly wrong, but I'm not sure what I get out before the blackness overtakes me.

Fourteen

EASTON

"EASTON! OH MY GOD, I LOVE YOU!"

"We saw you in concert last night!"

"Can we take a selfie?"

"Can you sign this?"

"Oh! There's Jordan! Jordan, can we take a picture?"

The screams start the second we step outside, but I'm expecting them. We had just sat down for lunch at a local restaurant, after doing a radio interview, when someone spotted us and posted it on social media. My team was notified, and my sister warned me, so I would know what to expect once I walked outside. This is nothing new. There's even a page dedicated to Easton Blackwood sightings. I'd be flattered if it didn't mean my location being leaked to millions of people at any given moment. I'm honestly surprised nobody has found out about Sophia yet. It probably helps that New York is a busy as fuck city and I haven't been seen in public, having kept to myself.

I nod toward Joel to let him know I'm going to take pictures and sign shit real quick before we head back to the bus. He nods back and immediately goes into security mode, along with my other bodyguard, Rex, asking the girls to calm down and step back so I can take pictures with them, as Jordan walks over and joins me.

While Jordan and I work together taking pictures and signing memorabilia, I feel my phone vibrating in my pocket. I haven't texted Sophia this evening, so I doubt it's her. She never initiates the conversation. But when it vibrates again, and again, I announce I'm signing one more thing and then I have to go, so I can check it. Only my close friends and family have this number, so for someone to be calling that many times can't be good.

I locate a young girl, who looks to be about Kendall's age, shyly standing to the side, and walk over to her. "Would you like me to sign something?" I ask, kneeling slightly so I'm at her level.

A CHANCE ENCOUNTER

She nods and thrusts a journal my way. I open it up and find a collage of some sort, me as the main subject. "I made it," she says, grinning.

"It's awesome. What's your name?"

"Jada."

"It's nice to meet you, Jada." I write out a quick note and sign the page, then pose with her so her mom can take a picture. Once we're done, Jordan and I thank everyone for stopping by to see us and make a quick exit.

"Easton, Mom just called me," Nicole says, as I pull out my phone. I glance up at the strain in her voice and immediately know something is wrong. "Sophia's in the hospital."

And with those words, my entire world tilts on its axis. "I need to get to her." She's already had one scare, and now she's back in the hospital. This can't be good. And of course I'm across the damn country.

"I know. I'm working on getting you a private flight out as soon as possible." She types away on her phone as we walk onto the bus. I dial my mom, needing to know what's happening, but she doesn't answer. I don't know what hospital she's at, and even If I did, nobody will give me any information over the phone. I'm not her person of contact.

A few minutes later, my phone rings with a number I've never seen before. "Hello."

"Easton," my mom breathes. "I don't have any service in the hospital. I'm quickly calling you from the nurse's station."

"What happened?" I ask, grabbing my duffle bag and shoving some clothes into it.

"They don't know yet. We just got here. I was coming over to check on her, and when I got there, she was passed out on the ground and Kendall was calling nine-one-one."

My heart both sinks and soars. That little girl is so damn smart, but the fact she was in that position makes me feel sick.

"Kendall let me in," Mom continues, "after I told her it was me through the door. I spoke to emergency and gave them her address. I'm with Kendall now in the waiting room, but we haven't heard anything yet."

"I'm on my way," I tell her. "Do you have Sophia's phone?"

"Kendall does…"

"Call Naomi and let her know what happened."

"Okay."

"Call me with any updates, please."

"I will. You just focus on getting here safely."

A CHANCE ENCOUNTER

I walk out and Nicole is typing away on her laptop. "I got you a private flight that can take off within the hour and a car is on its way to take you to the airport."

"Thank you."

THE MINUTE I STEP THROUGH THE DOOR TO SOPHIA'S PRIVATE ROOM AND SEE her eyes open and her face split into a soft smile, I take in a breath of relief. My mom updated me while I was on the flight here once the test results came in. She tested positive for the flu, and they said she was extremely dehydrated, which caused Braxton hicks, but she's okay. They checked the baby when she first arrived and everything was good, but I needed to see it for myself.

"Sir, we're in the middle of a—"

"It's okay," Sophia tells the woman, "he's the dad." She looks at me with glassy eyes. "She's showing me the baby."

I hurry over to her side and see the tiny baby on the black and white screen. He's floating in her belly, and you can hear the rapid beat of his heart. My own heart feels as though it's being pulled from my chest.

"I was just asking Ms. Davis if she'd like to find out the sex," the technician says.

"You can find out at sixteen weeks?" I ask.

"Depends on if the baby is cooperating."

I glance over at Sophia. "Do you want to know?"

"Do you?" she asks back.

"Yeah."

"Me too."

"It's a—"

"Wait." I glance around. "Where's Kendall?" It's already after eight o'clock, but my mom told me she and my dad were here with her.

Sophia's lips curl up. "She's in the waiting room down the hall. They didn't want her in here in case there were any problems. Naomi tried to bring her home to get some sleep, but she threw a fit." Her eyes water. "She was so scared. She hasn't left my side since they let her back here."

"I'll go grab her," I tell her, leaning over and kissing her forehead. "Be right back."

I find Kendall, my mom and dad, and Naomi and Dante all sitting in the waiting room. The second my mom sees me, she jumps up and throws her arms around me. "Oh, good, you're here. She's getting an ultrasound right now…"

"I know. I was just with her. I came in through the back, so I didn't see you guys here. I went straight to her room."

"Can I go see Mommy?" Kendall asks, looking far more stressed out than a six-year-old should ever look.

"That's why I came out here. We're about to find out if the baby is a boy or girl."

Her eyes light up. "I already know it's a boy, but I wanna see!"

Everyone laughs, appreciating the break in the tension.

"C'mon, K, let's go see your mom and the baby."

I give my mom a kiss on her cheek and hug my dad. "Thank you for being here," I say to everyone before I take Kendall's hand and walk her back to her mom's room.

When we walk in, Kendall runs straight to her mom and hugs her the best she can from the side. I grab a chair, sit down, and lift Kendall up so she can see and be near her mom.

The ultrasound tech walks us through all the body parts for Kendall's benefit, since it's her first time seeing the baby on the screen, and when she gets to the sex, she asks us all what we think. Kendall insists it's a boy, so we both guess the opposite just to mess with her.

"It's a boy!" the technician announces, making Kendall squeal in excitement.

"I knew it!"

"You did," Sophia tells her.

While the technician points out a few more things and then goes about shutting down the machine, I sit frozen in my place. Holy shit! We're having a boy. I'm going to have a son. A myriad of images hit me: a little boy playing in the dirt, martial arts, sports games, bonding over music, father/son trips like my dad and I used to take…

"You okay?" Sophia asks, wiping the goop off her belly.

"I'm perfect." I set Kendall down and kiss Sophia's cheek. "I can't believe we're having a little boy."

"I was so scared," she admits softly. "I'm just so glad he's okay."

"Me too," I agree. "I'm glad you're *both* okay. I'll go get everyone so we can share the good news."

When my parents, Naomi, and Dante come inside, Kendall immediately announces she was right and we're having a boy. Everyone congratulates us.

"How are you feeling?" I ask Sophia.

"I'm okay. Better now that I'm no longer dehydrated and they've given me medicine to stop the nausea."

"You're working too hard. You need to take it easy."

"It was the flu," she argues.

"That you tried to work through, to the point you got dehydrated and passed out."

"I'm okay now."

"The doctor would like her to rest," Naomi says. "I'm going to temporarily move back in."

"No, you're not," Sophia tells her.

"No, she's not," I agree. "Because you're moving."

"Not until I find a place. I still have a month…"

"You're moving into the house I bought."

"What?" She gasps. "That's not happening. I told you I need space! I can't live with you." Her heart rate monitor starts to ding faster and my eyes swing over to it, watching as the numbers increase, before turning my attention back to Sophia. She's stressed—because she needs space… She doesn't want to be around me. She's made that abundantly clear over and over again, but I ignored her, hoping I could convince her otherwise. I thought she was just scared, but looking at her now, her eyes wide with horror, it hits me like a wrecking ball. She needs space. *Real* space. From me.

"I know," I tell her calmly, not wanting to upset her more. "And I'm giving you your space. I'll—"

"Hey, guys," my mom says, cutting in. "I think someone is getting sleepy." She nods toward Kendall, who is curled up in the recliner, half-asleep.

"I can take her back to our place," Naomi offers.

"But I want to stay with Mommy," Kendall argues through her yawn, her eyes half-lidded from exhaustion.

"I have to stay overnight," Sophia tells her. "You won't be comfortable here. There's no bed, plus you have school tomorrow."

"Fine." Kendall sighs. "But I don't want to go to school. Please. I want to come see you." Kendall pouts, her eyes filling with tears.

"Okay," Sophia tells her, "you can skip school tomorrow and come see me." She turns her attention to Naomi. "You have an early morning appointment with your bride-to-be. Are you sure you can bring her back here and make it there in time?"

"I don't mind taking her," my mom offers. "I can stay with

A CHANCE ENCOUNTER

her at your place and bring her back in the morning."

"Are you sure?" Sophia asks.

"Spending time with this little princess is hardly a hardship," Mom says, smiling. And I know she means that. She told me about hanging out with Kendall and how much she enjoyed it. She misses having kids in the house and is looking forward to becoming a grandmother.

"Okay," Kendall says. "Let's go, Alicia. I'm ready to go home. I'm tired."

Sophia stifles her laugh. "Be good."

"Duh." Kendall hugs her mom from the side. "I love you."

"I love you too." Sophia kisses the top of her head.

"I love you more," Kendall volleys.

"Impossible," Sophia counters, making Kendall playfully roll her eyes.

"I love you, baby brother." Kendall leans over and kisses the side of Sophia's belly.

Sophia's eyes prick with tears. "You're going to be such a good big sister."

"I know," Kendall says, taking my mom's hand. "Bye, Aunt Naomi. Bye Uncle Dante. Bye Easton's daddy…"

My dad chuckles. "You can call me Sean, and I'm coming

with you. Gotta make sure you two get home safely." He steps over to Sophia and squeezes her shoulder. "I'm glad you and the baby are okay. If you need anything, we're here."

"Thank you. You're welcome to stay at my place with Alicia," Sophia offers.

"I have some work to do, so I'm going to drop them off and let them have a girls' night." He winks playfully. "I'll pick them back up in the morning and bring them to you."

"Thank you," Sophia says. "Thank you, everyone, for being here."

"That's what family is for," Mom says with a warm smile. "We'll see you tomorrow. Get some rest." She kisses Sophia's forehead and then she, my dad, and Kendall head out.

"I guess we'll get going too," Naomi says. "If you need anything…"

"I know, thank you."

Naomi leans in and kisses Sophia's cheek. "I know this is hard for you, but you have a lot of people who care for you. Maybe it's time to let them in."

Sophia closes her eyes and nods. "Love you."

"Love you more, Soph."

"Impossible."

A CHANCE ENCOUNTER

After Naomi and Dante leave, I pick up where we left off...

"As I was saying earlier, you're moving into the house I bought."

She opens her mouth to no doubt argue, but I shake my head. "No, we did this your way. Everything, from the moment I found out you were pregnant, has been on your terms, and you ended up in the hospital. Now we're doing it my way." Her eyes turn into small slits. "You've been in the hospital twice now with scares," I continue. "If you had to work, it would be one thing, but I have money... a fuck ton of it." I don't usually brag, but I'm at my limit with this woman. If she doesn't want me, I can't make her be with me, but she's carrying my baby, and as his father, I have every right to make sure they're both taken care of. "I'm done sitting back and watching you struggle, so you can sing to the tune of *Independent*."

She snorts. "Are we talking Ne-Yo or Destiny's Child, here? Oh! Or Kelly Clarkson? I love that song."

I grin, loving that she knows her music—even if she doesn't know mine. "None of the above. I'm talking Webbie."

"I haven't heard that one..."

Probably too rap for her. "I'll play it for you later. It should be your mantra."

She lifts her hand and pushes her hair out of her face and I itch to grab her hand and bring it to my lips to kiss it. I want nothing more than to show her how much I care about her, but that's not what she wants, and it's time I respect that. "We all get it, Dash. You're independent. You'd prefer to handle life all by yourself even if it kills you. But the thing is, you don't have to. I have the means and money to make sure you're taken care of and comfortable."

"East—"

"Nope, I'm talking." I hit her with a pointed look that has her huffing in annoyance. "Here's what's going to happen. You're going to stop being stubborn and move into the home I bought. You need a place to live, and I have one available. And you don't have to worry because I won't be there." Her brow furrows, and if I didn't already know how she feels, I would think she's upset that I won't be living there. "You're going to focus on school and Kendall and baking our little chocolate éclair…"

"Our what?"

"Chocolate éclair… It was that or a Blackberry." I shrug.

A CHANCE ENCOUNTER

"The old-school phone?"

"Yeah, but those are irrelevant, so I'm sticking with the dessert."

"Makes sense," she says with a light laugh before her face turns serious. "Easton, I can't just move into your home."

"I bought it for you." I actually bought it hoping one day we would be a family and would live there together, and I still hope that, but if I can't have her, if she doesn't want to be had, then the home is hers.

"No more stress, no more working more hours than you sleep. You want your space. I get it, and I'm going to give it to you, but you'll have it while being taken care of. What happened today never should've happened, and I'm going to make sure it never happens again. Because I can."

She swallows thickly and her eyes turn glassy. "Okay," she whispers, all the argument gone from her voice. "I'll move in with you."

Fifteen

SOPHIA

"I'LL BE BACK IN TIME," EASTON SAYS OVER THE PHONE. "AND WE'LL reschedule the concerts I had to cancel... I'll eat the costs myself if I have to."

I can't hear what's being said on the other line, but after a moment, he says, "Book me a flight for tomorrow morning... Okay, thanks." He hangs up and glances at me. "I didn't hear you come in. Is Kendall asleep?"

"She is. She loves her new room. I can't believe you managed to pull it off so quickly."

"Money talks." Easton shrugs.

He's not lying. It's been two days since I was released from the hospital, and in that time, Easton has been in boss-mode, handling shit, so when he leaves, I'll have no reason to stress—his words, not mine.

He's moved my entire apartment to the new house—well, the stuff Kendall and I wanted to keep—and had new furniture delivered as well—including turning Kendall's room into a room fit for a princess. At first, I refused to pick anything out, but when Easton told me it was happening whether I picked the stuff out or not, because the place needed furniture, I gave in, wanting the home Kendall will be living in to be nice.

He's hired a woman named Maria to come in every day to do all the cooking and cleaning—including the laundry. I tried to argue with Easton, but when I met her—she's in her early sixties and the family she used to take care of no longer needed her services because the youngest moved out to go to college—and her husband passed away last year—and she was so sweet and excited to take care of us, I gave in. She'll be arriving at seven o'clock every day and leaving after dinner is done.

He's also hired a driving service to take me and Kendall to school, as well as anywhere we need to go, so I don't have to walk, and a nurse to come check on me several times this week while I'm home. The doctor didn't put me on bedrest, only said I need to take it easy this week and rest, but to

A CHANCE ENCOUNTER

Easton, that meant I'm not to move unless necessary.

Tonight is our first official night in our new home and Easton's last night before he's back on tour. He's been so busy handling everything, we've hardly spoken. I could be wrong, but it feels like he's avoiding me. I'm hoping tonight we can spend some time together. I know it's a bad idea, but I can't help it. It's easier to push Easton away when he's thousands of miles away from me, but when he's here, near me, and I can see him smile and laugh, it's damn hard to do it.

"Are you settled in?" Easton asks, pocketing his phone and grabbing his coat from over the couch. Wait… is he leaving? He just told his sister to book him a flight for tomorrow.

"Everything is perfect. Where are you going?"

"To my parents' place. I'll be on an early flight out, so I won't be able to stop by before I leave, but Maria will be here at seven, so if you need anything, just let her know, and I'm only a phone call or text away."

"Oh…" I try not to sound deflated. I had assumed he would be staying here. It is his house. I thought we could hang out, maybe watch a movie. Then, it hits me—his words from in the hospital. "You're moving in after the tour is over, right?" When he said he wouldn't be here, I thought he meant because he's on tour.

He shakes his head. "We're not together, Dash, and if I were to live here the paparazzi would swarm the place." That's why none of his clothes are here.

"But—"

"Sophia, no stressing," he says. "Don't worry about me." He kisses my forehead. "Get some sleep." And then, without a backward glance, he's out the door.

I want to argue, chase after him and tell him this is his home, to stay, but he's right. If he lives here with us, we'll be in the spotlight. Once again, Easton is making sure we're taken care of.

ONE WEEK LATER

I CHECK MY PHONE FOR THE HUNDREDTH TIME. STILL NO TEXT FROM EASTON. Since he left to go back on tour, his texts have gone from flirty and sweet to robotic and to the point. And now, for the first time in the three weeks he's been gone, he hasn't sent me his good morning text.

A CHANCE ENCOUNTER

I'm sitting in class and should be focusing on the international economics lecture the professor is going over, but instead, I'm distracted by the lack of action my phone is getting.

It should be for the best that he's stopped trying to remind me how good things could be between us. It would definitely make my life easier. But what's that saying: you don't realize what you have until it's gone? Well, in my case, it's that I didn't realize what we *could* have until it was gone. Actually, that's a lie—I knew what we could have. I felt it every time he smiled at me, talked to me, kissed me. Our time together during the holidays was magical. We connected on a level I've never felt with anyone. But then he pushed for more and I pushed back, scared of what more would mean.

My phone dings with a Google update on Freeman—yes, I get updates on him. My goal is to always stay one step ahead. I click on the update and read through the article: Freeman Carmichael has announced he's running for senator. There's a picture of him, his wife, and their baby, and underneath the picture, there's a caption that says they're expecting baby number two.

My blood boils. Why is it that he gets to have it all—the

family, the life, the happiness—while I'm stuck hiding from the world? He hasn't contacted me since the day I left. Aside from our secret meetings—which at the time I didn't realize were secret—nobody can link us together or link Kendall to him. If they were going to do it, wouldn't they have already done it?

As far as anyone's concerned, the father of my daughter is dead, and I'll stick to that story. But I'm done passing through life, living in fear of the unknown. I'm done being weak and allowing bullies like Freeman to dictate my life choices.

Before I can overthink it, I swipe out of the stupid article and pull up the text thread between Easton and me and type out a message: **Hey, I hope you're having a good morning.**

I keep it simple to feel him out. If he isn't interested in me anymore, I don't want to make an ass out of myself. I still have to spend the next eighteen plus years co-parenting with him.

A few seconds later, bubbles appear and then a text comes in.

Easton: I am. Hope you are too.

My heart sinks. That's it? That's all he's going to give me? I consider giving up, but remember how much he tried for

A CHANCE ENCOUNTER

weeks while I didn't give him anything.

Me: I'm okay. In class listening to my professor drone on about financial law. I can't wait for class to be over so I can go home and eat. I'm starvvvviiiinnngggg.

I read over my text, realizing I suck at flirting, and delete it.

Me: Thanks! I'm in class thinking about how hungry I am.

Ugh! How does he do it? He opens his mouth or types and it's like insta-flirt. Meanwhile, I sound like a creepy guy with a cheesy pickup line.

Delete.

I'm about to type something else, when another text comes in.

Easton: Everything okay? You've been typing for a little while...

Oh. My. God. Face meet palm.

Fuck it. I'm a grown ass woman. Why am I beating around the bush?

Me: You never texted me this morning.

As I hit send, the professor concludes his lecture and

assigns the pages to read for next class. I pack up my stuff and head out. Since it's my last class of the day, I walk over to the front of the school where the car service Easton hired is waiting. They know what time I get out and are always here on time.

"Good afternoon, ma'am. Where to?"

"Home, please."

I buckle in and pull my phone out to see if Easton responded. He did.

Easton: It almost sounds like you want me to text you, Dash...

Damn him. He's good at putting that damn ball in my court.

Me: Maybe I do. I hit send then quickly type another text and send it. Maybe I'm hungry... And I'm not talking about food...

There! Take that! I can totally flirt too.

I hold my breath, waiting to see how he's going to respond, as my heart beats wildly in my chest. I don't think I've ever flirted with anyone before, and definitely not this forward.

I wait.

And wait.

A CHANCE ENCOUNTER

No response.

Shit! Did I say something wrong? Maybe his phone died... I click on the tracking app he downloaded onto both our phones, so he would be able to see where I am in case anything ever happened to me—his battery life is full. He's in Vegas, but it's early there, so he's not at a show.

Do I text him again? Maybe it didn't go through... Although, it does say delivered. The car drops me off in front of Easton's house and the gentleman tells me he'll be back in a couple hours so we can pick up Kendall from school. I thank him and get out, slinging my bag over my shoulder. Once I'm inside, I find Maria is in the laundry room folding some clothes—that woman is seriously a godsend.

"Hello, dear, how was school?" she asks, smiling warmly at me.

"Good."

"Are you hungry?"

I stifle a giggle at her question. "I'm—" My answer is cut off by the sound of my phone ringing. I pull it out of my pocket and see it's Easton. Holy shit! He's calling me. I expected him to text me back, not call me! "I'm tired. I'm going to go lie down," I say quickly, sprinting out of the room and up the stairs so I can answer the phone call in private. But before I can hit accept, the call ends.

Shit.

Then it rings again.

This time I answer it before the first ring has finished. "Hello?" I do my best to even out my breathing, so I don't sound like I just ran up three flights of stairs.

"What the hell was that?" Easton demands.

"What was what?"

"You're hungry, and not for food…" Oh, that. Duh! "What the hell is that, Dash? I'm in the middle of a radio interview and that's what you text me?"

"Um…" I can't tell if he's mad…

"I had to finish my interview so I could call you. I'd ask if you're drunk, but I know you're not since you're pregnant. Is that your idea of a joke? Because I have to say that shit ain't funny."

Oh no, I think he's mad…

"Sophia," he groans. "What's going on?"

"Nothing," I admit, suddenly feeling stupid. "I was just joking."

He's quiet for a long moment before he sighs and says,

"All right. I have to get going. You and the baby are okay?"

"We're good," I croak out.

"Kendall's good?"

"Of course."

"I'll call her later so I can tell her about Vegas."

"Okay."

There's an awkward lull in the conversation before Easton says, "I'll talk to you later."

He hangs up and I'm left staring at my phone, wondering what the hell just happened. I could be wrong, but he almost sounded sad. Was he hoping I was serious?

I shed myself of my coat and hoodie, since it's warm inside, and climb into my bed. I'm exhausted and I have a couple hours before I have to pick up Kendall. A nap will help give me a second wind.

But as I lie in bed, snuggling into my pillow, I can't stop thinking about Easton's and my brief conversation. That's not the way I wanted it to go, like at all. Instead of falling asleep, I grab my phone from my nightstand and type out a message:

I lied. I wasn't joking.

Easton: You said you wanted space...

Me: I know, but I've changed my mind.

Easton: What's changed?

And that's where the heart of the issue lies. Unless I tell him the truth about Freeman, I'm going to be keeping a secret from him. A huge secret. And while I've never been in a serious relationship, I imagine that's not the way to start one. My mind goes back to Easton's and my conversation on Christmas Eve...

"She was keeping secrets, hiding shit. And instead of being honest, she lied about it all."

If I have any hope of a future with Easton, I'm going to have to be honest with him... Completely honest. Can I do that? Can I let him in? I've never let anyone in regarding Freeman. Not even Naomi.

Easton: Sophia, what's going on?

I stare at his question, unsure what to type. What I need to tell him isn't something you type over a text. It's not even an over the phone type of conversation. It's one I need to have in person.

Easton: You obviously have a lot going through your head. I need to head to the venue. You asked for space and I'm giving it to you. So, maybe take some time and think, and we'll talk when I get back.

A CHANCE ENCOUNTER

I want to tell him that I don't want space anymore. I've made up my mind and I'm ready to go all in. I want to spend time with him, get to know him. I want what he wants... Well, what he wanted. I'm not sure if he wants that anymore. The problem is we need to have this conversation in person and he's on the other side of the country, which means I'm stuck... So, I type the only thing I can type: **Okay.**

Me: Good morning. What are you up to today?

I WOKE UP THIS MORNING AND DECIDED SINCE EASTON IS GONE FOR ANOTHER week or so, I can spend some time getting to know him. Even though a lot has happened in a short time, we still don't know a lot about each other.

Easton: Show tonight. You?

Okay, so he's going to make this difficult. No biggie…

Me: This morning Kendall and I are going to the library to check out books, but I was thinking tonight we could hit up a bar, get drunk, get jiggy on the dance

floor, then from there check out the local strip club... You know, the usual.

Easton: What vitamins does your doctor have you on?

I snort out a laugh.

Me: The good stuff...

I wait for a response to come through, and after several minutes when one hasn't, I give up for today.

Me: Good afternoon! Did you know the baby is the size of a pear? <insert image of a pear>

IT'S A NEW DAY AND TODAY I'M NOT GOING TO GIVE UP...

Easton: Actually he's the size of a roll of toilet paper.

Me: Single roll or double? Extra soft or firm?

Easton: single and soft.

Yes! I mentally fist pump. I'm getting somewhere.

Me: We could name him TeePee. T.P. for short.

A CHANCE ENCOUNTER

There's no way I would name my baby this, but I need to keep the conversation going.

Easton: WTF

Me: Yeah, you know...Like when you teepee someone's house with toilet paper.

Easton: I'm calling your doctor...

At this rate, he's going to think I'm crazy and run for his life.

Me: Real talk, what should we name him? I'm thinking Burt or Carl...

Don't worry. I wouldn't name him either of those names—no offense to anyone with those names.

My phone rings and Easton's name flashes on my screen. "Hello."

"So it is you... huh."

"Who's me?"

"You're you..."

"Of course I'm me." I'm so confused.

Easton laughs. "This sounds like a bad version of *Who's on Second?*"

"*Who's on First?*"

"No, nobody's on first. It's an episode from a show, called *Who's on Second?*"

"It's *Who's on First? Not Who's on Second?*"

"You sure?"

"Yes," I say with a laugh. "I did it in high school as a skit when I was on the debate team."

"I'll take your word for it."

We're both quiet for a moment, before I speak up. "You called me."

He laughs. "You have my head spinning. Yes, I called you to make sure it's you."

"Who else would it be?"

"I don't know, but you went from barely returning my texts for weeks to texting me weird ass shit, and we're not naming our son Burt or Carl."

"You have better suggestions?"

"Well, the middle name of all the boys on my dad's side of the family is Rocco, so I'm hoping you'll be okay with using that as his middle name. I don't really know your family situation, aside from your dad leaving when you were younger."

"I don't have anyone I want to name him after. Rocco is

A CHANCE ENCOUNTER

fine with me."

"Cool. So we need a name that goes with Rocco Blackwood."

I grab my laptop and open it, and once the internet is up, Google boy names, clicking on the first link.

"Dash, you there?"

"Yeah, I'm looking up names. I found a site that says top boy names."

"All right, hit me with them."

I read through each name and when I get to Camden, Easton says to stop. "I like Camden. It sounds strong. What do you think?"

"Camden Rocco Blackwood," I say out loud. "I love it."

"That's it? We have our son's name?"

"Should it have been harder?"

"I don't know. This is my first kid. Was it hard to come up with Kendall's name?"

"Nope," I squeak out, praying he doesn't ask—

"How did you come up with it?"—that.

I groan. "If you tell anyone what I'm about to say, I'll kill you."

Easton laughs over the line.

"I'm being dead serious. Nobody knows this and if it gets out, I'll be mortified."

His laugher comes to a halt. "You can trust me, Dash. Always."

God, I hope so... And I'm not referring to my daughter's name.

"I was binge-watching a reality show and one of them was named Kendall."

He cracks up again. "You named your daughter after *her?*"

"Shut up!"

"Well, if it's going to be after one of them, at least it's her. She's the most normal out of all of them."

"How would you know? And at the time she was a teenager. I thought she was sweet and I liked the name."

"She lives down the street from me," Easton says nonchalantly. "We've hung out a few times at mutual friends' parties. She's cool."

Of course he has, because he's freaking famous! He probably hangs out with all sorts of famous people.

"Soph, you there?"

"Have you ever dated anyone famous?" I blurt out.

He coughs lightly into the phone. "Umm... A few women,

A CHANCE ENCOUNTER

I guess. But nobody serious. What about you?"

"Oh, yeah, I've dated tons of famous guys. Last week I went out with Orlando Bloom."

He laughs and the sound, for the first time in a while, is carefree. I've missed that laugh… "I hope not," he says. "Katy wouldn't be too thrilled. But I meant, have you been with anyone serious? You mentioned before you weren't with anyone for a long period of time. Does that mean you've never been in a serious relationship?"

Shit. Last time I was vague, he let it go. Now, if I don't give him a clear answer, I run the chance of pushing him away. And I can't lie… "Once," I admit truthfully.

"With Kendall's dad?"

Oh, Jesus. How the hell did we go from talking about celebrities to my personal life? "Yeah. He was the longest relationship I was in…" And the entire thing was a lie. I was stupid and young and naïve. I gave him my virginity and he gave me a broken heart. But… he also gave me Kendall.

Someone says something in the background and then Easton says, "Hey, Soph, I have to get going. They need me in—"

"Of course, yeah. Sorry for keeping you…You must be

busy... You're working and—"

"You're not keeping me," he says softly. "I'm the one who called you. And I'm never too busy for you." Someone yells something and Easton yells back he's coming. "Have a good day, Dash. Tell Kendall I'll call her later."

Easton: Had to reschedule the shows I canceled for the end of the tour. I'll be gone an extra week or so. If you need anything, just let me know.

UGH. SO FORMAL. LIKE HE'S MESSAGING A COLLEAGUE INSTEAD OF THE MOTHER of his baby. I thought our conversation on the phone would've broken the ice, but I guess not. It's like every day is Groundhog Day with me starting all over again.

Me: I'm sorry. That sucks. Hope you have a good day and we'll be here when you get back! Xo Kendall, Baby Camden, and Sophia. <insert picture of Kendall and me lying in my bed with my newly protruding baby bump in it>

A CHANCE ENCOUNTER

I hover over the send button, unsure whether I should send this. I took this picture of Kendall and me last night when I was reading to her before bed. My belly seemed to pop overnight and now, instead of looking overweight, I look pregnant. Every day Easton and I have been texting, but it never goes below surface level. If I ask him a question, he answers. But he never starts the conversation unless he has information to relay to me, and then it's always straight to the point: your usual driver is sick. Someone new will be driving you... The furniture for the office is being delivered tomorrow between eleven and one... I spoke with your nurse and she'll be by when you get home to check on you.

Maybe it's because I'm pregnant and my hormones are out of whack, but it's starting to feel like he's more than giving me space—he's pushing me away. What if it's too late? No, I refuse to believe that, but I don't think I can go another ten days without seeing him face-to-face so we can talk. And then an idea forms!

I hit send on the text and then go in search of what I need.

A few minutes later a text comes through that has me grinning from ear to ear.

Easton: You look beautiful. Feel free to send me pictures anytime.

Hmm… maybe all hope isn't lost after all.

Sixteen

EASTON

"EASTON, OVER HERE!"

"Please, over here!"

"I love you!"

I grin at the fans who are jumping up and down behind the rope, thrusting their shirts, hats, phones, and other shit my way. I'm half out of breath from having just finished my set and dripping in sweat.

"I'll be right back!" I tell them, as I walk down the hall toward my dressing room. Before I meet with fans backstage, I always shower and throw on fresh clothes, so I don't sweat all over them and stink up the place.

I step through the door, wrenching my shirt over my head, when a tiny voice yells, "Easton!" I would recognize that voice anywhere. I put my shirt back down and come face-to-face with two of my favorite girls: Sophia and Kendall.

Sophia is dressed in a pair of holy jeans and one of my shirts that reads LOST across the front. Her hair is up in a tight ponytail and she's wearing a bit of makeup. She looks fucking beautiful. The only picture I've seen of her this last week is the one she sent me, and it didn't do her justice at all. My eyes rake down her body, landing on her belly, and I can't help but grin. I saw a bit of her stomach in the picture, but as she stands in front of me, in a tight shirt that accentuates her front, she actually looks pregnant, and hell if that doesn't make her that much sexier. To know she's carrying my baby is such a turn-on.

"Easton, you did so well!" Kendall squeals, knocking me out of my thoughts.

"Thanks, K." I step closer and Kendall throws her tiny arms around my legs for a hug.

"Eww," she whines. "You're gross." She backs up and scrunches up her nose. "You smell like the boys in my class."

Sophia snorts out a laugh.

"What are you laughing at?" I taunt, stepping over to her. Her eyes go wide. "I think you need a hug." She backs up, but

A CHANCE ENCOUNTER

I'm quicker, and before she can run, I pull her into my arms, making it a point to rub my sweat-filled hair across her neck.

"Easton!" She shrieks through her laughter. "That's freaking gross!"

I let her go and chuckle at the two girls both scowling at me. Thank God we're having a boy. We're going to need to even the gender playing field.

"What are you doing here?"

"Santa brought Kendall tickets," Sophia says with a smirk.

Oh, shit. That's right. With everything going on, I completely forgot.

"We flew on a plane!" Kendall says. "It was so cool."

"Should you be flying in your condition?" I ask, looking at Sophia.

"The doctor said it was fine. I spoke to Nicole and she helped set it up so we could surprise you." Sophia beams and my chest tightens. Shortly after I left after her hospital scare, she changed her tune. I told myself I was going to give her some real space, so she wouldn't be stressed out, and was shocked when the first day I didn't text her, she texted me. She pretty much told me straight out she's changed her mind and wants to be with me, but when I asked her what *made*

257

her change her mind, she couldn't tell me. And that sent up a red flag. I told myself after Ashleigh I wouldn't do secrets ever again. If Sophia wants to be with me, then she's going to have to talk to me.

I've kept her at arm's length the best I could, but I have to admit she's been persistent—texting me every day, joking around, and opening up to me. And now she's here...

"Easton, you need to get out there," Greg, my tour manager says, popping his head inside. "I've scheduled a car to pick you guys up, so you can take them back to your place once you're done."

"Oh, no, we're staying at a hotel," Sophia says.

"What? Why? I live here."

Sophia flushes and averts her gaze away from me. "I didn't want to intrude. You didn't know we were coming and—"

"Intrude?" I scoff. "This is the best damn surprise I've had in a long time."

"You said a bad word," Kendall says. "Mommy, what's his chore?"

Greg barks out a laugh. "While you think of his chore, I really do need Easton out here."

"I'll be back in a little bit. There's food and drinks in

A CHANCE ENCOUNTER

here..." I step over to Sophia and lean in so only she can hear. "You're not staying in a hotel. We need to talk about your text."

"My text?" she squeaks.

"Yeah, the one where you admitted how hungry you are for me... You didn't think I forgot about that text, did you?"

Without waiting for her to respond, I walk back outside with Greg. *Guess the fans will be getting the sweaty, smelly version of me tonight...*

I spend the next hour signing things and taking a million pictures. It's our third night in LA, but the show was completely sold out, including the VIP backstage passes that allow fans to come back and meet me. The entire time I'm meeting fans, half my mind is back in the dressing room with Sophia and Kendall. I'm shocked as shit that they showed up here, but also fucking elated. I wonder how long they're here for, and if they'll be here long enough for me to show them around. Will she want to be shown around? She said she's changed her mind about wanting space, but does that mean she's okay with being seen with me now? There's no way I'll get away with going anywhere in this city without being recognized. We're definitely going to need to talk tonight.

Once I've met with the final fan, I head over to Greg and Nicole. We usually have a meeting after the show to discuss how it went, but tonight it's going to have to wait.

"I already know what you're going to say," Nicole says. "Have fun. I'll see you Monday for the show. You have a flight scheduled out of LAX and I emailed you all the details."

"Thanks, sis." I pull her into a side hug and kiss her cheek. "See ya, Greg!" I yell back as I sprint down the hall.

When I get back to the dressing room, Kendall and Sophia are sitting on the couch watching something on Sophia's phone, each with one earbud in their ear. When they see me, they remove them.

"Sorry it took me so long. I hate leaving without greeting everyone."

"We're fine," Sophia says. "We were watching the videos Kendall took of you."

I walk over to the table with the gift basket of shit the venue provides. It has all the merchandise that's being sold, plus extras. I grab it and bring it over to Kendall, whose face lights up. "For me?"

"For my favorite VIP." I snag the VIP lanyard out of the basket and put it around her neck. "I'm so glad you guys are here." It's been a long as hell month without them. I now get why when my dad went on tour when we were little, my mom, Nicole, and I went along. I can't imagine not seeing them for months.

"Thank you," Kendall says, scouring through the basket.

"You ready to get going?" I ask them, excited to show them where I live.

"Yes," Sophia groans. "I'm exhausted. But we do have a hotel..."

"Is that where you want to stay?"

"Well, no, but I did pay for the hotel and—"

This woman. She just doesn't get it. "Whatever the hotel cost, I'll pay you back."

"No. I didn't mean it like that. It's just that I hate for it to go to waste when it's paid for..." She looks at me nervously and I know something else is going on.

"Can I talk to you over there for a second?" I nod toward the table, not wanting to talk in front of Kendall.

"Okay."

"Listen," I say once we're out of earshot. "I know everything between us is new, but in order for us to have a chance at working, you're going to have to let me in." Her face falls. "Whatever is going through your head, just tell me. I can't do anything about it if you keep it to yourself."

She releases a soft sigh. "I'm sorry. I'm used to it being me against the world and it's going to take some time to realize someone else is in my corner."

"You let Naomi in," I point out.

"Naomi's my cousin, and even she hasn't been let in completely," she mutters, her lips forming a slight frown. "I'm worried your house won't be child friendly and Kendall might mess something up or break something. I love my daughter, and she's a good kid, but she's still six."

"Everything in that house is replaceable. There won't be much for her to do there since I don't have any toys, but we're just going to sleep. How long are you staying?"

"Our flight leaves Monday morning when yours does."

Fuck yes. I have the entire weekend with them. "Cool. How about we go back to my place and get her to bed since she's already half-asleep." Kendall's eyes are drooping and her head is lulling to the side. "And tomorrow morning we can talk and figure out what to do this weekend."

"Okay," she says, suddenly looking nervous. She gnaws on her bottom lip, and I know something is wrong. We can't continue like this. One way or another, we have to figure this out, which means she's going to have to talk to me.

An hour later, we're back at my house and Kendall is fast asleep in one of my guest beds. Sophia is in my guest shower, rinsing off, and I'm taking a shower in my bathroom. Once I'm clean, I throw on a pair of basketball shorts and a T-shirt and head out to the living room to wait for Sophia to finish up.

While I wait, I go through some email reminders Nicole sent me for this week. After we do the two shows that were canceled, the tour will be over and I'll be on break until further notice—when I say break, I mean I'll be working on my next album, but I won't be going anywhere.

The sound of feet padding across my marble floor comes, and a second later, Sophia appears, dressed in tiny pajamas shorts and a tank top that has an image of a pregnancy test across her chest and under it, reads: *Sh*t just got real!* Her blond hair is up in a messy wet bun, and her gorgeous green eyes are staring at me with a bit of shyness.

"Did you have a good shower?" I ask dumbly since I don't know what else to say.

"Yeah, your home is beautiful."

"Thanks. You hungry? I was about to make myself a snack. I get hungry after a show."

"Sure. I'm always hungry." She laughs softly.

I walk into the kitchen, with her following behind, and open the fridge to see what's in here. Mrs. Burdette, the housekeeper, went shopping for the weekend for me before she left earlier.

I find some strawberry jam and brie cream cheese, and snag a package of water crackers from the pantry. I set them down on the counter and go about making them up. Sophia comes over and glances around me to see what I'm doing. When she reaches for one, I playfully smack her hand. "Not yet."

She huffs, and I chuckle. When she tries again, I set the knife down and lift her gently, setting her on top of the counter. "Wait until I'm done. I still need to add the jam."

I open the jar and scoop some out. "This is the best jam you'll ever find. I get it from the farmer's market, and nothing compares."

"Can I try?" she asks, hitting me with her sexy puppy dog eyes I have zero hope of saying no to.

"Fine." I go to scoop some more out, but before I do, she

A CHANCE ENCOUNTER

snags the jar and dips her finger into it. She brings her jam-covered finger up to her mouth and sucks, and my dick swells in my pants. She's doing that shit on purpose. She has to be…

"Mmm…" She moans. "Delicious." She dips her finger back in and scoops a bit more out. "Want some?" she asks, sticking her finger out for me.

I swallow thickly and drop the knife, stepping between her already parted legs. My plan was to keep my distance until we talk, but she's fucking that up.

She pushes her finger past my lips, and I suck the jam off her flesh. Her hooded eyes meet mine and I wonder what's going through her head. And then she grabs my shirt, pulls me toward her, and her mouth connects with mine. Her tongue pushes through the seam of my lips, and she tastes like strawberry jam. Her lips are soft, and her tongue moves in perfect sync with my own. It would be so easy to get lost in this woman, but then I remember we still haven't talked…

I back up slightly, but Sophia wraps her legs around me, holding me close to her. "Dash…" I groan.

She drags her fingers through my hair and pulls me back toward her for another kiss. For several minutes, we kiss, until her hands move from my hair and find their way under my shirt. Then I'm snapped out of my Sophia-induced fog.

"Wait," I rasp. "As much as I want to kiss you, we need to talk."

She sighs but nods, unraveling her legs from around me. "Okay."

I go back to making our food, and once I'm done, I grab one and bring it up to her mouth. "My mom always made us these as an after-school snack growing up. They are the best thing you'll ever eat." Her lips tilt into a smile and then she opens her mouth, but I don't give it to her yet. "But be careful, because they're addicting as fuck."

"Gimme!" She leans forward and opens her mouth again, and this time, I give her the snack. The cracker is small, so I pop the entire thing into her mouth. She chews for a few seconds and then moans. "Oh my God, this is so good."

"Told ya." I shove one into my own mouth and eat it. "The key is to buy the creamy brie. That, mixed with the jam, is the perfect combination."

"I'm going to steal some to bring home," she says, grabbing another cracker, while I get us a couple bottles of water. When she pushes it into her mouth, some of it gets on the side. Her tongue darts out to lick it off, and my dick,

A CHANCE ENCOUNTER

which is already half-hard from our kiss, stands at attention.

We eat and drink in silence until the plate is empty. Then I put it all away and throw the plate and knife in the dishwasher. When I turn around, Sophia is off the counter and leaning against the wall, watching me.

"What?"

She smiles softly. "Nothing. You're just so domestic. You have all this money, yet here you are, making your own food and doing your own dishes."

"I have a housekeeper who's here during the week, but while I'm gone, she only stops in once a week to clean. I had her pick me up some groceries since I knew I would be home this weekend. But growing up, even though my parents had money, they wouldn't let us get too spoiled. They would have the house cleaned but not our rooms. They had someone who cooked, but they would make us clean the table and do the dishes."

Sophia laughs. "I should do that with Kendall. She's been enjoying Maria picking up after her a little too much."

"It's okay to spoil her a little." I shrug, making Sophia laugh.

My house is two stories with all the rooms on the second

floor, so we both head up the stairs. When we get to the room Sophia is staying in, we stop. "Is there anything you need so you're comfortable?" She shakes her head. "All right." I step closer to her. "I'll see you in the morning." I kiss her forehead, and am about to walk away, when her fingers curl around my wrist.

"I know it's late, but do you think we could talk tonight?"

I turn around, my gaze meeting hers. She's pleading with her eyes, and even though I'm tired as hell, I nod. I want answers and I'll take 'em whenever she's willing to give 'em.

Once we're in my room, I sit on the love seat, expecting her to sit in the reading chair, but instead she sits next to me. Needing to say something before she begins, I start first. "I was already in a relationship once with someone who kept shit from me. She lied, kept secrets. It destroyed us. And I can't do it again."

"I know," she says softly. "When you told me that on Christmas Eve, it gave me a lot to think about. It's part of the reason why I pushed you away. I want so badly to tell you, but once I do, I can never take it back, and that's really scary for me."

Her voice is raspy, nervous, and I realize she's scared.

Not of me, or what I'll think, but of what would happen if the secret got out. I take her hands in mine and edge closer. "Whatever it is, I will do everything in my power to protect you. And not just because you're the mother of my baby, but because I care a lot about you. I've completely fallen for you, Dash."

"That's the thing," she says, her eyes going glassy with unshed tears. "Nobody can protect me." She squeezes her lids together and shakes her head, and when she opens her beautiful green eyes, she looks resolute. "But life is so short, and I want to live it and be in love. And in order to do that, I have to let you in and hope, no matter where the future leads, you'll never tell anyone. Because nobody knows, not even Naomi. And if it ever got out, I could lose my daughter."

Fresh tears fill her eyes, and my heart drops. Whatever she has to say must be pretty bad. She said she can't be protected, but I'll do everything I can to make sure she and her daughter are.

"When I was eighteen, I fell in love with a man, who I thought felt the same way about me. We spent six months together and I got pregnant. And then I found out that he was engaged to be married... I confronted him, and he told me I was just a hole to fill."

Sophia flinches, and when I look down, I see I'm squeezing my fists with her hands in mine. I loosen my hold. "He's an asshole."

"Yeah," she agrees. "I told him I was pregnant, and he told me to get rid of it. When I refused, he threatened me. Told me if anyone finds out about the baby or that we were together, he would destroy my family, making sure they lost their jobs. My mom had just started at a real good job for the first time. And…" She swallows thickly. "He told me he would take my baby from me."

"The fuck?" I bark out. "Who the hell does this guy think he is? He cheated and had the nerve to threaten you? Fuck him."

"You don't get it," she says. "Every threat he made he could make come true because…" She takes a deep breath. "He's Freeman Carmichael."

Seventeen

EASTON

*FREEMAN CARMICHAEL...*WHERE THE HELL HAVE I HEARD THAT NAME BEFORE? And then it hits me. "The fucking governor of California?"

"That'd be him. Although at the time, he was just a college student. And now he's running for senator. He has so many connections, Easton, which is why I was scared to be seen with you in public. When people find out who I am, they're going to dig, and I was scared they would dig up my skeletons. But I thought about it, and nobody knows I was with him. Kendall's birth certificate doesn't have a name on it, and I've told everyone from the beginning, her father is dead. I'm still scared, but I want to be with you," she says, placing her palms on the sides of my face.

"If people somehow find out, I'll figure out a way to fight

him, but I'm hoping it won't come to that. I just don't know what else to do." Tears spill over her lids and slide down her cheeks. "I've been alone for the last seven years and now here you are, and I care about you and want to be with you, and I know it's selfish, but I just want to be happy," she chokes out.

Holy shit. She was threatened by a powerful politician. That's why she can't live in California… and she's willing to put it all on the line to be with me.

I take her face in my hands. "I promise, your secret is safe with me. You have my word, Dash. And if it ever comes out, which won't be from me, I'll use every damn bit of my money and resources to make sure he never goes anywhere near you and K." My mind is whirling with this information. Fuck that guy for using his power to bully Sophia. I don't care what it takes…I'm going to make sure he never gets anywhere near her.

"Thank you," she says through her quiet cries. "I want you, Easton. I've always wanted you. I was just afraid of what being with you would mean." She climbs into my lap, straddling my thighs, and I grip the curves of her perfect hips to hold her in place. "I want to be with you. I'm sorry for pushing you away."

"Stop," I tell her. "You have nothing to be sorry for. Part of

A CHANCE ENCOUNTER

why I've fallen for you is because you're an amazing mother. You were doing what you had to do to protect your daughter, just like when Camden is born, I know you'll do everything in your power to protect him. But I promise, you will *never* need to protect either of them from me, and whatever happens, we'll face it together."

For the second time tonight, her mouth crashes against my own. When I kiss her back, her entire body sags against mine in relief, and I vow to keep my word, to always keep my family safe. Because that's what she is—my family. She, Kendall, and that precious little boy growing in her belly... They're my family, and it's my job to make sure they're protected... at any cost.

Quickly, our kiss turns heated, and this time when her hands find their way under my shirt, I break our kiss to remove it.

Her cool hands run up along my stomach, landing on my chest. "I've missed you so much," she murmurs, glancing down at my bare chest. She dips her head and places a soft kiss to my left pec, then swirls her tongue around my nipple before peppering kisses along my flesh to the other pec. She licks that nipple then bites on it playfully.

"Your body is so fit," she mutters. "You're hard... everywhere." As if to prove her point, she wiggles her ass along my *hard* as steel dick, and that's all it takes for me to take charge.

Lifting her by her ass, I carry her over to my bed and lay her on the mattress. I push my shorts down my legs, leaving me in only my boxer-briefs, and climb over her.

"I've been thinking about this for weeks," I tell her, kissing the corner of her mouth. "Waiting for you to let me in..." I plant a kiss on the side of her neck, and she shivers in anticipation.

"I've imagined every way I would take you once we were finally together again."

She stills at my words, and I stop kissing her flesh to look at her. "What's wrong?"

"Nothing. I—"

"Soph," I growl. "Don't you dare lie to me."

"It's stupid... and not my business."

"What?"

"Have you been with anyone else?" she blurts out. "I know I asked you for space, and you're this huge musician with all these women fawning all over you. And even though it would

A CHANCE ENCOUNTER

hurt, I'd kind of get it, because I'm the one who pushed you away, but—"

Has she lost her fucking mind? Then, I remember her only relationship was with a man who was cheating on his fiancée with her... This is all she knows.

"You asked for space," I say, cutting her off. "That doesn't equal me going out and sticking my dick in someone else." Using one arm to hold myself up, so my weight isn't on her, I use my other hand to rub my knuckles down her cheek. She's so beautiful. So special. And in a lot of ways, despite her age, she's young, naïve. She's sheltered her and her daughter from the world.

"I'm a grown ass man, Dash," I tell her, locking my eyes with hers. "I can control my hormones." She breathes a sigh of relief. "Since the day at the park, when that bee almost killed me and you saved my life, it's only been you. You're all I want."

I peel her tank top over her head, exposing her full breasts. Like she did to me, I give each nipple attention, licking and sucking. She squirms, moaning in pleasure, and I remember reading that pregnant women have sensitive nipples.

"Does it hurt?"

"No," she breathes. "It feels good."

I lick her nipple then blow on it, loving how it erects. I do the same thing to the other, and Sophia groans. "Easton, please. I need you inside me."

I tsk, shaking my head. "Soon, baby. But right now, I'm hungry." I plant kisses along her breasts one more time before I work my way down, stopping at her newly defined bump. I kiss right above her belly button, silently thanking God for this gift.

"Easton, please," she begs. "In case you forgot, I'm hungry too!"

I chuckle at her words, remembering her text. She's so fucking cute. I press a kiss just above the waistband of her shorts, then pull them, along with her underwear, down her thighs.

The last time I had the pleasure of eating her out, she was trimmed neatly. Now there's a bit more hair there. I tug on her pubes, and she gasps, sitting up on her elbows. "Oh my God, please." She shakes her head. "Don't look down there. I'm rounder and it's harder to reach down and see what I'm doing."

"Shh." I kiss the top of her mound. "I like it. But if you

need help cleaning it up, I don't mind helping." I shoot her a playful wink and she groans, plopping onto her back with her arm dropping over her eyes.

I spread her pussy lips and inhale her sweet scent. Fuck, I've missed this—missed her. I lick her clit, and her thighs tighten around my shoulders. I spread her legs back open and insert a finger. She's dripping wet. I pull my finger back out, then push two in. She groans and squirms in her place.

I go back to licking her clit, eating her pussy, while I fingerfuck her. Slowly, I work her over, tasting her, devouring her. I could live between this woman's legs. All too soon, her entire body tenses, as she detonates around me, coming all over my mouth and fingers. I suck up every drop of her orgasm, not stopping until she's pushing me away because her clit is too sensitive.

"My turn," she demands, sitting up and reaching for my cock with one hand while pushing me onto my back with the other.

As my back and head hit the mattress, my erection is pulled free of its confines, her warm, wet mouth wrapping itself around my shaft. She sucks and licks it like she's starving for it.

Needing to watch, I lift up slightly, as she takes me all the way down her throat. My dick twitches—yes, it actually fucking twitches—ready to shoot its load down her throat. But there's no way that's how this is ending. The only part of her body I'm going to be filling tonight is that tight fucking pussy.

I pull on the top of her bun, and her mouth pops off my dick. I groan as I watch saliva drip from her bottom lip and slide down the swell of her breast.

She glares at me, like I'm denying her her last meal, and even though we're in the middle of something intimate, I can't help but laugh. Cute. Sexy. Hot. Mine. All fucking mine.

"It's my turn." She pouts. "I'm supposed to be in charge."

"You want to be in charge? Then get over here and ride me, Dash, because I need your pussy wrapped around me now."

Her eyes gloss over with lust, and she quickly crawls up my body. Her hands land on my shoulders to steady herself, as she eases herself down onto my hard length. Slowly, too goddamned slowly, she takes me in, inch by inch, until my balls are touching her perfect ass.

And then she starts to move, up and down, circling her

A CHANCE ENCOUNTER

hips. My gaze drags down her body, starting at her beautiful face that's tipped back in pleasure. Her eyes are half-lidded and her mouth is slightly parted. Her breasts are bouncing up and down as she rides me. I lift my hands from her hips and pinch her rose-dusted nipples.

"Ohh, God," she rasps, grinding her pelvis against mine, bringing us both pleasure. "Do that again. Harder." I tweak both her nipples, twisting and pinching them. I rub the hardened peaks between my thumb and forefinger, and her pussy clenches around me. She's close to another orgasm. I can feel it.

My eyes drop a little farther, landing on her protruding belly. Jesus, I don't think I'll ever get enough of seeing her pregnant. I might have to knock her up again soon, just to watch her grow once more with my baby.

I imagine what it will be like in a few months when she's rounder, even softer. How she'll look riding me, stretched with my baby in her. And with that thought, I lose all control. My pelvis thrusts up, pushing her over the edge, and we both come hard. She shakes as her second orgasm overtakes her, and her pussy clenches around me like a vice as I fill her with my cum.

Yeah, I'm going to need to keep knocking her up… But first—

"What?" she breathes, cutting off my thoughts.

"What?" I say back.

"You're smirking. What were you just thinking about?"

"How fucking hot you look pregnant with my baby." Her one brow quirks up. "And how I'm planning to knock you up again and again so I can keep you like this…"

Her eyes go wide in shock. "You're crazy."

"About—"

She covers my mouth with her hand. "Don't you dare say that cheesy shit!" she says through a giggle.

I peel her hand off my mouth. "Here's something not cheesy." I grip her hips and flip her onto her back. "I want you, Dash. Every day, for the rest of our lives." I kiss her lips. "I want you pregnant with my babies, living under the same roof as me. I want to come home from work and spend my nights with you. Hell, I want to spend my days with you. Now that you've let me in, I want all of you, baby."

"You have me," she says. "You have all of me. When you come back, I want to live together. You can tell the world we're together and expecting a baby. I'm all in."

A CHANCE ENCOUNTER

Her words are the most exquisite music to my ears, but they're not enough.

"I want more," I admit. "I know that makes me selfish. But I want everyfuckingthing."

She frowns. "What else do you want?"

"You… as my wife."

Eighteen

SOPHIA

HOLY SHIT. HE WANTS ME AS HIS WIFE. SEVERAL THOUGHTS GO THROUGH MY head at once: is it too soon? Is he only asking because I'm pregnant? Do I love him? Does he love me? Shouldn't we be in love before we agree to get married? I care about him, and I want to be with him, but marriage… that's a huge commitment. My parents got married because my mom was pregnant and look how that ended.

My features must betray my thoughts because Easton's face falls. "Soph…"

"I want to," I tell him honestly. "But I want to make sure we're both certain. We haven't even dated or lived together. I need to know that when I say yes, when we say our vows, we both believe we have a chance at making it forever. I know there's no way of actually knowing that, and I get that everything can change in a blink of an eye, but I need to feel like we have a solid chance. Does that make sense?"

"It does." He kisses me softly. "So what you're saying is, I need to woo you to the point you're begging *me* to marry *you*."

He smirks, and I sigh in relief that he's not mad. "I will *not* be begging you to marry me," I scoff. "But yes, a little more wooing would be good. I want to get to know you, and I want you to get to know me."

"Ahh… so does that mean you'll be doing some wooing of your own?"

I can't help but laugh every time he says the word woo. "You want to be wooed?"

"Damn right, I do." He smirks.

"Fine, so I guess I'll be wooing you too." I roll my eyes playfully.

"All right then," he says. "Let the wooing commence."

"CAN I HAVE A HINT?"

A CHANCE ENCOUNTER

"Nope."

"Not even a little one?"

"Nope."

"But how about—"

"Dash, you're worse than the six-year-old sitting in the back seat," Easton says through a laugh. "Where we're going is a surprise and I'm not telling you anything a second before you see the signs and find out where we're going on your own."

I pout, crossing my arms over my chest, and huff. I hate surprises. I like to know what's happening, where we're going, so I can prepare. When Kendall and I woke up this morning, Easton was already awake and giddy as hell, ready to go. He said to bring the luggage we brought, in case there's anything we need, and insisted we get on the road immediately. We stopped at the donut shop for breakfast and coffee and then he jumped on the freeway, heading east. He had mentioned before he was excited to show us around where he lives, so I'm confused as to why it seems like we're leaving.

"Can you at least tell me how long it's going to take?"

Easton laughs again. "Wow, remind me never to go on a road trip with you." He reaches over the center console of his humungous Lincoln Navigator and squeezes my thigh. "What is it parents always say to their kids when they ask how long it will take?" He tilts his head to the side and smirks. "We'll get there when we get there."

Kendall giggles from the back seat in her pink booster seat Nicole had waiting in the vehicle that picked us up from the airport and Easton installed this morning into his SUV. "Mommy always says that to me."

Easton throws his head back, laughing harder. "What else does she say, K?"

"Umm, she says, 'You get what you get and you don't get upset.'" She mocks my voice, making both of us laugh.

"And she says, 'If you don't eat your dinner, no dessert.'" Her voice this time is deeper, like I'm reprimanding her.

"That's a good one." Easton nods. "My parents used to say that one to me too. What else?"

"Oh! She *always* says to Aunt Naomi, 'I'm going to be single for-ev-er.'"

"Hey!" I spin around in my seat, glaring at my little parrot. "Quit throwing me under the bus, kid!"

Her nose scrunches up in confusion. "I didn't throw you under the bus. I love you."

Easton snorts. "Forget the Kardashians, K needs her own reality show. Are all kids this funny?"

"Oh yeah, she's a riot," I say dryly.

"Well, at least you don't have to worry about being single." He shrugs. "You're officially taken."

His fingers intertwine with mine and I glance down at them, loving the way his strong hand envelops my smaller one. It reminds me how strong and protective he is and how safe I feel when I'm with him.

Out of nowhere, I feel a flutter in my belly and my hand instinctively goes to it.

"What's wrong?" Easton asks, his gaze darting between my face, my belly, and the road.

"I felt the baby," I say in awe. "It's not like a kick yet, but I could feel him tumbling around in there."

Easton grins. "He's the size of a pint of Ben and Jerry's ice cream this week."

"Mmm… My favorite is Phish Food."

"I think that's everyone's favorite," he agrees.

Two hours later we arrive at Big Bear Mountain. I've heard of the place but have never been here. Easton explains to Kendall there's snowtubing, sledding, and snowboarding, and Kendall shrieks in excitement, sticking her face against the window. Apparently, a friend of his has a cabin here and has lent it to Easton for the weekend.

"I thought you wanted to show us around where you live?" I ask, as we drive down the road where several cabins are situated on both sides of the road.

"There's nothing there worth seeing," he says with a shrug. I hear the hidden meaning behind his words and appreciate it more than he knows. "I had my sister contact a realtor. I'm putting the house up for sale."

I gasp. "But that's your home."

Easton glances at me for a second before he looks back out in front of him. "That place is just a house, a dwelling where I slept. My home is where you are, Dash. You and Kendall and that baby... You guys are my home."

My heart feels as though it's going to implode in my chest. Nobody has ever said anything like that to me before. To my parents, I was an accident, a burden. My mom was brought down by my presence and my dad didn't care about me enough to stay. I know Naomi loves me, but her home is with Dante. Kendall and I were only temporary—and I get it completely. We're part of her life, just like she's part of ours, but her *home* is with her soon-to-be husband.

But to Easton... I'm his home. The place where he wants to be. I'm the person he wants to be with. Not out of obligation, but because he cares about me. I've never had anyone feel that way about me and I didn't realize until this moment how badly I needed to feel wanted—*ached* to feel wanted.

"Hey," he says softly, lifting his hand from my thigh and swiping a tear I didn't know had fallen. "What's wrong?"

"Nothing," I tell him, reaching over and wrapping my arms around his neck—carefully, so he doesn't crash. "Everything is perfect." I kiss his cheek and feel him smile.

"Ohh, Mommy, you kissed Easton! That means you're boyfriend and girlfriend."

"That's right, Sunshine," I tell her. "That's exactly what it means."

"PINK! NO, YELLOW! WAIT, PINK!" KENDALL SAYS. "PINK!"

"You sure?" I ask, before I grab the snowsuit.

"Yes, pink, please."

"Okay." I grab it off the rack, then take it, along with her snow boots, mittens, and hat, over to where Easton's standing, talking to the gentleman about the snowtubing. It's cool in LA, but not as cold as it is up in the mountains, so we have to pick up some warmer clothes. I grabbed some gloves and a beanie, and a thicker jacket for me, but because I'm pregnant and won't be in the snow, I don't need the extra warmth Kendall will need.

Easton is wearing a hoodie and beanie to kind of hide his face the best he can, so he can last as long as possible without being noticed, but I've already seen a few people pointing his way. Thankfully, once we're done in here, he'll be on the courses with Kendall and away from everyone.

"Got everything you need?" he asks, grabbing the items from me.

"Yeah." I consider offering to help him pay for the stuff, since I've seen the price tags and they're not cheap, but I don't want to offend him. He made it clear when we got here this is his treat.

Once the items are all rung up, I take Kendall to the changing room to change her into her snow clothes. She looks adorable, like the cutest little pink snow bunny. After she's fully dressed, I insist on taking her picture and send it to Naomi with the caption: **Our little snow bunny.**

Naomi: OMG! She's so cute. Wait! I thought you were in LA??

Me: Easton took us to Big Bear Mountain to take Kendall snowtubing.

Naomi: Jealous! I miss you. Let's get together soon. The wedding is next weekend and then things will calm down.

Me: Miss you more. We'll do a girls' night soon.

"All right, Sunshine, you ready to go tubing?" I ask as we walk out of the changing room to meet Easton.

"Yes, but what will you do?"

"Your mom is going to sit and watch us, of course," Easton says, shooting a wink my way. "Ready?"

"Yep!" Kendall's so excited, she cheesy-grins.

Easton shows me to the viewing deck—where I can sit and drink hot chocolate, while watching them go down the slope—and then the two of them take off. I snap a picture of them from behind, and several more as they make their way up the mountain. While I wait for it to be their turn, I drink my hot chocolate and snack on a package of s'mores cookies I bought. When it's their turn, Easton places her on the tube and then gets in behind her. The guy manning the slopes gives them a good push and they fly down the slope. Kendall shrieks in excitement while Easton laughs the entire way down.

They do this over and over again for the next hour, while I take picture after picture and video after video. Since I've been keeping in touch with Easton's mom, I send her a picture of them.

Alicia: Big Bear Mountain? Easton loved that place growing up! How fun.

Me: Kendall is on cloud 9.

Alicia: She's so adorable. Keep sending those pictures! Next time, we should all go together.

Me: That would be fun.

Alicia: When you get back, let's do lunch. Xo

I smile at her text, getting a bit choked up—I blame it on the pregnancy hormones. She's so understanding and sweet. I wish my mom were more like her. But then again, Easton wasn't an accident who destroyed her world.

"What's wrong?" a masculine voice says from next to me, making me jump. I glance up and find Easton and Kendall standing there, both holding hot chocolates in their hands.

"Mommy, why are you crying?" Kendall asks. "Why are you sad?"

"I'm not sad, Sunshine." I place her cup on the table and pull her into my lap. "I'm crying because I'm happy." She looks at me like I've lost my mind and I laugh. "Sometimes people cry when they're very happy."

"I think your mom's pregnancy is making her crazy." Easton's eyes go wide, and he mimes the universal gesture for crazy, making Kendall laugh.

"I do too," she agrees, deadpan.

"I DON'T THINK SHE'S EVER FALLEN ASLEEP THAT FAST," I WHISPER, CLOSING the door to where Kendall is sleeping, behind us.

"I think she went up and down the slopes a couple hundred times." Easton laughs, shaking his head. "She killed it snowboarding. When she fell the first dozen times, I thought for sure she'd give up. You have one badass little girl. Fearless as hell."

I beam with pride, even though I can't really take the credit. I've lived the last seven years in fear, so I'm not exactly the model for badass, but I'm glad she hasn't been affected by my sheltering her. And hopefully, moving forward, I can show her by example what it means to be fearless.

"We'll have to come back when you're not pregnant so you can fully enjoy the place," Easton says, lighting the fireplace. Once it's crackling with flames and emitting heat, he joins me on the couch, grabbing a blanket and throwing it over both of us.

"I've never been snowboarding or tubing. They both look like a lot of fun. Kendall had a blast today."

Easton wraps his arm around me and I cuddle into the blanket and his side, sniffing his scent. He doesn't wear any cologne, but the mixture of his body wash and his unique smell has a way of relaxing me.

"Thank you for taking us away," I whisper into his chest. We needed this. To spend some time together without the stress of life, and I was scared of hanging out in LA—of course Easton knew exactly how to handle the situation.

A CHANCE ENCOUNTER

He takes my chin between his thumb and forefinger and tilts my face up to look at him. "You don't have to thank me, Dash. It's my pleasure. Thank you for talking to me. I know it was hard for you and it means a lot to me that you trust me enough to let me in."

He dips his face, and his lips gently touch mine. He tastes sweet, like hot chocolate and marshmallows, and I sigh into the kiss, loving the way his lips feel wrapped around my own. The kiss quickly goes from tender to impassioned. I crawl into his lap, my arms wrapping around his neck and my legs straddling his muscular thighs.

He breaks our kiss and rests his forehead against mine. "I missed you so much while I was gone," he murmurs, dragging the backs of his knuckles down my cheek. "Your smell..." He moves his face into the crook of my neck and runs his nose along my heated flesh. "Fuck, I can't get enough."

His hands glide down my sides and rest on my belly. "I think I'm addicted to you."

The most girlish giggle escapes my lips, but I don't even care. "You were just with me last night," I remind him.

"Yeah, but I spent weeks without you, wondering if you would ever give us a real chance. One night with you wasn't enough. I don't know how I'm going to let you go Monday morning."

His mouth connects with mine once again, and his tongue delves past my parted lips, tasting and coaxing my own. My belly does a flip-flop and my heart beats rapidly against my rib cage. The only other guy I've been intimate with was Freeman, and until Easton came into my life and showed me different, I thought how Freeman treated me was the norm. Not that he treated me so badly—up until I found out I was the woman on the side—but looking back, I can now see the difference. The way he was emotionally detached. He always had one foot out the door, never giving me his full attention. Never committing. Saying the right words to keep stringing me along…

With Easton, when he looks at me, it's as if I'm his entire world. He says what he means. He's all in, and he deserves to have someone who feels the same way. Who'll treat him the same way. And that's exactly what I'm going to do.

"Hey, Easton," I say against his lips. He pulls back, and I immediately miss his mouth. "I want you to announce that we're together and expecting a baby."

His eyes light up in surprise. "You're sure?"

A CHANCE ENCOUNTER

"Yes, I would rather it come from you than some trashy magazine, and I'm okay with everyone knowing. I'm not going to lie, I'm scared of how this might all play out, but..." I swallow thickly.

"Shh," he says, pressing his finger against my lips. "I know, but I promise you, you have nothing to be scared about. I've got you and Kendall. Always."

I believe him. It's written all over his face, threaded in his every word, and sealed in his tone of conviction. I can trust him. He'll protect us. The ball of stress in my body unravels and I sag against him. There's nothing more to say, so I kiss him to show him that I know he's got us. That I believe him and trust him.

He returns the kiss with equal passion. We're all teeth and tongues and hands as we strip each other out of our shirts. He kisses along my neck and then gives my breasts attention before kissing me once again. My hands roam his hard body, my fingers descending until I get to the happy trail that leads down to the Promised Land. I reach inside his sweats and pull his length out, stroking it from root to tip. He's already hard, but my touch makes him feel like a steel rod in my hand.

Since I'm in a maternity nightgown—that I received in my pregnancy box Easton got me for Christmas—it was so cute, filled with all types of pregnancy stuff—the only thing between us is my panties. I lift up slightly, my intention to pull them down my legs, but I'm left in shock when Easton grips the side and rips the material. I don't have any time to comment because seconds later, with my panties dangling off my leg, he enters me.

His fingers drag through my hair and he grips the back of my head, pulling my face to his for a kiss that has my head spinning. He moves in and out of me, his dick filling me in the most exquisite way, while his mouth never leaves mine. We make love, roughly, fervently, neither of us holding back—showing each other through our actions that we're all in.

"Fuck, you feel so good," he growls against my lips as we both find our release. "I could live right here, with you in my arms, buried deep inside you."

Satiated, I drop my head to his shoulder and sigh. "I'm completely okay with that."

Nineteen

EASTON

BUZZ. BUZZ. BUZZ. BUZZ.

I crack my eyes open and glance over at the nightstand. My phone is buzzing and lighting up with an incoming phone call. I snag it and look at the time: six in the damn morning. It's my sister calling, which means something is wrong. She would never call me this early unless there was a problem.

"Nic?" My voice is gravelly, laced with sleep. After Sophia was done riding me on the couch, we showered and went to bed. I wrapped myself around her with the intention of going to sleep, but I swear the woman is an addiction I can't control. One sniff of her sexy scent. One touch of her smooth skin. One look at her pregnant belly. And I'm a goner. I made her come two more times before she passed out from an orgasm-induced coma. I should've gone to sleep as well, but I couldn't stop watching her—how content she looked snoring softly next to me—one hand on her belly in a protective manner, with a slight smile on her face. And I silently vowed to make sure that look of contentment never leaves her face again. Which led me to hours of sending texts and emails to ensure just that.

"Sorry to wake you," Nicole says, actually sounding as such. "But we have a little issue." I hold my breath, praying what she says doesn't include Freeman Carmichael. I meant what I told Sophia—I will make sure he never goes near either of them—but I was hoping I wouldn't have to handle shit this soon. Sophia is finally coming around, has opened up, and the last thing I want is that asshole showing up in some way and her shutting down.

"What happened?" I whisper. "What's wrong?" I'm about to stand, so I can talk at a normal level, when a soft hand grips my arm. I look over and find Sophia awake, her eyes burning into my own. She's heard my question and she's scared. I pull her toward me and wrap my arm around her, so she knows I've got her back. Whatever it is we'll deal with this together.

"You were spotted in Big Bear and the paparazzi have

linked you and Sophia. They're using the images that went around when her friend was looking for you and are comparing them to the pictures of the three of you yesterday."

I put the phone on speaker and set it on my stomach. "Nicole, you're on speaker phone. So, they know Sophia and I are together?" Sophia audibly sighs now that she knows the issue isn't regarding that piece of shit sperm donor.

"They're speculating. We were able to remove the photos before and it died down, them thinking it was a photoshoot, and then you left for tour... But now they've got pictures of the three of you looking like a happy family."

I glance at Sophia and smile. "Isn't that what we are?"

She smiles back and nods. "Yeah, we are."

"They don't know she's pregnant," Nicole says. "Her jacket is puffy, hiding her bump, but we're going to have to do something... say something. I mean, we can ignore it, but now that they're connecting the dots, they're going to attack like vultures. Sophia's page is set to private and it doesn't have her last name on it, but it won't be long until they're digging up her info and chasing every lead."

My eyes stay on Sophia while Nicole talks to see how she responds. I look for any sign of her being upset about this, but I don't see any.

"Did you mean it when you said you're okay with us announcing that we're together and expecting a baby?" I ask her.

She nods.

"You're sure?" It won't be easy to spin this to hide it, but I'll do whatever I can if she isn't on board.

"I'm sure," she says with determination in her tone. "But, umm…" Her cheeks blush a soft pink. "Could we maybe tell a little lie?" Nicole and I stay quiet while she explains herself. "Maybe we could say we were dating and then I got pregnant?" She shrugs, her pink cheeks heating to a darker shade. "I know it's stupid, but women aren't exactly painted in the best light when they admit to a one-night stand with a stranger."

"Absolutely," Nicole says without missing a beat. "Nobody will ever know different. So, how do you want to do this? I'm thinking posting on social media is the best option. Make it personal with a picture of the two of you—"

"Three," I correct. "Kendall is just as much a part of this, and I would rather them learn about her from me." Sophia's head bobs up and down in agreement. "I'll post a picture we took yesterday with a caption."

"Okay," Nicole says. "You need to do it now. Send Preston what you're planning to post so he can tweak if necessary and approve."

"You got it. Thanks, Nic."

"Who's Preston?" Sophia asks, once I hang up.

"He's part of my PR team. He's in charge of my social media. You know how sometimes celebrities post shit they shouldn't, then later have to apologize? Preston makes sure I don't do that. I'm not allowed to post anything without his permission."

Her eyes go wide. "What if you do?"

I laugh. "I mean, I guess I could, but I trust my team, and I don't want to be that person whose career goes up in flames because he posted a dumbass comment out of passion or anger. So I never post without his approval."

I pull up the photos from yesterday and stop on one we had a resort employee take. It's of the three of us sitting on the couch. One of my arms is around Sophia, who is holding a cup of hot chocolate. Because it was warm in the restaurant, Sophia isn't wearing her jacket. It's obvious in this picture she's pregnant and not just a little overweight. Kendall is also holding a cup of hot chocolate and is leaning into her mother's side. We're all smiling happily in the picture.

"What do you think?" I nod toward the image.

"It's a nice picture. Is that the one you're thinking of posting?"

"Yeah. It's real. It's us."

I type up a post and then hand the phone over to Sophia to read and approve it.

For a while now it's felt like I was lost, stumbling through the dark, trying to find my place in this world. I had my family and music and friends—and of course you guys—but I longed for more. And then one day, several months ago, I met the most beautiful woman, who saved my life. That's right, she saved my life from a killer bee who was out to end me. With one slap of her flip-flop to my arm, she had me in her clutches. Then she looked at me, with her bright green eyes, and smiled, and I knew in that moment she was going to own my heart. Shortly after, I met her daughter, and by some miracle, the two of them welcomed me into their little world. Growing up, I watched my parents fall in love with each other over and over again and knew one day I wanted to have what they have. The love, the family. And I can finally say I've found that love with Sophia. With every day I spend with

A CHANCE ENCOUNTER

her and her daughter, Kendall, a bit of light brightens my life. I'm a lucky guy to get to call them mine. And now, we're excited to announce that we're expecting a baby. Camden Rocco Blackwood is due in June and we're beyond excited for this little guy to be added to our growing family.

"Oh, Easton," Sophia murmurs, handing my phone back to me. "Do you mean that? You love me?"

"Yeah, I do, Dash. I know it sounds crazy, but I'm almost positive I fell in love with you the day of the photoshoot. I know some people don't believe in love at first sight, but when you laughed, my heart felt like it leapt the hell out of my chest." I cradle her face in my palm and kiss her soft, plump lips. "I love you, Soph. Both you and Kendall. That girl…" I shake my head. "You both have me wrapped around your fingers and I love it."

Sophia's eyes fill with tears. "I love you too, Easton." She wraps her arms around my neck and slides onto my lap. "So, so much." Her mouth connects with mine, and just like that, the entire world disappears—leaving only me and the woman who loves me back.

"I CAN'T BELIEVE YOU HAVE CLOSE TO ONE HUNDRED MILLION FOLLOWERS ON Instagram," Sophia says incredulously, reading through the comments that have come in from my post. I warned her not all of them would be nice, but she said she didn't care and wanted to read them. She doesn't have any social media besides a Facebook page she never goes on, which made Preston very happy, since that meant he wouldn't have to worry about her posting anything—not that she would, but it's his job to worry about that shit.

"I have more on Facebook." I shrug. "What can I say? I'm a likeable guy." I smirk and she rolls her eyes.

"The comments aren't too bad." She hands me back my phone. "Most are actually really nice and supportive, congratulating us. You posted it thirty minutes ago and it already has thousands of comments. That's insane."

"Yeah, I have some amazing fans. Unfortunately, though, they can also be kind of crazy, and since this post confirms we're together, everyone will be out to get your picture. You and Kendall will be assigned a bodyguard to make sure you're safe."

Sophia's eyes bug out. "Why would they care about me? They already got the information in that post."

"Doesn't matter. The point of the post was to beat the paparazzi to the punch. Get it out there before they did. But now that they know, they'll be everywhere, especially since we're living together. It's not as bad in New York as California, but they'll be around. And once fans recognize you, they'll want to approach you because you're an extension of me. I told you I would do everything to make sure you and Kendall are safe, and I meant from everyone, not just that asshole."

"Will Kendall be safe at school?" I can see her starting to freak out, so I take her hand in mine and pull her close to me. It's almost 8:00 a.m. and Kendall is due to wake up soon. We're going to spend the day here and then head back to my place tonight.

"She'll be safe, but you'll have a bodyguard going everywhere with you. We can start with him just accompanying you when you're out and remaining in the vehicle, but if the paparazzi get bad, he'll have to stay with you at all times. I can't chance anyone bombarding you, especially with you pregnant. I have to make sure you're safe."

She nods in understanding. "I hope they leave us alone, but I get it. I've seen TMZ and how crazy they can be."

I sigh, thankful she isn't giving me a hard time.

"Mommy, Easton." Kendall appears, dressed in her pajamas, her blond hair a mess, and her tiny fists rubbing the sleep from her eyes. "Can we go snowboarding?"

Both of us laugh. The girl is obsessed with the snow.

"After breakfast," I tell her.

"I'm not hungry."

Sophia lifts a brow and pulls the mom card. "No food, no snowboarding."

"Okay," Kendall groans. "I guess I'm a little hungry."

After we get dressed, we head to the restaurant for breakfast. We're not even sat before a young woman approaches me.

"Easton, can I have your autograph, please?" She looks to be in her early teens, and has a restaurant napkin and pen in her hand.

I knew this was coming, especially since my whereabouts were posted, but I'm hoping it won't get so bad I can't spend the day with Kendall on the slopes. If the fans get too bad,

A CHANCE ENCOUNTER

since I didn't bring any bodyguards with me—giving them the weekend off before we head to Utah and Washington for the two shows I had to reschedule—we'll have to leave early and I know that'll break Kendall's little snowboard loving heart.

"Sure," I tell her with a smile. "What's your name?"

"Sammy. I loved your last album. My favorite song is 'Lost.'"

"Mine too," Kendall agrees, as if this girl is just here to discuss music.

The girl looks at her and smiles before turning her attention back to me. "I saw your post this morning. Does this mean your next album will be called *Found?*"

I chuckle. "I'm not sure yet, but once I know, I'll let everyone know." I shoot her a playful wink and sign the napkin before giving it back to her.

"Thank you so much. Could we, umm, take a picture?" She pulls her phone out and looks around.

"I can take it for you," Sophia offers, holding her hand out. After she takes the picture and the girl leaves, we're seated in a private area—at my request—so we won't be approached while we eat.

During breakfast, we talk to Kendall about how things will be a little different when they go home. She's little, so she doesn't really get it, and she doesn't see me as someone famous, so she doesn't seem fazed, more concerned with how much she has to eat before we can hit the slopes.

The day is spent like the previous one: snowboarding and tubing and drinking hot chocolate. Luckily, Nicole, even though I told her not to, sent a temp bodyguard to hang out just in case, and he actually came in handy a few times when we were approached. Despite being stopped on several occasions, we have a good time, and at five o'clock, when it's time to go home, Kendall whines she doesn't want to leave.

It's the first fit I've ever seen her throw, and Sophia handles it with patience. We get back and Kendall is passed out, so I carry her to bed and spend the rest of the night buried in Sophia, trying to cram a week's worth of time into a few hours.

Five a.m. rolls around too quickly, and our car arrives to take us to the airport. Since I'm flying on a private plane, where I enter is different than where Sophia and Kendall have to go. I'm worried about us separating, but Sophia tells me it will be fine. Nobody will recognize them without me.

Thankfully, that temp bodyguard—Dustin—is with us, and since Joel is back with me, I have Dustin go with my girls. I'm just climbing the steps to board, when Nicole meets me at the door, with a face that tells me something happened. We walk inside and Jordan is already sitting in one of the seats. We bump fists and I sit.

"They were spotted before they made it to security, but Dustin handled it," Nicole says. "I have a bodyguard meeting them at Arrivals to escort them, since they'll know they're heading home. He's been hired temporarily to see how it goes. If Sophia and Kendall like him, then we'll add him to the team full-time."

"How bad was it?"

"A couple dozen. They were asking her questions…" She flinches. "Asking who Kendall's dad is."

Shit. I knew this would happen.

"He's dead," I say, lying to my sister for the first time ever. The lie rolls off my tongue, though, because that's the story Sophia tells, and that's the story I'll tell until my dying day.

She nods. "Do you have a name?"

"No, no name. No information will ever be given."

She eyes me for a moment then nods. She knows I'm

hiding something, but she also knows I'm not going to tell her what it is. "Okay. So, we say it's a private matter and leave it at that."

"Are the rumors true?" Jordan asks. "You putting your house up for sale? Moving to New York?"

"Rumors?" I laugh. "You heard that shit from my sister."

"Didn't hear it from you, though," he notes. "That makes it a rumor."

"Yeah, it's true. I'm making New York my home."

He nods. "Well, then I guess Nic and I will be as well."

My gaze flings over to my sister. "Seriously?"

She shrugs. "With you and our parents in New York, that only leaves me on the West Coast. Jordan and I talked and we're moving too. When we get back next week, we're going to start looking for a place."

"Hell yeah."

My phone buzzes with an incoming text, so I check it.

Dash: We're on the plane. Miss you already.

Me: Miss you more.

Dash: Impossible.

This week without my girls is going to suck, badly.

Twenty

SOPHIA

I LOOK AT MY PHONE FOR WHAT FEELS LIKE THE MILLIONTH TIME. IT'S BEEN TEN days since I've seen Easton. It was only supposed to be seven, but he had a few interviews he had to do in California, so he decided to fly back and do them, as well as meet with the moving company to go over what to pack and get rid of, since his house is being put up for sale and he'll be living here with us. He wanted to make sure all of his loose ends were tied, so once he comes back, he won't have to leave again. Now that his tour is over, he's officially on break—no interviews or obligations, aside from him working on his next album, which he can do here.

We've texted and talked on the phone every day he's been gone. He even had a dozen pints of Ben and Jerry's Phish

Food ice cream delivered. A couple days ago, when I hit five months pregnant, he sent Kendall a whoopie cushion because apparently that's the size of the baby. She's been blowing it up and leaving it everywhere for me to sit on. I had Nicole buy him a beer from me since my chart says the baby is the size of a pint of lager. I think he won that round...

Today is Valentine's Day and I expected at least a *Good Morning! Happy Valentine's Day!* from Easton, but it's almost three o'clock and he's radio silent. I texted him wishing him a Happy Valentine's Day a couple hours ago, but it's showing as unread. I don't get it. He never goes this long without checking his texts.

Kendall comes barreling out of school, with a huge smile on her precious face, and flies into my arms. "Mommy! Look at all the candy and cards I got," she says, opening her cardboard mailbox we made and decorated for today. "So many people love me." She giggles, ripping a wrapper off a heart-shaped sucker, and pops it into her mouth.

"So many people do love you," I agree, walking us back to the black Escalade, where our driver and security detail await. Easton was right. While we beat the paparazzi at their game of *"Who is that woman?"* it hasn't stopped them from

A CHANCE ENCOUNTER

following us around and snapping pictures while throwing personal questions at me. Nicole got an injunction to stop them from going too close to our home, but the streets and sidewalks are free game. Thankfully, so far, Riggins, our security guard, has been able to wait in the vehicle when I pick Kendall up at school. He walks with me to class because he doesn't like not being able to see me, but he doesn't go into class with me, and he stays back so nobody knows who he is or what he's doing.

"I have an extra lolli," Kendall tells Riggins. "Do you want it?" She extends her hand and Riggins smiles—he's a serious dude, so it's more like a grimace, but it's his version of a smile.

"Thanks, Kendall," he says, "but I don't eat sweets."

Her eyes widen. "At all?"

"Nope. Only good fuel goes into this tank."

She shakes her head in confusion. "Fuel? Like gas?"

Riggins chuckles. "Yep."

She scrunches her nose up in disgust. "Gas is for cars, not people. You're going to get sick."

"He doesn't mean it," I tell her. "He means he eats food that's good for him, like fruits and veggies. Your body is like a car and food is like the gas. You need good food for it to run."

She nods in understanding. "My teacher said we couldn't eat our lollis until school was out because they make us run around fast."

Yeah, I bet she did…

When we get home, the guys wait until we're through the front door to take off. The second we walk in, I halt in place, stunned. Balloons—red, white, pink—everywhere. Roses, every color, are placed on every surface. And standing in the middle of the living room, holding the biggest heart-shaped box of chocolates I've ever seen, is the most handsome man.

"Easton!" Kendall squeals. "You're back! Is that for me?" She runs over and throws her arms around him for a side hug before she grabs the large box in both her hands. "Wow!"

"Happy Valentine's Day," he says to her, kissing the top of her head.

"Thank you!" She drops onto the ground and goes about trying to open the wrapped chocolates.

"And this"—he grabs a large red gift bag from the couch and hands it to me—"is for you."

I cut across the room and encircle my arms around his neck. "I missed you," I mutter against his chest, as he wraps his arms around my waist. My bump is bigger, so it's a bit

A CHANCE ENCOUNTER

awkward, but that doesn't stop us. "I thought something was wrong. You didn't answer my texts."

"I was on a flight back here. I wanted to surprise you."

"Well, I'm definitely surprised." I stand on my tiptoes and kiss him. "Thank you."

"Here, open your gift," he says, taking my hand and the bag and walking us over to the couch. I glance at Kendall, who's still working on removing all the plastic. She huffs and puffs, but she's determined to get it undone and get that box open.

Inside the bag is a box. I open it up and find the most exquisite red dress from a high-end maternity store.

"It's beautiful. Thank you." I kiss Easton's cheek.

"It's for tonight. I'm taking you out on our first date."

"What?"

"My parents are going to spend the night with Kendall, so we can go out. I realized this morning, everything we've been through, and we still haven't been on a single date."

I giggle at the absurdity because he's right. We've never actually been out, just the two of us.

"We don't have to go out tonight. Won't that ruin their Valentine's Day?"

"My mom offered. They went away last weekend to celebrate and she said they're planning to order in some food and hang out."

"I get to play with Alicia?" Kendall overhears. "Yay!" She tears the plastic off and lifts the lid. "Ohhh... Wow!"

"Only one," I tell her, bursting her chocolate-loving bubble.

"What?" She pouts. "But..."

"One," I repeat. "You've had enough sugar today."

"Fine." She picks one out and pops it into her mouth. "So yummy," she mumbles around her full mouth.

After showering and doing my hair, which I curl into large waves, I put on the dress Easton bought. It fits me perfectly, comfortable while showing off my bump. Since it's chilly outside, I pair it with my knee-high black boots that are perfect for the snowy walkways. I grab my new black puffer coat with its faux fur hood I got in Big Bear and throw it over my arm. It's too warm in here to put on.

I carefully descend the stairs, and when I reach the first floor, I find Alicia and Sean sitting with Easton and Kendall, chatting. At the sound of me entering, Easton glances up and stands, now sporting the most delicious suit—sans tie, with the top buttons undone.

"You look…" He shakes his head. "Perfect."

I flush, knowing we're in front of his parents. "Thank you. You look so handsome. I've never seen you this dressed up."

"Oh, Sophia, you look beautiful," Alicia gushes. "Stand together so I can take your picture."

We do as she says, and she takes several pictures. "I feel like we're going to prom," I joke.

Easton laughs. "Except I can't knock you up since you're already pregnant." He waggles his brows.

"Easton!" I playfully smack his chest, making his parents laugh.

"Mommy, you look so pretty," Kendall says, walking over and running her hand down the material of my dress.

"Thank you, Sunshine. Be good for Alicia and Sean, okay? I'll be home in a few hours."

Easton clears his throat. "Actually, they're spending the night. I set up the guestroom for them. We won't be home until tomorrow."

I open my mouth to question why, but he's already shaking his head. "Nope, no questions."

"More surprises?" I groan half playfully, half seriously.

The corners of Easton's lips curl into a mischievous grin. "Let's go, Dash. The night awaits."

After saying goodbye to everyone, I put on my coat, and we head outside. Waiting in front of our door is a large, sleek stretch Hummer limo. Easton takes my hand and helps me down the sleek steps, as several paparazzi flash their cameras and fling questions our way. Neither of us pays them any mind, but I do notice Easton's security team is situated on either side so nobody can come too close. A gentleman, who is standing by the limo door, opens it when we approach and greets us with a smile, then Easton helps me into the vehicle. I slide in and Easton follows, the door closing behind him.

"Happy Valentine's Day," he says, once we're situated inside and the limo pulls out.

"I feel like a princess," I admit, my grin almost hurting my face, it's so wide.

"Nah, baby, you're my queen." Easton takes my face in his hands and kisses me on my lips, his tongue thrusting into my mouth and swirling with my own. My blood warms at his touch and I have to undo my jacket so I'm not so hot.

"I know you're hungry for me, but not here, Dash," he jokes. "Wait until we're alone."

A CHANCE ENCOUNTER

"Shut up!" I smack his arm.

"Damn, woman. I never realized how violent you are." He chuckles, playfully rubbing his arm.

We arrive in front of a hotel I've seen plenty of times but have never been inside, and Easton helps me out. Once again, cameras are flashing, but we ignore them, living in our own little bubble. I briefly wonder how they knew we were coming here. They must've followed us. We enter the elevator and Easton presses the button to go to the top floor. The hotel must have a restaurant up there. We're greeted as soon as we step out and are brought back to a private dining room that's filled with balloons and roses like our house is. There's a table for two situated by the window that has the most beautiful view of the city skyline.

Like the gentleman he is, Easton pulls my chair out for me and I sit, unzipping my jacket and shrugging it off. He takes it from me and hangs it over the back of my chair.

The waiter comes over and asks what we would like to drink. Since I'm pregnant, I can't have alcohol, so I stick with water and Easton does the same.

"They have a set menu for Valentine's Day," Easton explains, "but I spoke to them and they're switching out a few of the items since you can't have them while you're pregnant."

My heart swells in my chest. He's been on tour for months, handles a million things on a daily basis regarding his career, and yet he still manages to always put Kendall and me first—i.e. taking us away to Big Bear and planning all of this—and on top of it all, he makes sure to double-check the menu. I am seriously one blessed woman.

Our drinks are brought out and a few minutes later, the first course. While we eat, we talk—about everything, nothing… the baby, Kendall, the house, his plans to get back in the studio to record. It feels good to just talk, without Kendall, without the craziness of the world. Just the two of us.

Each course is more delicious than the last, and when dessert is brought out, I'm not sure if there's any room in my belly for it, but when I see how good it looks, I force myself to have some.

"Are we staying here as well?" I ask Easton after he pays the bill.

"Yeah, I booked us a room."

Hand in hand, we walk back to the elevator. Easton holds a card to some scanner and a button labeled PH lights up.

A CHANCE ENCOUNTER

He's booked the penthouse for us.

Instead of the elevator going down, it goes up. Hmm… I thought we were already on the top floor. Guess not. The doors open a second later, and we step off. There are only a couple doors on this floor. We walk to the first one and Easton scans the card to let us in.

When we walk in, I take in our surroundings. It's less like a hotel room and more like a luxurious apartment. My old apartment could literally fit inside the foyer of this place. I take a calming breath, unsure if I'll get used to the extravagance that comes with Easton. I think one of the reasons why I don't mind it is because he doesn't flaunt or make a show of it. He uses it when necessary, but he isn't over-the-top.

We walk farther into the suite and I find fresh rose petals and lit candles scattered all over the place. Upon further inspection, I notice the candles are electric. Easton guides me through the main area. I assume he's going to take us straight to the bedroom—and I wouldn't be opposed—but instead, we end up outside on the terrace. It's cold outside, but the heaters are on, making the area toasty warm.

I step up to the railing and look out at the city. It's beautiful at night, and from up here, peaceful. We're too high up to hear the hustle and bustle down below.

Easton steps up from behind and envelops me in his arms, his hands landing on my belly. The second his hands touch my flesh, the most amazing thing happens: the baby kicks. Like a real, strong kick.

Easton gasps. "Did you feel that?"

I giggle. "If you did, I would hope I did."

He spins me around, so my back is against the wrought iron railing and I'm now facing him. "I love you being pregnant. Carrying my baby... I want more, so many more," he admits, not for the first time. The soft glow of the light from inside hits his face and his brown orbs sparkle. "I want a house full of little Blackwood babies running around."

He pulls a small box out from his coat pocket and gets down on one knee. "But I don't want them as your boyfriend, or even your fiancé," he says. "I want them as your husband. With you as my wife. The day at the park I knew you were the woman for me, and I don't want to go another day without you knowing I want to spend the rest of my life with you. And..." He swallows thickly. "I'd love to adopt Kendall. She has your last name, and it would mean everything to me if you both would share mine. When we bring that little guy into

A CHANCE ENCOUNTER

this world, I want it to be as a family, in every way possible."

He cracks open the box and nestled inside the black velvet is the most beautiful engagement ring. My heart stills and then picks up speed. It should be too soon, right? We're doing this all wrong. I mean, he's proposing on our first official date. A laugh bubbles up my throat and escapes past my lips. This is crazy. Insane. But it's also right. Because I know with every fiber of my being Easton is the man I want to spend the rest of my life with.

He extends his hand so I can see the ring better, and his eyes meet mine. "Will you marry me, Dash?"

He hasn't even finished his question and I'm already nodding my answer. The second he stops speaking, I find my voice. "Yes! Yes, I will marry you."

He slides the ring onto my finger and pulls me into his arms. He kisses me fervently, his tongue lashing out and dueling with mine.

When we come up for air, he takes my hand, which is now housing the beautiful light pink emerald cut diamond on a simple platinum band, and brings it up to his lips. I take a moment to admire it. It's so simple yet elegant. Perfect.

"I want to marry you soon," he says. "I meant what I said.

I want to bring this baby into the world as a family in every way possible, including legally. Talk to Naomi and have her plan whatever you want, but the sooner the better." He presses a soft kiss to my lips. "I can't wait to make you my wife."

His hands slide to my ass and he lifts me into his arms, carrying me back inside to the bedroom, where more candles and rose petals litter the area.

"Do you have any idea how much you mean to me?" he says, laying me on the bed and raining kisses all over my face.

I shake my head playfully, even though I know. He shows me in every word, every decision, every action how much I mean to him. "I think you're going to have to remind me…"

"Oh, I can definitely do that," he murmurs, kissing the corner of my mouth. "Consider it my first promise as your fiancé and soon to be husband: to show you every day just how much I want you…" He kisses the other corner of my mouth. "How much I need you…" He kisses the tip of my nose. "How much you mean to me… starting right now." His mouth presses against mine and for the next several hours Easton does exactly as he promised.

Twenty-One

EASTON

"ARE YOU SURE YOU'RE OKAY PICKING HER UP?" SOPHIA ASKS FOR THE THIRD time as she pulls her boots on.

"Yes. Go shopping, have lunch with your friend, plan our wedding." I shoot her a playful wink. "Kendall and I will be fine." This is the first time I'm in charge of picking Kendall up from school—the first time anyone, aside from Naomi, has ever been in charge of picking Kendall up—so I don't take offense to her overprotectiveness. One of the things I love about Sophia is how protective she is of her daughter. She's a damn good mom.

"Okay, if you have any questions, or if she needs to speak to me, I'll have my phone on me." She stands and kisses me. "Thank you."

"Dash, you don't have to thank me for taking care of Kendall. In a few short months she'll legally be mine, and even without that paperwork, I love her as such. I want to be part of this, and a great way to do that is for me to spend time with her."

Sophia's eyes water. Something that happens often these days. The further along in her pregnancy, the more emotional she gets. She's due in three months and our wedding is in two. After sitting down and discussing dates, we picked the weekend after she graduates from college so we can go on a mini honeymoon—while my parents keep Kendall—since Kendall will still be in school for another couple weeks.

"Soph, go," I say with a laugh, encircling my arms around her. "I love you, baby."

"I love you too." She takes a deep breath. "Okay, I'm going. You're taking Riggins, right? He knows where her school is and the proce—"

"Dash, I got this. Riggins is going with you, and I'm not taking anyone. I'll be fine." The paparazzi have died down, so I no longer need security with me, unless we're going to a big event. But I'm keeping Riggins on because Sophia is pregnant and Kendall is little. I've been doing this my entire

A CHANCE ENCOUNTER

life, so I can handle it, but I'm not taking that chance with my girls.

I can tell she wants to argue but doesn't. "Okay. I'll see you later." She kisses me again, then, grabbing her purse and slinging it over her shoulder, saunters out the door.

I have an hour before I need to head out to get Kendall, so I use the time to check my emails and get some writing in. The words have been flowing lately and I'm excited to get this album going.

I'm heading out the door, when my dad shoots me a text asking if I'm coming into the studio today since I'm scheduled. Shit, I forgot. I wrote a new song I want to work on putting music to. I consider telling him I need to reschedule, but Kendall and Sophia have been to the studio with me a few times and Kendall loves it there. She spends the entire time between the sound booth and control room, messing with the equipment and singing her little heart out. The girl loves music. So, instead of canceling, I let him know I'm going to pick up Kendall and then we'll be on our way.

I arrive at her school a few minutes before the bell is due to ring and pull around the pickup line, finding a parking spot. Sophia said she has the driver park, so she can walk up and greet her, but if I want to wait in the carline so nobody recognizes me, I can do that. Since this was last-minute and Kendall isn't expecting me, I park and walk up. It's an elementary school. I doubt anyone is thinking about who I am...

But the second I step onto the sidewalk where parents are allowed to wait, I realize my mistake. Apparently, based on the way the group of moms are staring at me like they want to devour me, kids, teenagers, and people in their early twenties aren't the only ones who listen to my music.

Thankfully, the bell rings, and the school quickly becomes a madhouse. Doors swing open and kids fly out. My pulse picks up speed as my eyes dart all over looking for Kendall. There's no way they would just let her find her own way out, right? If that's the case, we're going to be looking into private school.

Quickly, I notice the kids aren't actually going anywhere they want, but are lining up along the painted lines to wait to be called. Cars drive up and teachers call out the kids' names. I breathe easier, seeing it's ordered chaos.

A few minutes later, another group of kids come out and I spot Kendall in the mix, looking around for her mom. The

A CHANCE ENCOUNTER

second she sees me, her face lights up and she runs over to me. She jumps into my arms and hugs me tight. "Easton, you're here!" Her tiny hands squeeze my cheeks. "Ms. Kelly told me Mommy called and said you're picking me up."

"I'm here. You ready to go?"

"Good afternoon, Mr. Blackwood?" a young woman says.

"Yeah."

"I'm just going to need to see your ID, so you can take Kendall. It's standard procedure since you've never picked her up before."

"Absolutely." I set Kendall down, pull my wallet out, and hand her my driver's license.

"Kendall, is that your daddy?" a little girl asks. Her mom is one of the women who were staring at me.

"No," Kendall says softly. "He's my baby brother's daddy. I don't have a daddy."

Her words have me darting my gaze down to her. Sophia and I have confirmed with an attorney that I can legally adopt Kendall because there's no one on her birth certificate as the dad, but we were waiting until it's all legalized to tell her. Looks like we're going to need to say something sooner because I can't have her thinking like that.

"Oh," her friend says. "I have two, but one is my stepdaddy."

The teacher hands me back my license and I scoop Kendall up, taking her away from here. "What do you say we go by the bakery to get cupcakes and then go to the studio?" I ask, changing the subject.

I know it works when her face lights up. "Yay!" She cheers. "I love cupcakes and the studio! Can I sing?"

"Of course." I load her into my SUV that I had brought here from LA—the rest of my vehicles are in storage since there isn't much use for them in New York—and head over to the studio. The bakery is right around the corner, so we park in the parking garage and then walk over to place our order for the cupcakes, so we can take them to the studio.

My parents are both in the studio when we walk in, and Kendall runs over to give them a hug. "We brought cupcakes!" she tells them excitedly. "And Easton said I get to sing and make music."

Mom lights up. She loves Kendall as if she were her own granddaughter. "Have you been writing any music?"

"Yes. Me and Easton wrote a song. Right, Easton?" Kendall looks at me with wide eyes. Every night when I'm writing music, she'll join me and help. It's so damn adorable.

A CHANCE ENCOUNTER

"Yep, Reggie and I are going to work on the instrumentals for it today." Reggie is one of Blackwood Records' producers, and in my opinion—aside from my dad—the best. "You going to help us?"

"Yes." Kendall takes the box of cupcakes into the control room and climbs onto a stool next to Reggie. "Want a cupcake?" she offers. "They're super yummy."

Reggie grins and takes one. "Thanks, Little Miss."

"Hey, Easton, check out what came in today," my dad says, handing me a box. "Your mom wanted to save it for the baby shower—"

"But your dad is too excited," Mom finishes, playfully rolling her eyes.

I open up the box and inside is a tiny onesie. I pull it out and read what's written on the front out loud. "My daddy makes music at Blackwood Records." I flip it over and, on the back, it reads, "Future musician in the making."

I can't help but tear up. I have a picture of me in the same onesie when I was little. My mom had it made when my dad first started Blackwood Records. "Thanks, Dad." I give him a hug. "This is awesome."

I put it back in the box and sit on the stool next to Kendall, who is staring out at the empty sound booth instead of eating her cupcake.

"Hey, something wrong with your food?" I nudge her side.

"No," she whispers. "I'm tired. Can I go lie down?"

Her not devouring her cupcake is the first red flag. Her head down and not looking at me is the second. And the fact that she rarely takes naps anymore without her mom making her is the third. "Hey, K. Look at me."

Her glassy eyes slowly meet mine and the sadness in them has my stomach roiling. "What's wrong?"

"Baby Camden has a daddy, and you have a daddy, and my friend Tiffany has two, but I don't have a daddy." She shrugs.

"Can you guys give us a minute?" I say to everyone in the control room. They quickly exit, leaving Kendall and me alone. This conversation was supposed to happen later, with her mom, but I can't spend another second with her thinking she doesn't have a dad.

"K, do you know what a daddy is?"

She thinks about it for a second before she says, "A daddy loves his baby like your daddy loves you and you love baby Camden in Mommy's belly."

"That's right. A daddy is someone who loves their

A CHANCE ENCOUNTER

children, but they don't have to be babies. Do you know that I love you?"

Kendall's eyes widen slightly. "You do?"

"I love you very much, just like I love Camden and my dad loves me. How would you feel about me being your daddy too?"

"You can be my daddy?"

"Of course I can. I love you, and when your mom and I get married, I want you both to have the same name as me."

"My name won't be Kendall anymore?" She gnaws on her bottom lip nervously.

I stifle my laugh. "I meant your last name. Your first name will still be Kendall, but instead of Davis, it will be Blackwood."

Her little mouth breaks into a smile. "Like my brother? Camden Rocco Blackwood?"

"Yep, we'll all have the same last name. You'll be Kendall Naomi Blackwood and your mom will be Sophia Marie Blackwood. What do you think?"

"Can I call you Daddy?"

"You absolutely can," I tell her, lifting her into my lap. "As a matter-of-fact, it would make me very happy if you did."

"Can I tell people you're my daddy?"

"You can tell anyone you want, as long as I can tell people you're my daughter."

Her smile widens. "You can tell people."

"Good, now eat your cupcake. We have some music to make today."

Dash: I need your help. What time will you be home?

Me: Within the hour. Everything okay?

Dash: Yeah.

"CAN I STAY WITH GRANDMA AND GRANDPA?" KENDALL ASKS. THE SECOND MY mom heard K call me Daddy, she jumped on the name train and insisted Kendall call her Grandma, which led to her calling my dad Grandpa.

"Please, Daddy." She bats her lashes and between that and her calling me Daddy, I don't stand a chance. Plus, it's Friday night and I'm okay with having some alone time with my fiancée.

A CHANCE ENCOUNTER

"All right, you can spend the night."

"Yay! I get to spend the night!"

"I'm going to get going," I tell my parents. "Sophia texted she needs help with something. Want to meet tomorrow for breakfast? We're going shopping for the nursery."

"Sounds good." My mom kisses my cheek.

"I'm really loving that song," Dad says. "Keep writing like that and your album is going to kill it."

"Thanks." I give him a hug then fist bump Reggie. "Good work today, man. Those instrumentals were on point."

He grins. "You make my job easy."

Twenty minutes later, I walk through the door to find Sophia sitting on the couch flipping through a magazine.

"Did you have a good lunch with Naomi?"

"Hey, yeah. Almost everything is planned for the wedding. Thank you for being okay with keeping it small."

"Of course." I sit next to her and pull her into my arms. "The only thing I care about is making you *mine*."

"I'm already yours. Umm, where's Kendall?" She sits up straight, realizing her mini-me isn't with me.

"She begged to spend the night at my parents, and I couldn't say no... Especially when she batted her damn

337

eyelashes, like you do, and called me Daddy."

"What?" She gasps. "She called you Daddy?"

I explain what happened at school and at the studio, and by the time I'm done, she's practically in tears. "I know we were going to talk to her together, but—"

"No," she cuts me off. "It's okay," she chokes out, hugging me. "Thank you, Easton."

"You don't have to thank me, baby."

"I know, but it's just... everything you've done. The house, your love, the way you make us feel safe, and how much you care about my daughter."

"Our daughter," I correct. "She's mine too."

"See? That's what I mean. I feel like I'm living in some kind of fairy tale." She swipes away her tears. "I just feel so lucky."

"It's me who's the lucky one. I meant what I said on that post. I was lost and now I've found my way. Finding you was a game changer, Dash. And I'm going to spend every day showing you how much I love you and our daughter." I kiss her forehead. "So, what is it you needed help with?"

"Oh! This." She grabs a huge box and opens it, exposing several small pieces of... cake?

A CHANCE ENCOUNTER

"You need my help eating dessert?"

"Not eating dessert… Picking out the flavor for our wedding cake."

She doesn't have to tell me twice. Everything else she's asked my opinion on was hard as hell—linens, color scheme, invitations, the venue. So many decisions to make. All I want is to say 'I do.' Everything else is just details. But I also want her to have her dream wedding, since it's the only wedding she'll ever have, and according to my mom and sister, the wedding is important to the woman.

"Try this one." Sophia lifts a piece of cake up to my lips and I open, making it a point to bite down on her flesh before she can retract her hand. I chew for a few seconds, tasting it. The flavor is chocolate with peanut butter filling. It's moist as hell and melts in my mouth.

"Delicious."

She smiles and grabs another piece. "Try this one."

It's vanilla with some cream filling. Also moist. "Delicious."

She smiles again.

"Okay, how about this one?" she asks, after I take a gulp of the milk she grabbed for me.

I take a bite. Red velvet with cream cheese frosting.

Perfect mixture of sweet and tart. "Delicious."

Her brows dip. "How about this one?"

Marble with fruit filling. Very refreshing.

"Delicious," I tell her, making her glare.

"Easton, they can't all be delicious."

"But they are." I shrug.

"Which one tastes the best?"

"Hmm, I'm not sure…" I pluck one of the samples from the box and swipe it across her lips. Her eyes widen, and then my mouth is on hers, sucking and tasting her. "Mmm… this one is the best."

She snorts out a laugh. "Everything is done but the cake. Help me pick. I can't decide, and Kendall is with your parents, so she's no help."

"Let me try them again," I tell her, snatching up another piece and smearing it across the side of her neck. "Don't move," I say, my voice serious. "I'm on a mission to determine which cake tastes the best." I growl playfully and attack her neck, nipping the sensitive area just above her pulse point. "Yep, that's it. This one is the best."

I back up, just in time to see her roll her eyes. "You're no help." She pouts, leaning back and crossing her arms over her chest. The movement causes the swells of her breasts to rise, and my eyes gravitate toward them.

"No way!" She shrieks with laughter, jumping up. "You are not spreading cake across my entire body." She tries to run, but I grab ahold of her before she can and carefully push her back onto the couch.

"You told me to pick, so you don't get to judge my process." I pull her shorts and underwear down and fling them to the side. "Now, hush your mouth while I finish sampling the goods." I spread her legs and go about taste testing another part of her.

"Mmmm," I moan, once she's come all over my fingers and tongue. "That's it. That's the flavor."

"What's the flavor?" she breathes.

"Pussy. The most delicious flavor of all."

Twenty-Two

SOPHIA

Easton: Send me a pic.

Me: I'm in class!

Easton: I don't care. I miss you.

Me: Fine... <insert eye-rolling emoji>

I GLANCE AROUND TO MAKE SURE NOBODY IS PAYING ATTENTION TO WHAT I'M about to do, then quickly snap a selfie and send it to Easton, secretly loving that my man is missing me after only a couple hours of not seeing me. Last week was spring break and we spent the entire week together. We finished up the nursery, spent time at the studio, and took a weekend trip to The Hamptons for Kendall's birthday, where his parents have a beach house. Everyone met us there and we had a barbeque to celebrate my little girl turning seven years old. It was nice and relaxing, and when I woke up this morning and had to threaten Kendall to get out of bed and get ready for school, I wished we were still there. But at the same time, I'm excited for everything that is to come. It's crazy to think that in a few weeks' time I'll not only be a college graduate but a wife, and shortly after that, a mother once again.

Easton: Fuck, you're beautiful.

Me: <insert blushing emoji> Your turn!

A few seconds later, a sexy selfie of Easton graces my screen. His hair is on the longer side, since he hasn't gotten it cut in a while, and his chocolate brown eyes are sparkling with a mixture of laziness and mischief. He's at home on the couch and I can see a hint of his naked chest. Damn, I wish I were at home with him, snuggling up against his hard—

"And that's all for today," the professor says, cutting off my thoughts. "Read over chapter thirty-two and come to class ready to discuss your take on Political Theory." The professor closes his briefcase and exits out the side door, which leads to his office.

I type a reminder into my digital planner and shut down my MacBook before stowing it away. I have one more class

A CHANCE ENCOUNTER

this morning and then I'm picking up Kendall from school and meeting Naomi, Alicia, and Nicole for my final fitting for my wedding dress—unless my belly grows too much in the next few weeks, in which case the seamstress assured me she can take it out a bit more at the last minute.

I am definitely looking forward to the wedding. For one, it will mean Easton and I are legally married. He'll also be adopting Kendall. But also, because he's planned a mini getaway for us. It will be our last trip before the baby comes. He hasn't told me where we're going, but I've hinted that I hope it's somewhere with sun, warmth, and sand. Winter has been long and bitter. We're in April and the high has been in the sixties. Even in The Hamptons it was too chilly to go swimming. I'm over it.

After gathering my stuff, I head out to meet Riggins, so he can walk me to my next class. I swing the door open and walk down the hall, toward the exit, where I know he'll be waiting for me, when a firm hand grips my wrist and tugs me into an empty room. I don't have time to scream before my mouth is covered and I'm shoved against the wall. The back of my head hits the wall hard, and a feeling of dizziness momentarily overcomes me.

When I open my eyes, my vision clearing, I'm standing face-to-face with the man I prayed on too many occasions I would never see again: Freeman Carmichael.

"What the hell are you doing?" I hiss, after smacking his hand away from my face.

"What the fuck are *you* doing?" he barks.

"The last I checked I was leaving class and going to my next one. Why are you even here?"

"I'm here because I warned you if anyone finds out about that bastard child you insisted on keeping, I would destroy you!" He smacks his palm against the wall next to me and I jump.

"Go fuck yourself!" I spit. "My daughter is not a bastard. She's a beautiful, smart, perfect little girl, and fuck you for even speaking about her." My hands are shaking, and my body feels numb from the adrenaline rush, but it feels good to finally stand up to this bullying asshole.

"No, fuck you!" he booms. "What are you hoping to get out of this, huh?" He pulls something out of his back pocket and shoves it into my face. I home in on it and all the blood in my veins goes ice-cold. It's an image of Freeman and me laughing. It was taken at the club I used to work at. We were

A CHANCE ENCOUNTER

both so much younger and looked carefree. I'm on one side of the bar and he's on the other. Whoever took this picture must've been sitting at the bar as well.

"Where did you get that from?" I whisper in shock. It's been almost eight years. This makes no sense. And there's no way this image has gone public. Easton has an entire team of people who stay up to date on anything that exposes him— and now me.

"You tell me!" he barks. "It was left with my secretary with a note warning me that all my secrets will come to light."

"It wasn't me." The last thing I want is anyone finding out about my past.

"If it wasn't you then who the hell was it?" His eyes look manic, out of control, and out of instinct, my hands go to my belly to protect my baby, unsure of what he's capable of. I've never seen him this mad and it scares me.

"Maybe someone else you fucked over." Uncomfortable with his close proximity to me, I shove at his chest to get him away from me, and since he's not expecting it, he stumbles back. "As far as I'm concerned, my daughter's sperm donor is dead. I have *never* mentioned your name"—except to Easton—"nor have I seen that image." I shove him again, but this time he's prepared and doesn't budge.

There's a chair by the table and I pick it up and fling it at him. "Nobody knows we were together, so go back to whatever hole you crawled out of and stay the hell out of my life, and I'll continue to do the same. If someone is threatening you, that's your damn problem." I step closer to the door, needing to get away. I don't know what he's capable of and I don't want to find out.

"That's where you're wrong!" he shouts, shoving the chair out of his way. "It's your problem too. Everything I worked my ass off for is about to go up in flames because of you! A fucking whore I made the mistake of sticking my dick into a few times." He stalks toward me and I move back, inching closer to the exit. "I can tell you right now, if it gets out what happened between us, if whoever sent me this picture opens their mouth, my campaign is fucked, and then I'm going to have nothing to lose. And I promise you, I'm going to come after that kid, and if you think for a second any judge will grant a stripper custody over me, you're fucking delusional."

My eyes go wide at his words. He's been watching me. That's the only way he would know my old job. "You're not going anywhere near my daughter!" I scream, refusing to cower to this piece of shit. "She's mine!" I grab another chair that's near me and kick it at him. "Over my dead body will you get anywhere near her!"

"If I find out it was you who sent that fucking picture, I'll make sure you're buried six feet under," he sneers, throwing the chair to the side and stalking toward me. Thankfully, I'm now near the door and before he can catch up to me, I push it open.

"Go to hell!" I yell as I hurry out of the room and down the hall. I see Riggins on the phone, his features etched with worry.

"Where were you?" he asks, glancing around the hall. "You can't just—"

"Let's go," I say, cutting him off. "We need to go, now."

I fly out of the building and head straight to the parking lot, needing to get away from here. I need Easton. I need to tell him what happened. I need him to hold me and tell me it's going to be okay.

Riggins follows me out, staying on my heels. The second we're in the SUV, I feel like I can breathe a bit easier. He drives us to the house in silence. When we pull up, I grab my backpack and laptop case and exit the vehicle.

I'm up the sidewalk and into the house, screaming Easton's name and praying he's home. When he hears me, he comes flying down the steps. "What's wrong?"

I rush over to him and loop my arms around his waist.

"What's going on, Dash? Is it the baby?"

I glance up at him and our eyes lock. "It's Freeman," I choke out. "He came to see me. He's going to take Kendall."

"Like hell he is," Easton growls. He walks us over to the couch and sits us down with me situated in his lap. "Talk to me, baby," he says, tucking strands of hair behind my ear.

Through my sobs, which I try and fail to contain, I explain from beginning to end my run-in with Freeman. The entire time Easton listens, his jaw is locked in anger. When I finish, he kisses me softly and says, "Thank you."

"For what?" I ask, confused.

"For letting me in. For not running or pushing me away." He lifts me off him and sets me on the couch. "I'm going to handle this." He walks over to the counter where he keeps his keys and wallet and shoves them into his pocket.

"You're leaving?"

"Yeah, I—" His words are interrupted by the buzzer going off. Where we live, those who don't live here, or have the access

A CHANCE ENCOUNTER

code, have to buzz to be let into the building. From there, they can come to our door. Easton insisted wherever he lives has this feature, since his crazy fans have been known to stalk and find him. In California, he lived in a gated community. In New York City, it's a little different, but at least this way, there's a second barrier between us and the outside world.

My eyes meet Easton's, my stomach bottoming out. There's no way it's Freeman...

"Hello?" Easton says over the intercom.

"Hello. I'm looking for Sophia Davis."

"And you are?" he asks.

"Rachel Deluca. I would like to speak to Sophia regarding a personal matter."

He looks at me and I shake my head, having no clue who she is.

"Regarding what matter?" he asks.

"Freeman Carmichael."

What. The. Fuck.

"You can come up." He buzzes her in.

"Oh my God, Easton," I cry out. This can't be a coincidence. I was just with Freeman a little while ago and now a woman is wanting to discuss him. "Do you think she's his lawyer? She could be coming to serve me, to try to take Kendall away."

"Stop," he demands gently. "You're stressing yourself out and it's not good for you or the baby. Nobody is taking that little girl from us."

There's a knock on the door, and Easton opens it. Standing on the other side is a redheaded woman with pale skin and freckles, dressed in business attire.

"Good morning," she says, her eyes focusing on me. "Sophia Davis?"

"Yes," I say, as she steps over the threshold.

"I was wondering if we could have a word…" She glances quickly at Easton then back at me. "In private."

"Anything you have to talk about can be done in front of my fiancé."

She purses her lips, not liking that answer. "Very well." She hands me what appears to be a business card. "I would like to ask you a few questions about your association with Governor Freeman Carmichael."

"I don't know who you're talking about," I insist, trying with everything in me to come across as nonchalant, but my voice gives me away.

"I saw you with him," she accuses, her eyes narrowing. "Is

he scared?" She smirks evilly. "I knew the second he saw that picture of you two he would go running straight to you."

"Who the hell are you?" Easton asks, placing himself in front of me protectively.

"I am a journalist, doing an exposé on Freeman Carmichael."

"Where did you get that picture from?" No point in denying it. She already knows, and it's clear she's the one who sent it. "Do you have any idea what you're doing? Who you're messing with?"

"Oh, I know exactly who I'm messing with, and if I have it my way, when I'm done, he'll never be able to mess with another woman again."

Something about the way she says it makes my stomach roil. Freeman's obviously screwed her over and it's clear, unlike me who's trying to stay out of his way, she's out for his blood.

"How did you get that picture of them?" Easton asks.

"From another woman he fucked over," she says matter-of-factly. "Something he's done to a lot of women over the years. I'm going to write my story and expose him for the piece of shit he is, whether you cooperate or not, but I'd prefer if you'd cooperate. You're a victim, just like the rest of us."

My gaze darts over to Easton. She knows and she's going to put my business out there. Easton's eyes meet mine and he shakes his head slightly, only enough for me to see.

"Does the woman who took the picture know anything?" he asks.

"Other than the fact that you two had a summer fling, no. I dug and found out the result of that fling."

"How much will it cost for you to sign, agreeing not to use Sophia's name, story, and that image in any story you write?"

"Easton," I gasp. He can't seriously be considering paying her off.

"How much?" he repeats.

Her eyes light up, and I want to scratch her eyeballs out. Victim, my ass. Freeman might've screwed her over, but the money signs flashing in her eyes tell me her true motives.

"One million."

"No—" I begin.

"Done," Easton says. "I'll have my attorney draw up the paperwork that will state if you ever speak of or write about Sophia or her daughter in any way, or share that photo, you will not only have to pay back the money I gave you, but I will

A CHANCE ENCOUNTER

sue you. Do you understand?"

"Understood." She plucks the business card out of my hand and gives it to Easton. "Call me when the contract is drawn up." Then she saunters out of the house, with swagger she didn't have walking in.

Twenty-Three

EASTON

"HOW COULD YOU DO THAT?" SOPHIA ASKS THE SECOND RACHEL IS OUT THE
door. "A million dollars? That's a lot of money."

"I would've given her double, hell, triple that," I admit, roping my arms around her. "I told you I would protect you and Kendall, and I meant that."

"But—"

"No buts, Dash. A million dollars is a drop in the bucket. The last time Forbes checked, I was worth over six hundred million dollars. A measly one mil is worth knowing she'll keep her mouth shut. I'm smart with my money, I don't overspend, and my financial advisor makes extremely profitable investments. I doubt I'll ever be able to spend what I'm worth in my lifetime."

Her jaw drops. "I can't even imagine…"

"Well, you better start, because once we're married, what's mine is yours, and whatever we can't spend in our lifetime will go to our kids."

"Easton," she breathes. "I don't… I assumed I'd have to sign a—"

"Don't even think about finishing that sentence. We're marrying for love, and there's no way in hell I'm starting our marriage signing a paper that stipulates what happens if we don't work." I kiss her hard on the mouth. "You're mine for life, Dash, so you better get used to it."

THE NIGHT BEFORE THE WEDDING

"WE'VE BEEN CONTACTED BY MR. CARMICHAEL."

"And?"

"He's agreed to meet this afternoon."

I glance at the clock. I can't postpone this. I've been waiting for this. "Fuck, all right, I'm on my way."

"You're on your way where?" Sophia asks, walking in and

A CHANCE ENCOUNTER

catching the end of my statement. I hang up and pocket my phone.

"I have a meeting I have to get to… in California."

Her eyes go wide. "Today? Our wedding is tomorrow."

"And I'll be there, I promise." I fist the back of her head and pull her face toward mine for a kiss. "If it weren't important, I would put it off, but I have to go. I'll be there, Dash. I promise. I'll be the one in black." I pull back and wink.

She rolls her eyes. "Very funny. You better be there, because I promise you if you're not… If I walk down that aisle and you're not standing there…"

"Stop." I kiss her one more time. "There is nothing that will keep me from marrying you tomorrow."

The flight to the West Coast is long, but I spend the time jotting down some notes for my vows. Sophia and I agreed to say our own, and for the most part I'm planning to speak from the heart, but I'm afraid I'll get up there, see her in her dress, and all thought will leave me.

When I arrive at LAX, a town car is waiting for me. I head straight to my attorney's office, not wanting to waste a second. If all goes well, I can be back in New York before nightfall.

I walk past the receptionist, giving her a slight head nod, since she already knows Daniel is expecting me. He's been my family's personal attorney as well as a close friend for years.

"Mr. Maxwell." I step into his office and shake his hand, ignoring the asshole sitting in the chair in front of Daniel's desk. "How are you?"

"I'm good, man." There's a twinkle in his eye because he'll be attending the wedding tomorrow, but he's not mentioning that.

"Enough with the bullshit," Freeman says from behind me. "You asked for this fucking meeting. Made your threats. I'm here."

I stifle my smirk. "I did. Thank you."

"Get to the point. I don't have time for this."

"Mr. Blackwood is requesting you relinquish all your rights to Kendall Naomi Davis." Daniel pushes the papers across his desk.

"In exchange for what?" he scoffs.

"Nothing," I tell him. "You're going to do it because you're a piece of shit and I want to make sure you can never threaten my soon-to-be wife again."

A CHANCE ENCOUNTER

Freeman glares. "That bitch—"

I'm on him before he can finish his sentence, my fist connecting with his ugly fucking face. "That beautiful woman is my fiancée," I bark, taking a step back. "And you will speak about her with respect. Got it?"

He wipes a bit of blood from his lip. "I don't have to do shit! Like I told her—"

I yank him up by the front of his suit and slam him into the wall. "I know what you told her. I know you threatened her. Had her up against the wall, scaring the shit out of her. Not only did she tell me, but I saw it with my own eyes. On video."

His beady eyes bug out.

"Don't worry, it's in my safe."

"What the fuck do you want?" he barks.

"My attorney told you. I want you to relinquish your rights."

"Is that why she sent me that fucking picture? To blackmail me?" He barks out a humorless laugh. "Are you seriously blackmailing a politician?"

I want to laugh and tell him he's a dumbass, but I keep my mouth shut regarding the truth. "You're a dirty, corrupt, poor excuse for a politician," I tell him, tightening my hold on his neck. "We're just using what you know... what you can relate to. Just like all those times you blackmailed and threatened her. The difference between you and me, though, is that I have money. Tons of it. And money talks."

I loosen my hold on him slightly so I can look him in the eyes. "You have some bullshit sense of power, but when the world finds out the shit you've done, and trust me, I know everything you've done... That power will, poof, vanish." I smirk, knowing I've got him. "And then I'll fight you with every dime I have until your life is destroyed. So, are we going to do this the easy way or the hard way?"

He knocks my hand away and stalks toward the desk where the papers rest. "Fine, but this means you keep your mouths shut."

"Absolutely," I agree, laughing to myself. "Sophia and I will never say a word..." We won't have to because that bitch Rachel is out for Freeman's blood, and she won't stop until she gets it. She won't be using Sophia to get it, but she has enough to blow up Freeman's entire world—I made sure of it.

"Hey, Daniel, you got this?" I ask, walking toward the door. "I have a wedding I need to get to. Two beautiful girls I need to officially make mine."

Daniel grins. "I got this. And I'll see you tomorrow."

"I WAS A LITTLE SCARED YOU WEREN'T GOING TO MAKE IT," SOPHIA WHISPERS, her arms wrapped around my neck as we sway to "A Thousand Years" by Christina Perri. We've said our I dos and now we're at our reception, dancing to our first song.

"And miss the most important day of my life?" I chuckle. "Not a chance, Dash." Because of the tradition of not seeing each other the night before, she didn't know until this morning, I was back in New York last night.

Sophia lifts her face and I drop a soft kiss to her perfect, lip-glossed lips. Her hair and makeup has been done for the wedding, and she's donning a gorgeous white, sequin dress that accentuates her belly.

"You're so damn beautiful," I tell her, kissing her again. "I can't wait to peel this dress off you and make love to you as my wife."

Her cheeks flush pink. "You must really love me to want

to see me naked. I feel like a whale."

"No fucking way," I argue. "I wasn't kidding when I said I plan to keep you pregnant. I love you like this, carrying my baby, growing a life inside you. You're perfect."

She sighs and rests her head back against my shoulder. "You going to tell me where you went?" she murmurs.

"To see Freeman." Her body freezes. "He relinquished his rights to K. No matter what happens in the future, he can never come after either of you."

She raises her face and her watery eyes meet mine. "Oh, Easton," she chokes out. "How did you—"

"Not tonight, Dash. Tonight is about us, about saying our vows in front of our friends and family. It's about agreeing to spend the rest of our lives together before God. I want to finish this dance with my wife and when the song is over, I'm going to dance with my daughter. Tomorrow we can talk."

We spend the rest of the night dancing and eating and enjoying our family and friends. When it's late, and Sophia is exhausted, we kiss Kendall good night, since she's going to stay with my parents, thank everyone for coming, and then bid our goodbyes.

We're staying in the hotel where the reception is being

A CHANCE ENCOUNTER

held, so the walk to our suite is short. Tomorrow, we're going to leave for our mini honeymoon, but tonight I'm going to make love to my wife.

Sophia asks for a few minutes to clean up, so I use that time to light some candles and undress out of my tux. When she steps out, no longer in her dress, I pout, annoyed I didn't get to take it off her myself. But then my eyes home in on what she's wearing: a white lacy bra and panty set with those sexy as fuck garters that come up to her mid-thigh with clasps on the front of each thigh, connecting them to her panties. Her belly is big—there's no other way to describe it. She's due soon and you can tell our boy is stretching her. And holy shit, she's never looked so goddamn stunning.

"Don't move," I tell her, grabbing my phone and pulling up the camera app.

"Easton!" She shrieks.

"No, don't move." I snap several pictures. "I need a visual, baby."

I throw my phone onto the nightstand and stalk toward her. My mouth crashes against hers, tasting her sweet tongue. I guide us over to the bed and she lies down in the middle, spreading her thighs for me.

"Jesus, Soph. Do you have any idea how fucking delectable you look like this?" I drop small kisses all over her full breasts and down her stomach, then place an open-mouthed kiss to the top of her mound, inhaling her sweet musk. "You smell delicious."

I pull her panties down her creamy thighs, loving how smooth she is everywhere. She was a bit hairy before the wedding, having had trouble shaving. I offered to do it for her, but she insisted on going to the salon.

I spread her lips and devour her pussy, licking her clit like I know she loves. Her fingers dive into my hair, tugging on the strands as she climaxes all over me and the bed.

"Oh shit, Easton!" she screams.

"Fuck, woman. You're so wet."

"That's because... my water broke!" She darts up. "Oh my God!" She backs up and we both look at the soaking wet bed. "My water broke!" she repeats, panic in her eyes.

"Your... water—" Oh shit! Her water broke.

"We have to go," she says, scrambling off the bed. "The baby is coming... now."

After we're both dressed—her in a hoodie and sweatpants that read "Just married!"—we call for a car service to take us

A CHANCE ENCOUNTER

to the hospital.

Two hours later, Sophia gives birth to a healthy little boy, and shortly after, our family and friends show up.

"Daddy!" Kendall squeals, running over to me. "Is he here?"

"He is, K. Your baby brother is here."

Everyone hugs and congratulates us and spends some time passing around the baby, while Kendall lies with her mom and listens to the story of Camden being born. Once everyone has held him and taken some pictures, they say their goodbyes so we can have some time with the baby and Kendall. Since my parents are keeping Kendall, they let us know they'll be in the waiting room.

Carefully, I pass Camden over to Kendall, who gently holds him in her lap, stroking his fuzzy baby hair while he sleeps soundly.

"Wow," she breathes. "Today is the best day ever. I got a daddy and a brother."

"Today is definitely the best day ever." I lean over and kiss both of my girls on their foreheads.

Who would've thought a chance encounter at the park in a city filled with millions of people would end with us getting our happily ever after?

"Thank you," I whisper to Sophia.

"For what?"

"For saving me from that killer bee." I press a kiss to her lips. "For finding me."

Epilogue

SOPHIA
ELEVEN YEARS LATER

"JUST LET ME STICK IT IN, DASH."

"No way." I shake my head.

"C'mon, baby," he croons. "Just the tip."

"Hell. No. Every time you say that, I end up pregnant. I just got on birth control and it has to kick in. I'm not taking any chances."

Easton pouts. "Are you saying you don't want to have my baby?" He slides his hard length up and down the slit of my wet pussy, knowing what it does to me.

I bark out a laugh. "I'm saying I don't want to have *another* baby. I told you four is my limit and I meant it."

Yes, we have four children: Kendall, who's eighteen,

Camden, who just turned eleven, Bailey, who recently turned ten—yep, she's only eleven months younger than Camden because Easton pulled the same stunt he's pulling now—and our most recent little bundle of joy, Phoebe, who is only six weeks old. I had an issue with my IUD and had to have it removed. Easton, of course, swooped in the first chance he got and knocked me up before I could switch my birth control.

"You said three was your limit too... Just one more, baby, please," he murmurs, leaning over me on his elbows and kissing his way down my neck. My insides clench and my brain goes fuzzy. He uses my momentarily loss of brain cells to push into me. He's thick and long and fills me so full and deep. I groan, arching my back at the feel of him inside of me. It's been six weeks since I felt him.

"Yes," he hisses. "Fuck, you're so warm and tight and—"

"Mom! Dad! I'm leaving," Kendall says through the door. Her words slice through my dick-covered fog and I push Easton away.

"Not happening." I hit him with a glare and roll off the bed, grabbing my robe and throwing it on.

"Oh, it's going to happen," he says, falling onto his back on the bed. "And soon. There are too many damn girls in this

A CHANCE ENCOUNTER

house. We need to even out the gender playing field."

I laugh. "You're so full of shit. You love having all these girls."

A grin spreads across his face. "True. Maybe we'll have another one." He shrugs and stands. He grabs his boxer briefs and pulls them up, then throws on a pair of sweats.

"No more babies," I groan, swinging open the door. "Morning, Sunshine."

"Did you just say no more babies?" Her eyes go wide. "Mom, tell me Dad is not convincing you to have another baby."

"Another baby?" Camden asks, walking down the hall with his sleeping baby sister in his arms. "Hopefully this time it's a boy."

Easton chuckles and Kendall rolls her eyes.

"Nobody is having another baby. Your dad *will* be getting a vasectomy as scheduled when we get back." I shoot a pointed glare Easton's way before heading out of the room. "Are you all packed?" I ask the kids.

"Yep, I ready," Bailey says.

"I'm pretty much ready," Camden says, setting Phoebe in her bassinet and kissing her forehead.

371

"I'm good to go," Kendall says. "I just need to go by Steven's house so I can say goodbye."

Easton growls but keeps his mouth shut. Steven is Kendall's boyfriend, and while he's a good guy, very sweet and respectful, Easton still hates him for simply being a guy.

"All right, go ahead and go. We're leaving at eleven, though, so be back before then, please."

"Will do!"

Since I'm taking time off from work to be home with Phoebe, we've decided to do something crazy and go on one last road trip before Kendall leaves for college in the fall. Easton had this tour planned before I accidently— insert glare—got pregnant, so instead of canceling it, we've purchased a massive tour bus and will be hitting the road. I'm not sure how long the six of us will last on a bus together, but we figured what the hell. Worst-case scenario, the kids and I come back early and Easton finishes his tour. This isn't our first time traveling with him—though more often than not, we prefer taking a plane—but it is our first time traveling with a baby this young.

I sit down at the table, and Maria, who is still with us, brings me over a cup of coffee and a plate of pancakes.

A CHANCE ENCOUNTER

"Thank you," I moan, taking in a whiff of the hot, caffeinated beverage. Phoebe is breastfeeding every two hours around the clock, which means I'm getting little sleep right now. "Are you sure you don't want to come with us?" I joke.

Maria laughs. "Oh no, but I'll be here when you get back." Here, meaning her private suite in our home. After I found out I was pregnant with Bailey, we decided to purchase a bigger brownstone. As much as I wanted to stay in the same area, we made the decision to move our family to Brooklyn Heights, where it's a bit more family-friendly and the homes have backyards. Since we had the space, I suggested she move in with us, and Easton agreed. She's more like a grandmother to our kids, which works out well since my own mother passed away a few years ago—without ever speaking to me again after she found out I was pregnant with Camden—and Easton's parents semi-retired, spending a lot of their time at their house in The Hamptons. Don't get me wrong, we still see them often, but having Maria around is like having a mom and grandma in one all the time. She dotes on the kids and they love her so much.

My phone dings with an alert from Google and I glance at it. It's been a long time since I've seen that name on my phone. I should turn the alerts off, but like I said, it's been a long time, so I forgot they're on there. I click on the article and read the headline: Former Governor Freeman Carmichael Dies of a Heart Attack.

After he signed the papers, we never heard from him again. But we did hear about him. Rachel did what she set out to do and exposed all of his secrets: from sexual assault, to paying off women to have abortions. His wife divorced him, and he lost the election. After that, it was as if he disappeared, which was fine by me. He got what he deserved, and I have zero sympathy for him. I skim the words, trying to feel some kind of sadness toward his sudden death, but I can't seem to muster up an ounce of care.

"Hey, Dash," Easton calls out from somewhere in the house. "Before we go, do we need to go by Blackwood to handle that contract?"

"No," I yell back. "I took care of it yesterday." Technically, I'm on maternity leave from work, but since my job is at the record label my husband part-owns, I'm always on the clock.

When I was trying to decide which way to take my career, I interned for a few different firms. I learned quickly that family law wasn't for me. I had envisioned all the children I

A CHANCE ENCOUNTER

would save, but I didn't consider all the nasty people I would have to deal with. A few weeks in and I was ready to bolt. I tried out a few other firms, but nothing felt right.

And that's when Easton's dad mentioned Entertainment Law. Three years, a law degree, and a bar exam later, and I was hired by Blackwood Records. I love my job and what I do there, and most of all I love that I get to spend plenty of time with Easton.

Phoebe whines and Easton walks into the room, scooping her up into his strong arms. He comes over and presses a kiss to the top of my head, then hands me my baby girl, so I can feed her, watching in awe as she latches on and sucks.

"What?" I ask.

"Nothing," he says, "I just can't imagine what my life would be like had you not found me."

It's funny, to this day Easton says what we have is because I found him, but he has it all wrong. He might've been lost, but I was alone. In a city filled with too many people, I felt like I didn't exist. Sure, I had Naomi… I still do—she's married to Dante and they have a beautiful son who's close in age to Camden.

But it wasn't the same.

With one look, one moment, one kiss, one touch, he *saw* me.

He says I found him, but the truth is, we found each other.

About the Author

Reading is like breathing in, writing is like breathing out. – Pam Allyn

Nikki Ash resides in South Florida where she is an English teacher by day and a writer by night. When she's not writing, you can find her with a book in her hand. From the Boxcar Children, to Wuthering Heights, to the latest single parent romance, she has lived and breathed every type of book. While reading and writing are her passions, her two children are her entire world. You can probably find them at a Disney park before you would find them at home on the weekends!

Printed in Great Britain
by Amazon